SECRETS OF A WALLFLOWER

Amanda McCabe

MILLS & BOON

First published in Great Britain 2018
by Mills & Boon, an imprint of HarperCollins*Publishers*
1 London Bridge Street, London, SE1 9GF

Large Print edition 2018

ISBN: 978-0-263-07500-7

MIX
Paper from
responsible sources
FSC C007454

This book is produced from independently certified FSC™ paper to ensure responsible forest management. For more information visit www.harpercollins.co.uk/green.

Printed and bound in Great Britain
by CPI Group (UK) Ltd, Croydon, CR0 4YY

Amanda McCabe wrote her first romance at the age of sixteen—a vast epic, starring all her friends as the characters, written secretly during algebra class. She's never since used algebra, but her books have been nominated for many awards, including the RITA®, Romantic Times Reviewers' Choice Award, the Booksellers' Best, the National Readers' Choice Award and the HOLT Medallion. She lives in Oklahoma with her husband, one dog and one cat.

Also by Amanda McCabe

A Stranger at Castonbury
Tarnished Rose of the Court
An Improper Duchess
Betrayed by His Kiss
The Demure Miss Manning
The Queen's Christmas Summons

Bancrofts of Barton Park miniseries

The Runaway Countess
Running from Scandal
Running into Temptation
The Wallflower's Mistletoe Wedding

Debutantes in Paris miniseries

Secrets of a Wallflower
And look out for the next book
Coming soon

Discover more at millsandboon.co.uk.

To my mom, because we'll always have Paris!

Prologue

Spring 1888—Miss Grantley's School for Young Ladies

'By this time next year I will be a famous authoress,' announced Miss Diana Martin as she lay in the grass with her two best friends and stared up at the clouds sliding across the pale blue April sky. They were only a few days from leaving their schooling for ever, presumably as polished young ladies of eighteen, ready to grace society, and had thus been allowed a rare afternoon picnic unchaperoned in the school's lush park.

'How can you do that, Di?' murmured Lady Alexandra, a duke's daughter, the sweetest, shyest and most beautiful girl in all of Miss Grantley's. 'There are no great lady authors. It must be so hard. Everyone knowing who you are, staring at you wherever you go. If anyone would buy the book at all. I would be so terrified.'

'Oh, Alex,' laughed Emily Fortescue, the most sensible of the trio that everyone in the dormitory corridors like to call The Three Musketeers. 'You would be terrified if a mouse even looked at you, though you must get used to it. You are a duke's daughter *and* you look like an angel. Everyone will stare at you when you make your debut.'

Alexandra's face, which was indeed heart-shaped, all ivory and roses crowned by spun sil-ver-gold hair, blushed bright red. 'Please, Em, don't remind me. I wish we could stay here for ever, just as we are. Right at this moment.'

Diana could definitely see what Alexandra meant. It was a perfect day, the sun soft and warm, the grass like a velvet blanket beneath them, the smell of honeysuckle on the breeze. The solid, Georgian red brick of Miss Grantley's main build-ing was in the distance, watching over them, keep-ing them safe as it had done for the last few years of their education.

She *had* loved it here. The teachers had taught them so many things—geography, mathematics, philosophy, as well as the more usual French, wa-tercolours, music, and how to curtsy to the Queen.

They had one of the finest libraries in the county thanks to their founder, the daughter of a famous rare book collector. At Miss Grantley's, Diana had found the stories that took her out of herself, the poetry and novels and plays. She knew she wasn't pretty—she was too thin, too gangly, her hair too red—but here she had found a place for herself. Here she could start to see herself, unlike at her parents' house where she always felt so awkward, out of place, and—wrong. Miss Grantley's had changed all that, at least for a while.

Best of all, she had found Emily and Alexandra. From the very first day, when they sat next to each other for the school's formal dinner in its vast, intimidating great hall, they had been bonded fast in friendship. None of them had their own sisters, so they became sisters of the heart. They studied together in the library, whispered in the night as they shared chocolates, wandered the gardens, shared hopes and dreams and stories.

And now it was all coming to an end, rushing towards them faster than a railway train, sweeping them into the unknown future. It was frightening—but also very exciting.

Alexandra would surely marry. She *was* a great beauty and, as a duke's daughter, could probably find a prince—if she could bring herself to speak to him. She was so very shy, which was why her ducal parents had sent her to school, hoping she would come out of her shell, make new friends.

Emily, the daughter of a prosperous merchant in Brighton, could marry a wealthy factory owner her father knew, or she could run her very own business empire. She was clever enough, strong enough, brave enough, to do anything.

But Diana—she had no idea what she could do. Her father was a respected diplomat, well-to-do but not hugely wealthy, long retired from a military career that had once taken him to India and South Africa. She knew her parents expected her to find a country gentleman to settle into a fine home with, or maybe a vicar, if he was from a good family, or even an army officer, as her father had once been.

Yet marriage, despite all the wonderfully romantic French novels all the girls at Miss Grantley's passed around and devoured along with their chocolates, seemed quite terrifying. Once a lady was married, her own ideas seemed finished.

She knew she wasn't shrewd enough to run a business, as Emily could do. The one thing Diana really loved, the one thing that could take her out of herself and into other, stranger, beautiful worlds, was writing stories.

Miss Merrill, their literature teacher, told her she had a rare gift for creating vivid atmosphere with her words. She couldn't play the harp very well, could barely add sums above three digits, hopelessly mixed up the borders on globes and who should sit beside who at dinner parties. But she could write well enough.

Couldn't she?

She propped herself up on her elbow and studied her friends. Their hats were all off, their faces turned to the sun, their shoes discarded, Emily's chestnut hair spread on the grass beneath her. Miss Merrill would lecture them if she could see! Diana tucked a loose strand of her red-gold hair back into her unruly plait.

'There *are* great women writers,' she said. 'Jane Austen. Mrs Gaskell.'

'Charlotte Brontë,' said Emily. 'Plus all those anonymous books by A Lady, the ones Ann Parkinson is always bringing back from Paris. Plenty of lady writers, though few are as good as you, Di.'

Diana felt her cheeks turn warm, maybe from the sun, maybe from the compliment. She had always longed for praise, but when it came she didn't quite know what to do with it. She laid back down in her spot on the grass.

'Do you want to write one of those French books, Di?' Alexandra asked.

'I don't know.' Diana thought of what they found in those smuggled books: wonderfully vivid descriptions of gowns and balls, kisses, elopements, scandal. They *were* fun. But she also loved the more realistic worlds found in George Eliot and Thackeray, so full of deep truths. 'Maybe I'd like to do something like Mr Dickens. Something to make a bit of difference in the world. Or at least distract people from their troubles for a moment, as Miss Austen does, and give a bit of joy.'

'You do that just by being—well, you,' Alexandra said. 'I've never known anyone to make me laugh as you do.'

'Only because I fall down in deportment class and show my petticoats every week,' Diana answered.

'You only do that because it *does* make us laugh!' said Emily. 'Otherwise dreary old Mrs Percell would have us all asleep in boredom every week. We've seen you waltz when we practise our dance steps at night.'

Diana had to admit that was somewhat true. When Miss Merrill, their floor chaperon as well as the literature teacher, had gone to sleep, the girls would often have their own little dance parties. It *was* fun to dance then, using the frilled hem of her dressing gown as a train, pretending she was dancing with a prince in a grand ballroom. They would all spin and spin, and then collapse into giggles before they ate their hidden stash of teacakes.

But she still had the dratted tendency to topple over in curtsies. What she really liked about those classes was learning what to wear to various social events. She pored over the Parisian fashion magazines avidly and liked to sketch her own ideas for gowns and hats when she was supposed to be reading Cicero. Usually those imaginary gowns ended up on heroines in her short stories.

Stories of young ladies like her friends. Ladies who could change the world.

'And even if you were clumsy,' Alexandra said, 'no one is more stylish than you.' She reached out to touch the elaborate floral embroidery on the pale blue muslin sleeve of Diana's dress. The local seamstress had made it to Diana's own design, with puffed shoulders and a narrow skirt in the latest fashion.

Maybe she could use that style to make her mark. But how? Once she went home to her parents and their rules, she wouldn't have many more chances.

Diana sat up on the grass and stared over the rolling lawns, the bright reds and yellows of the flowerbeds, the tennis court where girls in white were wielding their rackets, their merry laughter echoing on the breeze. The sun glinted on the windows of the main building, dazzling and golden.

It was a wonderful place. But Emily and Alexandra were right. Soon they would have to fly away. Where would they all go?

'No matter what happens,' she said, suddenly feeling quite urgent, almost frightened, 'we must never lose each other.'

Emily sat up beside her, a tiny frown between her amber-brown eyes, and Alexandra reached for their hands.

'Of course we'll never lose each other,' Emily said. 'We're sisters, are we not? We have to support each other through our horrid Season next year, all those ghastly teas and receptions. Curtsying to the Queen in her black veils…'

'Or worse, the Prince of Wales,' Alexandra said with a giggle. 'My cousin Chris says the Prince tries to grab ladies' backsides if they don't move away fast enough.'

'Alexandra!' Emily cried. 'That is quite the naughtiest thing you've ever said. But if Mr Blakely said it, I'm sure it's true.'

Alexandra's cousin, Christopher Blakely, was a bona fide member of the Marlborough House Set, a group that centred around the Prince of Wales and loved horse races, music halls, card games and beautiful, married ladies above all else. Chris was a handsome bon vivant, favouring carnation boutonnières and gold-headed walking sticks, and he made all the girls giggle and blush when he came to the school's family visit days, which he often did, since he was Alex's favourite relative. Diana also quite liked him. He had style and humour, and was impossible to take seriously. She had been looking forward to his visit today for weeks.

Chris's older brother, Sir William Blakely, on the other hand, was the very portrait of solemn respectability. A member of the Foreign Office, he seldom visited his cousin at school, and they said he was soon to go to India. While Sir William was certainly handsome, with his glossy dark hair, fathomless dark eyes and tall, lean figure in his perfectly cut suit, he was quiet. He so seldom smiled, yet always seemed to be watching everything around him so closely.

He made Diana feel so—so frivolous. Silly. Young. And so strangely, well, fluttery. Those dark eyes that seemed to see so much…

Diana pushed away thoughts of William Blakely's handsome eyes. It was very unlikely she would ever see him again, anyway. Bombay was far away and she had more immediate things to worry about. Such as what to do when she left Miss Grantley's.

'Where *are* your cousins, Alex?' Emily said, turning her face up to the sun. 'It's almost time for tea.'

'I think they went fishing in the lake or something like that,' Alex murmured dreamily. 'Surely it's ages before tea. I don't think I can bear to move just yet. I feel so wonderfully lazy.'

'I think I had better move about a bit,' Diana said, 'or I will never want to leave this spot! Maybe I'll go draw. I'm supposed to add some landscapes to my portfolio for art class, so it won't just be filled with drawings of gowns and hats.'

She took her sketchbook and made her way along the winding pathways that led between the groves of trees beyond the picnic grounds. She soon found herself lost in the work, as she always did when sketching, and barely noticed the time passing, the light changing overhead. Until she heard a loud splash, a shout. Startled, she spun around to stare at the lake in the distance.

There were two men on the mossy bank, one was Alex's cousin Christopher, laughing as he tried to push the other man into the water, to the loud encouragement of the people already splashing in the waves. Chris was laughing, as he usually was, his golden hair damp and standing on end, his expression full of mischief.

The man he tried to push was his brother William, he of the dark eyes and solemn smile. When Diana had first met him, she had been barely able to speak when he looked at her, she had felt so foolish. She was sure he hadn't even noticed her then, but she had certainly noticed him.

Now, she instinctively ducked down, even though the men weren't looking in her direction at all. She knew she should leave right away, but she couldn't seem to stop watching. Stop staring at William Blakely.

He looked very different to the way he had in the school drawing room, his coat gone, his fine linen shirt damp and showing the lines of his muscled shoulders, his dark hair rumpled, his face alight with laughter. Yet he seemed so still within himself, so perfectly in control even in his dishabille against Chris's silliness. Diana found herself utterly unable to look away.

William gave Chris one light push back and Chris toppled into the water. William laughed and his face, all sharp, elegant angles, like a classical statue when it was still and watchful, glowed.

Diana reached for her sketchbook and quickly drew in the lines of his face. She couldn't seem to stop herself from trying to capture it; he was so fascinating with his elegant looks, that smile that transformed him into something younger, glowing like the sun. She had never seen anyone quite like him.

She hadn't got as far as she would have liked on the sketch when the bell rang for tea. The men glanced up and she flattened herself on the grass, afraid to be seen. There was a burst of more laughter, rippling splashes as they climbed out of the water. She knew she had to get back to the school before she was missed. She quickly closed the book and leaped up.

She had to glance back one more time before she left, to take in the sunlit scene. William Blakely seemed to be looking in her direction, a small frown creasing his handsome face, and she gasped and broke into a run, not stopping until she tumbled back on to the lawn behind the school.

The bell rang from the school's main building again, a deep, brassy gong that signalled the end of the picnics and that precious, golden day. The end of her small fantasy of William Blakely. The tennis players gathered up their rackets and flocked inside, and Diana and her friends stood up to pack away their glasses and plates. Diana shook the bits of grass from her ruffled blue skirts, relishing the last vestiges of the flower-scented spring air. The last dream of school and of a handsome man who seemed like a fantasy.

'No matter what happens, all will be well,' she said to her friends, trying to reassure herself. 'Because we will always have each other.'

Chapter One

Spring 1889—Duchess of Waverton's ball, London

'What are your plans now, William, since you have returned from India?' Harold Blakely, William's father, asked from the head of the dining room table. 'They must be glad to have your expertise once more at the London office, but surely they won't want you to stay behind a desk there for long. I was always eager to be on to the next task myself, when I was at work there.'

William's mother didn't even look up from the plate she was listlessly picking at. 'I'm sure we all well remember those days,' Beatrice Blakely muttered. 'William has plenty of time to decide what to do next. At least he has returned from that pestilential India.'

'Hmmph,' Harold said with a scowl. He gestured to the footman for more wine. 'You've certainly worked hard enough of late, William. That's a great deal more than can be said for that useless Christopher. Takes after his mother, does that one. No direction at all.'

Beatrice didn't even answer, merely sighed and studied the curtained windows across the room as if she was in her own little world. She had been that way for as long as Will could remember and he was appalled to find nothing had changed in the Blakely house while he'd been abroad.

Ever since he and Chris were children, their parents had alternated between quarrels and icy silences. The only respite was in the long periods when their father was gone for his mysterious work and Beatrice would laugh a bit again. But her pale, fragile beauty had faded and her laughter was rare, and some times, as her sons grew older, she would complain to them of her loneliness. Her wasted youth.

She pushed her food from one side of the Wedgwood plate to the other, as Harold drained his wineglass. William longed to take his mother's hand, to give her a reassuring smile, but he knew from experience it would be like touching a ghost.

'Where *is* Christopher?' Harold demanded of no one in particular.

'He's here somewhere,' Beatrice answered vaguely. 'Aren't you meant to go to my sister's ball with him, William?'

'Yes,' Will said. 'He was meant to meet me for dinner and we would go to the Wavertons' after.' He did wonder where Chris had vanished to and meant to scold his brother for leaving him alone with their parents for a whole meal, but he found he couldn't entirely blame Chris for disappearing again.

'No use at all,' Harold grumbled. 'Can't even get himself to a duke's party and he's related to them. Some people would give their eye teeth for an invitation like that. The boy's been given everything and he's throwing it away.'

William ignored him and smiled at Beatrice. 'Why don't you come with us, Mother? I'm sure Aunt Waverton would love to see you. Alex was saying you hadn't called on them since the beginning of the Season.'

Beatrice gave him a startled glance. 'A ball? Oh, no. It will be so very crowded. I couldn't. My nerves.'

'This family,' Harold snorted. 'Weak blood. Except for you, I hope, William. What *are* you going to do now you're in England again?'

William took a long drink of his own wine, gathering his usual quiet control. He needed it when it came to dealing with his parents. 'I haven't decided yet. The office will decide where I'm ultimately needed.'

'Of course they will. And I'm sure you'll do us proud. I do miss those days of work.' Harold sighed. 'Perhaps you'll use this time to find a proper wife, set up a house where you can entertain. That's the best way to make contacts for the long run.'

Beatrice perked up a bit at those words. 'Oh, yes, William. A marriage would be lovely. There are so many pretty girls out this Season, or so I hear. I'm sure my sister would be happy to introduce any of them to you in a trice.'

William glanced around the gloomy dining room, the burgundy-red silk walls, the gold curtains muffling everything from the outside world, the dark portraits and still lifes staring down at them. The very cushions of the dark, carved furniture seemed seeped with years of loneliness and unhappiness. So filled with bitterness. He certainly had no desire to replicate such a life, to make a lady miserable as his mother had been.

'I'm not ready for such a step,' he said. 'But as soon as I am, Mother, you and Aunt Waverton will be the first to know.'

Before his parents could answer, the dining room door opened and Chris staggered in. His blond hair was rumpled, his cravat half-tied, and he gave them all a crooked grin.

'Good evening, Blakelys all!' he said, waving his arm. He grabbed his mother's still-full wine-glass and drained it. 'Well, Will, are we going to this ball or not?'

Lady S-T was wearing a gown of yellow...

No. No, marigold.

...marigold silk taffeta and velvet, with rust, olive-green, and beige lily bouquets of satin, with a floral pattern of pearl and gold beads on the hem.

Diana studied the lady's gown again, jotting down one last detail in her little notebook.

Smaller bustle at the back, falling in beaded pleats, according to the new fashion for narrower skirts.

Lady Smythe-Tomas, a young, wealthy widow, was widely known as one of the most fashionable women in London and tonight, at the most fashionable ball of the Season, she didn't disappoint. Was it from the House of Worth? It had to be, Diana decided, with that wonderfully intricate beadwork and unusual colour combination in the bouquet trim.

She glanced down at her own gown, a debutante's pale pink organza, with only the tiniest edge of white-lace frill along the short, puffed sleeves. Her pearl necklace was fine enough, but she knew the wreath of pink rosebuds in her hair was wrong for her red tresses. How dull it all was! Surely if she could visit Monsieur Worth in Paris, look at his sketches, feel the fine lengths of fabrics, cool satins and rich velvets, choose some daring design of her own...

She sighed. It would be heaven. And if she could get these descriptions just right, get them to sound perfect, it could all come true.

In the meantime, she had the next best thing. She could sit here in the corner at one of the most fashionable events of the London Season and observe everything going on around her. All the ladies vying with each other to have the finest, most unique, most up-to-the-minute gowns, and the most glittering jewels.

She could do it—if only her mother didn't catch her. Diana peeked carefully around the gardenia-and-white-rose-draped trellis she was hiding behind and studied the ballroom. The Duke and Duchess of Waverton, Alexandra's parents, had one of the largest ballrooms in London and the Duchess never spared any expense in her party arrangements. Tonight was no exception.

The ballroom, a glittering jewel case of a room in ivory and gilt, crowned with crystal chandeliers and furnished with gilded satin chairs and sofas, sparkled even more when crowded with the satin and gemstone kaleidoscope of dancers on the polished floor. More white roses and wreaths of gardenias were draped everywhere, turning the space into a garden bower.

Oh, that was good. *Garden bower*, she wrote in her notebook.

The Duchess stood beneath a full-length portrait of herself by Mr Sargent, clad in a gown of midnight-blue velvet and tulle embroidered with a dazzling pattern of stars and crescent moons that matched the famous Eastern Star sapphire from India in her tiara.

The Duchess smiled brightly as she greeted each new guest, even though her husband was probably hiding in the card room, and the Prince and Princess of Wales, who were rumoured to be attending because the Princess was Alexandra's godmother, had not yet arrived. Alex herself, who the ball was nominally in honour of, was nowhere to be seen. Diana was sure she must be hiding just like her father, maybe still in her chamber or in the ladies' withdrawing room, as Alex so often was at large balls and soirées.

Luckily, Diana's mother was also nowhere to be seen. She was safe for the moment.

She glanced at Lady Smythe-Tomas's gown again. The lady was laughing, her golden-blond head thrown back as she languidly waved her rust-red feather fan. She always seemed to be one of those ladies who walked about constantly back-lit by an invisible amber sun. She would make a great heroine in a novel—or maybe a villainess.

The heroines of novels, at least novels of the sort she and the other girls at Miss Grantley's passed around secretly, never realised how beautiful they were. Lady Smythe-Tomas was fully aware of her looks. After all, her photographs were often displayed in shop windows, along with Mrs Langtry and Lady Warwick. All of them always clad in the latest fashions.

'What is that you're writing, Diana Martin? It doesn't look like a dance card,' a high-pitched voice said behind her, startling her out of her fashion dream.

She gasped and whirled around, her heart pounding. She was sure it was her mother and she did *not* want another lecture about how she needed to stop writing and find a suitable husband. That her time was running out. She was nineteen! Almost twenty and ancient! And she was wasting her chances.

But it wasn't her mother. It was Alexandra's cousin Christopher Blakely, using the falsetto voice that served him so well in amateur theatricals. He burst out laughing at the appalled look on her face and his green eyes sparkled. Or maybe they sparkled from the champagne glass in his hand, which Diana was sure wasn't his first of the evening. Chris was well known in town for his love of a fun time. Unlike his brother, who was off pursuing some very important career goal far away in India. Though it was William Blakely whose dark eyes were in her dreams.

'Christopher Blakely, you scared the ghost out of me,' she hissed. 'I thought you were my mother.'

'Fear not, I just saw her in the card room playing a wicked hand of piquet,' he said, downing the last of his champagne. He leaned out from their hiding place to gesture to one of the liveried footmen carrying silver trays around the ballroom. He took two fresh drinks and handed one to her.

'Oh,' she whispered, staring down into the shimmering gold liquid. Maybe champagne was the inspiration for Lady Smythe-Tomas's gown, with all that iridescent glow. She had to put that in the essay. 'I shouldn't.'

'I won't tell if you won't,' he said, leaning against the flower-covered trellis. 'My aunt gave me strict instructions I could only have two glasses before the midnight supper.'

Diana smiled as she thought about what happened last time the Duchess had a party, a tea in honour of Princess Alexandra. Chris had stolen the large, elaborate hat off the head of the Princess's lady-in-waiting and given them a wonderful recital from a music hall selection after sneaking rum into the tea. It had all been very amusing, if not strictly proper for a deb to see. 'And how many glasses does this make?'

'Four. But they *are* very small.'

She laughed and tucked her notebook into her reticule before she sipped at her own drink. Heavenly, so bubbly and sweet on her tongue. 'The Duke does know how to put together a wine cellar, everyone says so.'

'And the money he spends on it could support ten families for a year, I'm sure,' Chris muttered.

Diana studied him over the rim of her glass, a bit worried. There had been rumours that he had lost more than he should on horse races. She had dismissed such things as gossip before, but what if he *was* in trouble? 'Chris, if you're in need of a bit of income…'

'You would come to my rescue with your dowry?' he said with a comical leer.

Diana laughed and pretended to study him ostentatiously. He was handsome, of course, with his dark golden cap of hair and green eyes, his ready smile. And very funny and always up for a lark. She could see why so many of the other debs sighed over him. He came from a good family, even if he had no career, and was always house-party-visiting with the Waleses. And he was the nephew of a duchess, the cousin of her good friend. Even Diana's parents would approve of him.

But she could only see him as a friend, someone who made her laugh, helped her and Alex hide at parties. Brought her champagne when debs were meant to stick with lemon squash. He didn't make her feel all stammering and blushing, didn't make her daydream as his brother had.

'There are plenty with better dowries than me. But surely you don't have to worry about such things?' she said.

'Of course I don't,' he said. 'And what *are* you writing in that little notebook of yours? Scandalous secrets you overhear from your flowery hidey-holes? Are you a spy?'

Diana laughed and shook her head. 'Never you mind, Chris. It wouldn't interest you at all. And shouldn't you be dancing? I'm sure your aunt expects you to do your duty as a single gentleman?'

He grinned. 'Why do you think I'm in hiding, too? There's no one else worth dancing with here yet, except for Emily, and her card is full.'

Diana glanced back to the dance floor and saw Emily waltzing past with a young viscount something or other, her mint-green silk skirts swirling. Usually Emily, the daughter of well-to-do Brighton wine merchant, would never be in the Waverton ballroom. But it was Alex's party, sup-

posedly, and her best school friends were invited.
And Emily had proved to be most popular with
the fashionable set, indulging in her love of dancing and music, her open-hearted good humour.

They liked her father's wine, too. Just look at
the Duke's cellar.

Diana smiled to see her friend having such a
good time. She turned back to Christopher and
was startled to catch an unguarded look in his
eyes as he stared at Emily. A raw, solemn instant
of—was it longing?

But it was quickly gone and he laughed, back
to his usual careless self. 'Did you hear? William
is back from India for good.'

Diana blinked at the sudden change of subject
and remembered the scene of William by the
lake, laughing in the golden sun. 'William—your
brother?'

'Yes, or St William, as my mother would call
him if she could, now that he's been given a
knighthood at only twenty-eight. Above and beyond in service to Her Majesty.' He took another
glass of champagne from a passing footman. 'And
he's returned just in time to be sent off to Paris,
the lucky beggar.'

'Really? Paris?' All the talk in London for

weeks had been of the upcoming Exposition in Paris. Eiffel's great iron tower, the Turkish villages, the art pavilions, the American Wild West show. Just like everyone else, Diana was wild for stories of the Exposition.

And, if she was very lucky, she might just get to see it, too. She tried not to imagine William Blakely strolling along the river at her side, smiling down at her, his dark eyes glowing. That would surely never happen, not after she had been so stammering and gawky the few times they met before. But it *was* a lovely image.

'What sort of work does a diplomat do there?' she asked. 'Eat at the café atop Monsieur Eiffel's tower? Deliver letters from the Queen to other visiting monarchs? Ride a horse in the Wild West show?'

Christopher laughed. 'I have no idea. Will is infuriatingly tight-lipped about everything. He's here somewhere, I know, but I doubt dancing or playing cards. Probably working. He's always working.'

Diana suddenly glimpsed her mother at the other side of the ballroom. Lavinia Martin was hard to miss, tall and stately, prematurely white-haired, clad in beaded bronze satin. 'Oh, no. Speaking of cards, I think my mother's hand of piquet is over.'

'Let's dance, then. We shall both do our duty and escape a lecture.'

Diana nodded. She had already been able to hide out much longer than she had expected. She put down her empty glass and took Chris's hand, letting him lead her out on to the dance floor.

It was a polka, lively and quick, and he spun her around and around until she was dizzy with laughter. 'Maybe we could take ourselves to the Exposition and do dance demonstrations!' he said. 'The Whirling English Pair.'

She giggled. 'I doubt they would pay us for our dance skills. Toss us out and tell us never to darken France's door again, rather.'

'It's all in the attitude, my dear. Pretend you know how to dance and you will do it.'

'Excellent advice.' She would have to remember it. Pretend she knew what she was doing and others would believe it. Eventually she might even believe it herself.

As they spun around, Diana saw that Alex had appeared at last, standing beside her mother as the Duchess whispered to her through a gritted-teeth smile. Alex wore a beautiful gown of white tulle and pale blue satin, perfect with her angelic looks and spun-gilt hair. A wreath of red roses and pearls was woven through her upswept curls, matching the triple strand of pearls with a large ruby clasp at her throat.

Yet Diana could tell that her friend was unhappy. Alex bit her lip, her eyes downcast as she nodded to her mother. Her gloved hands twisted at the ivory handle of her fan. Diana wanted to go to her, but Christopher spun her around again and Alex and the Duchess were lost to view. Instead, Diana found herself facing the last person she wanted to see at any party.

Lord Thursby.

She hadn't seen him in a few days, not since a tea her mother had given. She'd hoped he had left town, but there he was, chatting and laughing with one of the Duchess's friends, a marchioness famed for her dyed red hair and diamonds. The lady's cheeks were glowing pink as she waved her fan at him.

Ladies did often seem to like him and Diana could see why. He was handsome, with thick blond hair and bright blue eyes, along with a dashing moustache and perfectly tailored, stylish clothes.

He was charming and well connected as a relation to Lord Lansdowne, the Viceroy of India.

That was how he first appeared at her parents' dinner table when he returned to London for the Season, with a letter from the Viceroy and questions for her father about his time in India. It was rumoured that Lord Thursby sought a career there himself. Her parents liked him and invited him back. Her mother seemed especially fond of him, laughing at his jokes, watching him carefully.

And, for some reason, he seemed to have taken a liking to Diana. He made such a point of sitting beside her at tea and at musical evenings, bringing her refreshments at the interval at the theatre. Smiling at her, even touching her hand as he mentioned how very much she looked like a 'Titian goddess' with her hair.

At first, she had been flattered. Who wouldn't be? A handsome, sought-after man who sought *her* out and complimented her red hair, which had always been the bane of her life.

Yet then something changed. She didn't even know what it was, for he was as complimentary as ever. Perhaps it was the way she some times noticed his conversation never included questions to *her*, only tales of his life, his career hopes. His compliments were all about her hair, her gowns, her way with the piano—which she knew was mediocre at best, despite the best efforts of Miss Grantley's fine music teachers. He sat closer, his touches lingered. He had even sent her a bouquet before the ball, which she 'accidentally' forgot.

She had no time for such things, not with a man who made her feel so strangely—itchy. As if she wanted to jump up and run away.

Just like now. He hadn't yet seen her. She tried to pull Chris deeper into the crowd of the dancers as she noticed Lord Thursby was scanning the crowd over the Marchioness's head.

'Oh, no,' Diana whispered.

'What is it?' Chris asked.

'Just someone I would rather not talk to at the moment.'

'An unwanted suitor? That sounds interesting,' he said, infuriatingly contrary. 'Which one is it? Should I call him out for pestering you? I will, if he's not too large and intimidating.'

Diana laughed. 'It's that man over there, the one talking to your aunt's friend, the Marchioness. And no duelling yet. All he's really done is send flowers and compliment my non-existent musical skills. I just—can't like him, somehow.'

Chris frowned as he studied the man. 'Thursby? Really? He has some kind of investment scheme in India he says he can let some of us in on later.'

An Indian investment scheme? Was that why Thursby had started coming to her father's house so often? That sounded strange to her. Surely such ideas always ended in calamity? 'Oh, no, Chris. You aren't thinking of doing that, are you?'

'It sounds simple enough and Thursby says we're sure to double our money very quickly.'

'I don't think…'

The dance ended and as they swirled to a stop at the edge of the dance floor, they found themselves next to Emily and her partner.

Emily looked quite pretty, with her cheeks pink with enjoyment and laughter, her amber-brown eyes glowing. Diana quite envied her gown, too, for with only a father, Em had far more control over her own wardrobe. Her mint-green gown, trimmed with black-velvet rosettes, with black and green plumes in her hair, made her look far more elegant and sophisticated than other ladies their age.

'Oh, Di! Isn't it splendid?' Emily said. 'Such a wonderful orchestra.'

'Only because you're the best dancer here and could find rhythm in any old tune,' Christopher said.

Emily laughed. 'As can you. Shall we, then, Chris? Show them how a *schottische* is done?'

'We shall,' Christopher said and took her arm to swirl her away.

As they disappeared back into the sparkling melee of the dance, Diana looked around. Her mother sat along the row of gilded chaperons' chairs by the silk-papered wall, gossiping with two of her friends. At the other end of the room, glimpsed between flower arrangements and groups of laughing people, she saw Lord Thursby. She felt suddenly trapped, caught between two forces she didn't want to face yet.

On impulse, she spun around and dashed out of the ballroom via the nearest side door. She found herself in a small, domed hall, also draped in carpets of flowers but blessedly quiet. There were only a few people there, whispering together, sipping champagne, the music muffled beyond the door.

She hurried down a flight of stairs to the next floor down, where there was the card room, the billiards room, and a large sitting room that had been turned into the ladies' withdrawing room. She heard a burst of giggles from that chamber and she knew she could easily join them, but she suddenly only wanted to be alone. To hear her own thoughts for a minute.

Unlike most London houses, including her own parents' narrow dwelling on Cavendish Square, Waverton House was vast, four storeys of chambers like a series of jewel boxes, sparkling with treasures. She went down one more set of stairs and peeked through a half-open doorway to find a library. Perfect.

The silence was heavy, deep and echoing after the hum of the ballroom. She could almost hear herself think again. She wandered along the rows of books, studying the gilt titles on the leather spines, the paintings on the panelled walls between the shelves.

Next to the curtained window nook was a table laid out with the day's newspapers. She studied the headlines. They were all about the Paris Exposition, of course, swooning praise for the delicious cafés, the wonders of the pavilions for the arts, the exotic mock-souks, the fashionable ladies arriving to parade along the Champ de Mars.

A loud voice suddenly burst the silence, making Diana jump.

'Oh, please, just listen to me this one last time! Don't you owe me that at least? For all we were to each other?'

It was a woman's voice, low and urgent, filled with choking tears, and it was coming from the corridor outside. Moving closer to the library with every word. Diana held her breath, hoping whoever it was would just keep moving past.

'Laura, what we had was over long ago,' a man answered, weariness barely hidden in his soft, kind tone. 'We can't revive it now. You know that.'

'Why not?' the woman demanded. 'Everything has changed this time. It could be even better! I have missed you so much…'

To Diana's horror, the quarrel wasn't moving away. The door swung open and she instinctively dived behind the heavy velvet window curtains before they could see her and they all faced a most embarrassing scene. It seemed to be a night for hiding out.

'We should return to the party,' the man said, still so calm and steady, so horribly quiet. Diana couldn't help but wince for the woman. 'Neither of us wants a scandal.'

'Of course that's not what I want! Some horrid, shabby court case like Bertie Wales and the Aylesfords. That won't happen now. We're both free!' the woman said sweetly. 'Oh, my darling Will, don't you remember what those heavenly days at Beresford Hall were like? It could be that way all the time now.'

Quite against her will, Diana found herself rather curious. It sounded like one of those delicious French novels they had once passed around at Miss Grantley's! She cautiously peeked around the edge of the curtain.

The couple stood near the carved onyx fireplace, the lamplight throwing them into silhouette. The woman was Lady Smythe-Tomas, Diana could tell that from her luminous champagne gown, the golden swirl of jewel-bedecked hair. She reached out with her elegant gloved hands to grasp the man by his lapels, her fingers curling against him sinuously. Diana was quite surprised she would have to beg any man for his attentions; they all seemed to fall right at her feet.

Who was this man? He surely had to be vastly attractive. Her curiosity growing, she pushed the curtain back just a bit more so she could see his face.

She gasped and quickly stifled the sound with her satin-covered fingers. It was Sir William Blakely.

Sir William *was* handsome, of course, arrestingly so. The perfect counterpoint to Lady Smythe-Tomas's golden, sunny beauty, with his glossy dark hair and fathomless brown eyes. If Diana was a casting agency for the theatres, she could do no better than those two for looks. But he was so solemn! So dedicated to his career.

Or maybe he wasn't always so solemn. She remembered him laughing by the lake, his damp shirt clinging to his shoulders, all bright and full of youth in the sunshine. Surely *that* man could have a passionate affair.

'Laura, this can't go on,' he said, still so calm, so cool. Diana wondered why the lady hadn't slapped him yet, for staying so unruffled about the whole passionate business.

'Why not? Do you not still find me beautiful?'

'Of course you are beautiful. Your photo in every shop window tells you that. And you deserve more than a man buried in his work.'

'But surely I could help you with that, too! Every diplomat needs a hostess.' She leaned towards him with an enticing smile, her fingers smoothing the satin lapel she had crushed. 'And there is always this…'

She went up on her toes and tried to press her lips to his. But the promised kiss didn't last long at all, the merest brush. He pushed her away, gently but firmly, his hands unwinding her arms from around his neck and holding her away. 'I need to return to the ballroom.'

Lady Smythe-Tomas's pretty face creased in a fierce pout. 'Why?' she cried. 'Because some young, sweet deb is waiting to waltz with you? Or, no—it's Lady Lammington, isn't it? She's always wanted you for herself!'

'Because I will be missed soon and so will you. Please, Laura. Be reasonable.'

'Very well.' Her tone turned cajoling again. She ran one fingertip up his arm. 'But only if you agree to have tea with me one day this week.'

'I've been quite busy since I returned to London, you know that.'

'Just one tiny little visit. You can even bring your brother Chris if you need a chaperon.'

'No, Laura,' he said, very firmly. Then he added something too low for Diana to hear. Whatever he said must have pleased Lady Smythe-Tomas, or at least placated her, for Diana heard the library door slam and there was silence again. They were gone.

Perhaps she had been right in her very first assessment of him on his visit to Miss Grantley's—he was gloriously handsome but rather chilly, intimidating. Only—only once he must have known passion, if he'd had an affair with a woman like Lady Smythe-Tomas. People were always so strange. It was easier to capture them in fictional stories than in real life.

She waited for a few more breaths and then slipped out of her hiding place. Only to find she was not quite alone.

Sir William stood by the fireplace, starring into the empty grate, a frown pressing his handsome lips together, his eyes narrowed as if he was deep in thought. He glanced up, and those dark eyes widened. He seemed as startled to see her as she was to see him. She dropped her reticule, flustered, and quickly scooped it up again. Her heart pounded to see him again, so loud she could barely hear anything else. She feared he could hear it, too, that her chagrin showed on her face.

'Miss Martin,' he said. She dared to glance up at him and saw that he was just as handsome as he had been at Miss Grantley's, but he had changed, too. His face was bronzed by the Indian sun, set in harder lines, his eyes shadowed. It only made him even more intriguing, blast him. 'Whatever are you doing in here?'

'Oh, I—just needed a breath of air. And, um...' She gestured around the room helplessly. No etiquette class at Miss Grantley's had ever taught her what to do in such a situation. She was angry at him for brushing off a woman who obviously had deep feelings for him. All the romantic novels she had read told her the heartbreak a woman like Lady Smythe-Tomas must be feeling in the face of such carelessness! She was also burningly embarrassed to have been caught watching the scene. And she wanted to burst into strange, hysterical laughter. All at once.

Maybe it was because she had seen the effect William had on Lady Smythe-Tomas, on the poor woman's sad feelings. It was all most confusing.

'I was reading about Paris,' she said weakly.

'Paris?' he asked. And she finally saw some emotion in those dark eyes that always seemed to see everything without giving anything away. She saw a flicker of—bafflement.

'Yes. The tower, the art displays, the Turkish souk.' She remembered that Christopher had said

Sir William was soon to be sent to Paris himself. 'But you must know all about that.'

'Indeed I do. And I can see why that might be more attractive than a crowded ballroom. But why hide here?'

'I just—came across it. I thought it was empty. So it was, for a while.'

'You just came across it?' he asked doubtfully.

Diana suddenly wondered if he thought *she* was there for an assignation, as well. She felt her cheeks burn brighter, one of the banes of her life to blush so fiercely that it clashed with her hair. 'Yes. Your aunt's house is a rather confusing place, though you seem to know your way quite well.'

'As you said—some times quiet is what a person needs.' He stepped closer and Diana noticed his eyes were not entirely brown. They glowed with flecks of green and gold, like a primeval forest. *Poor Lady S-T.* 'I suppose your mother must be looking for you, Miss Martin.'

The room suddenly felt much too warm, too close. Diana looked away, clutching her hands tightly in the folds of her skirt. 'So she will. I hope—well, perhaps you needn't mention you saw me here?'

A smile tugged at the corner of his lips, but he seemed unable to quite let it free. Diana wondered what would happen when he *did* smile. Probably his good looks then reached dangerous levels, so he had to keep it reined in. 'I suppose I needn't. But secrets can go both ways.'

Diana suddenly remembered why he was there—Lady Smythe-Tomas, past love affairs. She blushed even more. 'I don't know Lady Smythe-Tomas and have no desire to gossip about her.'

'Thank you. It was an—unfortunate matter that was over a long time ago.' His words were strong and steady, but he tugged at his tie a bit, as if he was embarrassed by any loss of control.

She could tell he was not a man accustomed to having to explain himself. He had a reputation for steadiness and discretion in his work and in his family. 'I'm sure.' She felt a sudden burst of courage and added, 'You should be kind to her. She seemed very upset.'

He gave her a small, startled quirk of a smile. 'I dare say she will soon get over it.'

Diana doubted it.

To her surprise, he held out his hand as if to shake hers, quite as if she was his peer and they were sealing a bargain. She rather liked that small gesture, as she was so tired of being dismissed as just a silly deb. She wanted to do a job and be taken seriously at it, just as he was.

She laid her gloved palm against his and for an instant, their fingers tightened around each other. His grasp was strong and gentle, warm, and she found she wanted to hold on to him just a bit longer. Just a bit closer. It was just like their first, fleeting meeting at Miss Grantley's, she felt so flustered, so silly. She didn't want to look away.

'Thank you,' he said, letting her go.

Diana nodded and turned towards the door. As she reached for the handle, she glanced back at Sir William to find he watched her. His face was mostly in shadow, his hands clasped behind him, and she couldn't read his expression.

'Perhaps you really are being a little unfair to her,' she said impulsively. 'She does seem to care for you.'

A frown flickered over his brow again. 'Care for me? Miss Martin, I fear you mistake the situation.'

'Do I? I *am* young and haven't seen the world as you have, but I'm not entirely ignorant.'

His brow arched as if he was surprised. As if she had startled a reaction out of him. 'I never supposed you were. You went to Miss Grantley's

school with my cousin, didn't you? Alexandra
says you are very clever.'

'She's a good friend. I was only clever in French
and lawn tennis. But I do read a great deal and
Lady Smythe-Tomas does seem—well, very fond
of you.'

He laughed and it sounded rusty and sharp-
edged, as if he hadn't used that laugh in a long
time. But it sounded so warm and soft, she wanted
to hear it again. Make him laugh again.

So *that* was what Lady Smythe-Tomas saw.
Diana could tell he was trouble.

'Oh, Miss Martin. I suppose that is one way of
putting it.'

'Well,' Diana said again. Her vocabulary seemed
to have shrunk considerably in his presence.
'Thank you. For not telling on me.'

She hurried through the door and let it close
behind her. Only once she was safely away from
the library did she let herself stop and take a deep
breath of air, or at least as deep as her new corset
would let her.

She closed her eyes, and saw *him* there, his
rueful smile, his intriguing eyes. What an unusual man he was indeed. She could really see
why even a sophisticate like Lady Smythe-Tomas
would be so infatuated with him.

Chapter Two

What a very strange girl, William thought as he stared at the closed door of the library where Diana Martin had stood only a moment before. Her hurried patter of heeled shoes had faded, but he thought he could still smell the trace of her sweet lilac perfume, feel the satin of her glove on his palm.

He stared down at his hand, remembering the warmth of her touch, her slender fingers curled around his for the merest instant. He felt something he hadn't felt in ages. An urge to laugh. For just a moment he had forgotten Laura, forgotten his work, forgotten everything but Miss Martin's smile. He remembered her from his visit to Alex at Miss Grantley's. She had been so sweet, a blush on her face, her words stammered a bit, a slightly gawky, charming schoolgirl. Now she

seemed to have blossomed into an autumn goddess with her red hair, her bright eyes, her enthusiasm that seemed to make everything turn new
again. At least in looks. When she talked, she became that awkward schoolgirl again and he feared
for her in the ballroom jungles of London. The
poor, sweet girl.

He only wished she hadn't seen him at his very
worst. His country-house party tryst with Laura
seemed so long ago now, after India and all that
had happened, a memory shrouded in wine and
youthful passion. He had almost forgotten about
it, until he saw her in the ballroom. To his surprise, she had begged to talk to him in private.

Much to his shock, she wanted to renew their old
liaison. She was still beautiful, of course, maybe
even more than she had been at that house party.
Yet there was something strange about her, about
the over-bright glow in her catlike eyes, her desperate grasp on his arm. He wanted to help her,
but he knew very well he couldn't go back to her.
He was a much different man now.

The man he had been back then, younger and
wilder, just starting his career, probably would
have looked at someone like Diana Martin and
seen a pretty but shallow deb. Indeed, he *had*

thought that when he and Chris visited Alex at school.

He found he didn't want to return to the crowd just yet. Didn't want to lose the fleeting, bright, silly glow Miss Martin had left behind, as sweet and summery as her lilac perfume. He wandered over to the table where the newspapers were displayed and scanned the headlines about the Exposition.

William did see how an eager, enthusiastic young lady like Diana Martin would be fascinated by it all. The whole world gathered in beautiful Paris, the art and fashion, the food and theatre. He hoped she would get to see it.

Then he glimpsed a grainy photograph in one corner of the *Mail*. A tall, bearded man in a pale tunic and loose trousers, standing on the deck of a ship with three ladies in elaborate embroidered saris.

The Maharajah Singh Lep with his wives, boarding HMS Princess Augusta *to make his way to the Paris Exposition, where he will visit the Indian Pavilion and see the wondrous sapphire, the Eastern Star. On display thanks to the generosity of the Duke of Waverton.*

The Star was once worn by the Maharajah's grandmother...

Singh Lep—who was no doubt trailing trouble in his wake, as he had in Bombay with his investment offers, his proffered and then withdrawn friendship. His grandmother had once ruled for him in his kingdom and had sold the Star to William's uncle and then sold the kingdom. The man was understandably angry at what had happened. But did he blame his grandmother—or someone else?

And now he was going to be in Paris. The article said it was merely a pleasure trip and listed other dignitaries on their way to climb Eiffel's tower and eat ices at his cafés—including the Prince and Princess of Wales. But William was sure there was more to it than that.

He stared out the window where Diana had been hidden and for a moment he didn't see the rain-soaked London street. He saw the baking sun of India, smelled the spices and heady perfumes of a world he had left far behind. A world no one could even begin to fully understand.

The door suddenly opened, and William glanced over his shoulder, ready to send Laura away again if had she returned. Or maybe he was half-hoping it would be Miss Martin?

In any case, it was neither lady, but his brother who stood there. Will laughed at himself and folded the paper away.

'Hello, Chris,' he said. 'Come to hide out here, too?'

Christopher grinned and closed the door behind him. 'Our parents have arrived,' he said and that was all that was needed to explain the fact that even Christopher, who rarely cracked a book if he could help it, would hide in a library. William had taken lodgings since returning to London, only taking a few dinners at his parents' town house as he had done earlier that evening, but Chris still lived there, in that suffocating place that hadn't changed a bit since they were boys.

'Sorry about that. Mother must have changed her mind after all,' William said.

'She sent me to find you,' Christopher said, carelessly scanning the paintings hung on the walls, a series of indifferent landscapes and a few really fine French pieces. 'One of the footmen said you came this way.'

Will wondered if the footman had told Chris

who he was in the library *with*. Perhaps his hope for no scandal was misplaced.

'You visited Alex at school more than I did,' he said. 'Did you come to know Miss Diana Martin very well?'

Christopher looked at him with a surprised expression. 'Di? She's a corker. Lots of fun, but sensible. Our aunt thinks she's been a good friend to Alex.'

Chris knew her well? William frowned as he wondered if his brother was fond of her, had designs on her. 'You're friends, then?'

Christopher shrugged and William felt unaccountably relieved to see no spark of passion in his brother's eyes at the thought of her. Chris was always quite open about his interests and always had a beautiful woman to write poems to. 'I suppose we are. I see her at these boring old bashes with Alex and their friend Emily Fortescue, and they make it all a little less dull.' His bored expression suddenly changed, his eyes widening. 'Why? The footman did say you came this way with a lady. I hope it wasn't Miss Martin.'

'No, I didn't come here with Miss Martin. I saw her in the ballroom. She seems quite charming.'

'Charming? I guess she is. Pretty, too.' Chris

stepped closer, as if he thought he could read Will's mind. But Will had too much experience hiding his thoughts; his job depended on it. 'Are you interested? You could certainly do worse and Mother's matchmaking fever could go to you for a while.'

His brother's avid expression was so comical William had to laugh. 'Does she want you to marry so much, then?' He had hoped that maybe his parents' own wreck of a marriage would have cooled their mother's ardour for matchmaking, but it seemed not. Maybe she wanted company in misery.

'She begins to say that if I won't go into law or join the army, an heiress is the only way to set me up in life.'

'Maybe an American dollar princess?'

'I don't have a title or a crumbling ancient castle to offer a lady like that. And the ladies I *do* like...' He suddenly turned away. 'Well, Mother will just have to go on thinking I'm just a terrible wastrel who can't even marry properly.'

'She doesn't know about your work?'

'Of course not. I wouldn't be much use if anyone *did* know, would I? But you and Diana...'

'I hate to disappoint, but I'm not in a position

to marry now, either. We both saw the effect our father's work had on his marriage. No one needs a repeat of that. I shall have to admire Miss Martin from a distance.'

Christopher spun a globe, watching its oceans and continents blur in front of them. 'Better for her, I'm sure. I think Thursby is after her, but she doesn't seem to like him much.'

William frowned. 'Thursby?' He certainly hoped not, not with what he had recently learned about the man.

Chris shrugged. 'Then if it wasn't Di in here earlier, who was it?'

'Just a bit of unfinished business.'

'Really?' Chris's golden brow arched. '*You*, Will? Whoever could have guessed there were such skeletons in your wardrobe. I suppose it's finished now?'

'Quite,' William said shortly.

Chris seemed to realise he wouldn't learn anything more and turned back to the door. 'We should get back to the party, then, before our aunt sends a search party for both of us.'

William nodded, and started to follow. He noticed a small, pale square on the floor near the window. Curious, he picked it up. It was a leather-bound notebook, stamped with the gilt initials D.F.M. Diana Martin, maybe?

He flipped through the pages, glimpsing pencil sketches, mostly of hats and gowns, and snatches of words.

Champagne...pearls...peacock colours.

From the back, a small newspaper clipping fluttered out.

Writer wanted. Paris assignment. Must be fashionable and have a way with words. Portfolio preferred. Please apply to the Ladies' Weekly *offices.*

Well, well. William remembered Diana saying how much she wanted to see Paris. Maybe she was doing something about it. How very modern of her.

He smiled and tucked the notebook inside his evening jacket. He would have to make sure it was returned to its owner. Very soon.

'There you are, Di! Where did you go off to?' Emily called as Diana slipped back into the ballroom.

She hoped she hadn't been missed by anyone but her friends. She scanned the crowd and was quite relieved to see her mother still in her chair and Lord Thursby nowhere to be seen. Neither was Lady Smythe-Tomas.

She turned to smile at Emily, whose cheeks were pink from all her dancing. 'Just needed a bit of air.'

'Well, you didn't miss much, except the fact that this ballroom has become even more of a crush and someone tore the ribbon on my hem with their clumsy dancing shoes. But no drunken fisticuffs or dramatic broken engagements yet.'

Diana laughed weakly and took an offered glass of liquid. She sipped a bit and winced in disappointment. Lemon squash, not champagne. 'That sounds rather dull.'

'Yes, but the dancing is lovely. I'll say this for the Duchess—she always hires the best orchestras.' Emily reached out and plucked something from Diana's hair. She held it up; it was a shred of newsprint. 'Where did you find this bit of air?'

Diana thought quickly. It was always best to be honest, even if it wasn't all the way. 'Oh—in the library. It was nice and quiet, and I was able to read a bit about Paris in the Duke's newspapers.'

Emily leaned closer, her eyes wide. 'Any word yet?' she whispered. 'From the magazine?'

Diana shook her head, feeling the sick excitement, fear and hope deep in the pit of her stomach that had sat there ever since she mailed off the letter of application. 'I have an interview tomorrow with the editor. Isn't it amazing?'

'An interview?' Emily clapped her hands in delight. She knew more about running a business than anyone Diana knew, male or female, after years of helping at her father's offices. She took it all very seriously and had given Diana a great deal of advice ever since Di decided she was the best confidante. 'Shouldn't you be at home resting, then? You have to be sharp tomorrow.'

'Oh, I know. But Mama would never have let me miss the Waverton ball and I'm much too nervous to sleep. I was hoping to get a bit of fashion news to add to my portfolio. I did write a bit, you see...' She opened her reticule to take out the notebook to show Emily. To her shock, she found only a handkerchief and her discarded dance card. 'Blast,' she gasped, remembering dropping the bag.

'What is it?'

'I've lost the notebook.'

'What's amiss?' Alex asked as she appeared

from the crowd and hurried to their side. She always did seem to sense the feelings of the people around her, especially if they were distressed, even from across the room.

'Di lost her notebook,' Emily said.

'No!' Alex cried. She and Emily knew all the bits and pieces in that book, so carefully gathered and recorded. They had even helped with much of it. 'Here in the ballroom? But anyone could find it.'

Diana shook her head. 'I had it in the library. I must have dropped it in there.' In the library— with William. What if *he* found it? What would he think?

'Diana! There you are at last,' she heard her mother call. This time there was no evading her.

Diana forced a smile on to her lips and turned to see her mother making her way towards them. With her was Lord Thursby.

Diana had to admit he was handsome, with his fair hair pomaded to a shine, his stylish moustache and well-cut clothes. He smiled charmingly and was solicitous as he led her mother through the crowd. But she wished he would just—just go away!

Yet she knew very well there was no chance of that.

'I will go look for it,' Alexandra whispered. She and Emily vanished beyond the dance floor.

'Diana,' her mother demanded again, 'where on earth have you been?'

'I was just—dancing. We're at a ball, you know, Mama,' she said, trying to laugh carelessly. She fanned herself vigorously, wishing Lord Thursby was not watching her so closely.

'Lord Thursby was looking for you. He says you promised him the supper dance,' her mother said, reaching out to fuss with Diana's tulle-edged sleeve. She drew away, wondering if she had newsprint caught there, too.

'The supper dance?' she said. That meant spending the midnight meal by his side. 'Oh, Mama. I'm afraid my head rather aches and I was hoping we could go home soon.'

Her mother's eyes narrowed. 'Diana...' she snapped.

But Lord Thursby intervened smoothly, smiling politely. 'That is a vast disappointment for me, Miss Martin, but I would never wish to cause you a moment's discomfort. Please, let me send for your carriage. I can also ask our hostess if she has a headache powder.'

'That is kind of you, Lord Thursby,' Diana said cautiously.

'Indeed,' her mother said. 'Thank you.'

Lord Thursby bowed and hurried away. As he spoke quietly to the Duchess, Diana saw William and Chris come back into the room. For just an instant, before the crowd closed around them, she saw how much Sir William stood out from everyone around him, an island of watchfulness and dignity, so dark and handsome. Was this really the same man Lady Smythe-Tomas was so ardently chasing? Such intriguing contradictions.

He caught her eyes and gave her a small nod, making her feel suddenly flushed and fluttery. She spun around, waving her fan in front of her face.

Her mother grasped Diana's arm, her fingers hard through her satin glove. 'Mama,' Diana gasped and yanked her arm back.

'You should make a tiny bit of an effort, Diana,' her mother said through a gritted-teeth smile. 'He is quite nice, you know, with a fine future ahead of him.'

Diana rubbed at her arm. She glanced back to see if she could see Sir William again, but he was gone. 'Mama, perhaps there are things I want to see before I'm married.'

'What sort of things? You can see whatever you like, go wherever you like, after you're married! Just as I did. What choice is there?'

Diana thought of men like her father, like William Blakely, travelling, doing their bit for their country, seeing the world. Making a difference. 'I could be like Miss Bird, or Miss Butler. Travel, write. Do good works.'

Her mother snorted. 'Such hoydens. That wouldn't work for you, Diana. You have been well brought up. Did we not send you to the best school? Make sure you had the best friends? Now we only want to see you happily settled before we are old. Is that too much to ask?'

'I want to be happy, too,' Diana said, but her mother wasn't listening. Lord Thursby had returned to tell them their carriage was on its way.

'Oh, how kind you are,' her mother said with a laugh. 'So reassuring to have someone to rely on thus.'

'It is the least I can do, Mrs Martin, for how kind with his advice your husband has been.' Lord Thursby offered Diana his arm and she saw no choice but to take it. She held it lightly, trying to smile, as he led them to the staircase hall where a footman waited with their cloaks.

'I hope you will be recovered enough for me to call on you tomorrow,' Lord Thursby said.

Diana suddenly remembered her interview the next day. Nothing could be allowed to stop that! 'Perhaps in the afternoon?'

'The afternoon?' he said. 'Not the usual morning hour?'

'Yes. I—I shall probably need to rest and recover my strength in the morning.'

He nodded solicitously. 'Of course. I know how delicate you ladies can be after such a busy evening as this.'

'How understanding you are, Lord Thursby,' her mother chirped, practically pushing Diana out the door towards their waiting carriage. 'We shall look forward to seeing you tomorrow.'

Just as they were leaving, a procession of carriages arrived behind them. From the grandest stepped a man unmistakable in his healthy girth and greying blond beard, a beautiful lady in an ivory satin and ostrich feather cloak on his arm. The Prince and Princess of Wales. Diana just hoped her mother did not see them and make them go back.

* * *

On the journey home, Diana knew her mother was chattering about Lord Thursby and his 'gentlemanly behaviour', and the splendours of the ball. But Diana only paid enough attention to nod and smile at the right moments. Her real thoughts were far away—with tomorrow's interview, with plans to persuade her parents to let her go to Paris if she got the job. It would be a very delicate task.

And, she had to admit, her thoughts wouldn't seem to leave William Blakely. How wonderful it had been in those few moments alone with him in the dimly lit library, so far away from everyone and everything else. How she wished she could have stayed there longer, listening to him talk! Those dark eyes watching her...

Once they were home, she managed to plead her headache and escape to her room. There she took out the portfolio she had managed to compile: sample essays about fashion, etiquette and bits of society gossip. Losing her notebook at such a moment was a consternation, but hopefully not a disaster. She could remember enough to reconstruct the evening's observations and hopefully Alexandra would find the notebook itself.

She found another folder, stuffed full of old drawings and notes, and beneath a stack of flower studies was her old sketch of William Blakely at the lake behind Miss Grantley's. His smile still glowed from the faded paper, the lines of his face still elegant, classical. He hadn't changed so much after all, yet so many other things seemed to.

She took out another copy of the job listing and carefully read over the words.

Writer wanted. Paris assignment. Must be fashionable and have a way with words. Portfolio preferred. Please apply to the Ladies' Weekly *offices.*

She closed her eyes and whispered, 'Please let it happen,' as she envisaged in her mind what it could all be like. Walking by the Seine, sipping wine at a café on the famous new tower, visiting Monsieur Worth's studio itself.

But now, much to her shock, when she imagined dancing at the Moulin Galette, her partner wasn't some faceless, dashing Frenchman. It was William Blakely, smiling down at her in the red and gold lights of the lanterns, spinning her through the night.

Which was most strange, for Sir William didn't seem at all like a spinning sort of gentleman…

Chapter Three

Diana hurried down the pavement, clutching at the leather valise containing her sketches and the portfolio of 'articles' she had cobbled together to try to impress the magazine editor. She could barely hear the commotion of the London streets around her, the clatter of carriage and omnibus wheels, the shouts and cries and laughter, the shriek of the bobby's whistle. All she could focus on was getting to her interview on time and what she would say when she got there.

She waited on a corner to cross the street, caught a glimpse of herself in a shopfront window and straightened her hat. She had dressed in the most stylish yet simple thing she owned, a tailored russet-red suit with leg-o'-mutton sleeves and narrow lapels, with a patent-leather yellow belt that matched the colour of her shirtwaist. Her felt hat was a matching red with a yellow-checked ribbon. She felt terribly crisp and efficient, which she hoped covered up her giddiness from not being able to sleep a wink after the ball.

If only she hadn't lost her new notes about the fashions at the Waverton ball! She had stayed up until dawn writing new descriptions, but she worried they weren't quite as vivid as they should be.

She also worried that William Blakely seemed to slip too much into her memories of the ball, always getting in the way of everything else! The dratted man. How had he come to be so—so distracting?

The crowd surged forward and Diana went with them as they flowed towards Trafalgar Square. The *Ladies' Weekly* offices were there, and she felt her excitement flutter even higher as she glimpsed the stone tower of its office building. Everyone around her seemed intent on their own errands, all black suits and tailored dresses, leather cases and intent expressions.

The difference between that workaday crowd and the people at the Waverton ball was amazing. Diana felt at the same moment out of place and exactly where she belonged. It was most strange.

She rushed around the corner and nearly

bumped into a man hurrying in the opposite direction. His bowler hat tumbled to the pavement.

'Oh, I'm so sorry!' she cried and bent to retrieve the hat before it could roll into the street. He reached for it at the same time and they almost knocked each other to the ground. Diana's own hat tilted over her eyes.

Flustered and embarrassed, she pushed it back and glanced up at the man, who was laughing. To her shock, she saw it was William Blakely, looking not at all dignified and solemn now. His hair, rumpled by the loss of his hat, waved over his brow in an unruly dark comma and she glimpsed a dimple—a dimple!—in his cheek as he laughed even harder.

'Sir William,' she gasped. 'What a surprise. I do beg your pardon. Again.'

'Good day, Miss Martin,' he said, his laughter fading to a wry smile. 'You are looking quite well this morning.' He took her arm and helped her up, gently brushing the dust from her sleeve. She felt her cheeks turn warm under his gaze, his touch.

'It was quite a lovely party last night,' she said, feeling rather silly. A *lovely party*? After she had run into this man in the most ridiculous circumstances now—twice? 'In the end.'

'You're up quite early. I see dancing 'til dawn couldn't tire you.' He gave her a teasing smile and there was that dimple again.

Diana laughed. She just couldn't help it. 'Well, I admit I do have an early appointment. I really should be on my way.'

'Let me escort you, then.'

Escort her? Then she really never would think clearly at her interview! 'That is kind, but I'm sure you must be getting to your own work.' Then a terrible thought suddenly struck her, making some of the smiling glow fade. Maybe he was not on his way to work. Maybe he had a meeting, an assignation, with someone like Lady Smythe-Tomas.

His smile turned quizzical, as if he sensed her thoughts. 'Indeed I should, but I'm glad to be delayed in such a delightful way. It gives me a chance to return this.' He reached into his coat pocket and took out a small book.

'My notebook!' Diana cried. So that was where it had been. Had he found it when she dropped her reticule in the library? Had he *read* it? Even the silly gossipy bits? How ridiculous he must think her, then.

'You seemed to have misplaced it last night. I meant to give it to Alexandra, but I'm afraid she was rather distracted by the Prince and Princess's arrival. I'm glad I could return it to its rightful owner so quickly.'

'That's kind of you,' she said again. Diana quickly replaced it in her valise. 'I did wonder where it went.'

'I shouldn't keep you any longer. If you won't let me escort you, perhaps I could give you a cup of tea after your errand? There's a rather nice little teashop around the corner from here. To make up in small part for knocking you to the ground.'

Diana peeked up at him from beneath the brim of her hat, curious and excited and unsure all at the same time. She knew she shouldn't, that her confused feelings towards him made him rather dangerous at such a moment in her life. But she found herself smiling and saying, 'That sounds most pleasant. Thank you.'

After all, it was a day to be daring, to leap before she looked. What was a cup of tea after a job interview? A cup of tea with Sir William Blakely. After a job interview. Two things she would never have thought she could ever do.

He smiled, though there was no dimple that time. Diana felt a pang of disappointment. 'Excellent, Miss Martin. Here is my card. My office

is just on the next street, you can see it from here,'
he said, indicating a quiet, discreet Georgian mansion, all elegant red brick and white stone, plain
except for the bright flag above the doorway. 'Just
call on the receptionist in the hall when you've
finished your errand.'

'I will.'

His gaze flickered behind her, a small frown
creasing his brow. 'Is your maid with you?'

'I…' Diana made herself laugh. A maid would
have been in the way at the magazine—and would
run right back to her parents with the tale before
she could decide how to frame it all. She hadn't
been thinking of what would happen if she met
an acquaintance, especially not Sir William. 'No,
not today. It is nearly the twentieth century, Sir
William! We must step into the modern era some
time.'

He smiled wryly and placed his hat back on his
head. Diana rather missed his glossy dark hair,
that wonderful air of informality. 'Indeed. Good
luck on your errand, Miss Martin. I do hope to
see you later.'

She nodded and he tipped his hat as he took his
leave. She watched him walk towards his office,

his stride strong and confident though not at all showy.

What a strange man, she thought. So hard to read. Strange, and—and quite wonderful, too. A puzzle. And she did like puzzles.

But she couldn't worry about Sir William at the moment. She had a task to complete, one she had been waiting to do for ever, it seemed. She squared her shoulders and marched ahead, clutching her valise in both hands, trying not to knock anyone else down in her path.

She did wonder, though, if he *had* read the notebook. If so, what had he thought? She wavered between wanting his advice on her work and being rather blush-faced to think he had seen her scribbles. Did he think her frivolous for such detailed descriptions of gowns and party arrangements? Maybe he wouldn't, if he knew what she was really doing with them.

The offices of *Ladies' Weekly* was on the third floor of a rather nondescript but solid building, in a corner tower. She made her way past rows of young women at typewriters and stacks of papers and photos waiting to be made into articles. The click of the typewriters blended with shouts and cries, and the warm air smelled of newsprint and coffee. It was unlike anything Diana had ever seen before, entirely different from the flower-scented hush of her parents' house, and it was utterly thrilling.

She was led to a small corner office, where a be-whiskered, harried-looking man sat behind a cluttered desk, dictating to an equally harried-looking lady in spectacles and a pink-striped shirtwaist.

'Ah, so this is the Paris girl!' the man shouted. 'Not before time, I'll say. Come in, come in.'

'I...' Confused, Diana glanced at the clock on the wall. 'I thought my appointment was at ten?'

The woman chuckled. 'You are quite punctual, Miss Martin. He means on time for Paris. Our last correspondent there decided to get married instead of going to the Exposition and has rather left us in the lurch. We need a replacement right away.'

'You're not engaged, are you?' he barked.

'I—no,' Diana murmured, thinking of Lord Thursby. And of Sir William.

'It would mean you would be in charge of the coverage rather than assisting,' the woman said. 'We do have such a small staff. I hope that would not be a problem?'

Diana swallowed hard. She had never written

professionally before, but she had wanted this so much for so long. Surely she could do it. 'Of course not.'

'*The Lady* and the *Mail* are already there, curse them,' the man said, shoving a stack of papers on to the floor. 'We need to scoop them and soon! You look like a young lady who knows the fashions of Paris.'

'I do have lots of ideas for articles,' Diana said quickly, digging out her portfolio from her valise. 'The new sporting clothes, for tennis and bicycling. Worth and Doucet…'

'But do you have connections?' he demanded. 'That's the question. Can you get into all those fancy parties in Paris? Give our readers the inside look?'

'I…' she began. Of course she could. Couldn't she? After all, as her mother said, she had gone to the best school, made the best friends. Surely she knew how to get what she wanted, no matter what her parents said.

'What he means is—can you tell our readers things no one else can know? Describe gowns no one else has yet seen, things like that?' the woman said.

'I do have an invitation to the opening of the

new Gordston's Department Store on the Champs-Élysées,' Diana said. It was actually *Alexandra's* invitation, but her friend had passed it on, too shy to face it. Malcolm Gordston was a dashing celebrity, handsome beyond words they said, a man who had risen from poverty in Scotland to the height of elegant riches because he knew how to give the stylish world what it craved. 'And I know how to get to the very top level of Monsieur Eiffel's tower for a moment all alone. Only a very select few are allowed there, you know.'

The man and woman exchanged a long glance. 'Excellent,' he said. 'You're hired, Miss Martin. Can you start next week?'

Diana quickly accepted and floated out of the building on such a glittering cloud she hardly knew how her feet carried her down the street. The crowd on the pavement swirled past, buffeting her on all sides, yet she barely noticed them.

She was going to Paris. She was going to write. Never mind that she now had to persuade her parents. She had a job.

She walked a few more steps and glanced around. The crowd was the same as it had been earlier, a hurrying, sombre group in dark suits, not paying her any more attention than the stone lions on the square. She wanted to dance, to twirl, to shout out her excitement. But everyone else had their own work to get to and it was still too early to call on Emily or Alexandra, even though she would have dearly loved their advice. She needed someone to tell, someone to give her sensible words about her situation.

She suddenly remembered William Blakely. He had asked her to tea! When they first met, his seriousness, his quiet watchfulness, had made her feel uncertain, too girlish, too giggly. But then she had seen that other side to him, that flash of humour, those hidden depths. Maybe someone like that was just what she needed right now?

And she would get to see him again.

She turned the corner towards that elegant Georgian mansion, and hurried up the stone steps before she could change her mind and run away. It did seem like a day for bold moves. She had a job now! Surely a cup of tea with William Blakely would be only one more daring step?

She pushed open the door and found herself in another new world. This one was completely different from the crowded, ever-moving river of the street, or the bustle and dust of the magazine. The hall was all cool marble and hush, portraits of stern old men staring down at her from the azure-painted walls, potted palms looming tall in the corners.

What was it exactly William did in that place? she wondered. She knew he had something to do with diplomacy and that he had just returned from India. Maybe the building was an outpost of the India Office her father had once worked for?

She glanced back over her shoulder, uncertain. But he *had* invited her. And she found she really did want to see him again, tell him her news and hear what he thought about it all. How very odd; he was really a stranger to her, yet she was quite eager to see that smile of his again.

She nodded resolutely and marched up to the only living being in that silent hall, a young man with pomaded hair and spectacles in an old-fashioned black suit, who sat behind a dark oak desk. He glanced up from the papers he was sorting, a frown on his face.

'May I help you, Miss...?'

'Miss Martin,' she answered with a smile and far more confidence than she felt. After all, she would have to learn to march in and take what she needed now, or she would never get the articles she wanted for the magazine.

'I am here to see Sir William Blakely,' she said calmly, adjusting her gloves as if she did this sort of thing every day. 'He is expecting me for tea.'

The young man stared at her for a long moment, his face growing redder, but she just kept smiling. Finally, he gulped and nodded. 'If you will just wait here, Miss—Miss Martin,' he said and hurried away up a curving staircase.

Well, Diana thought, *that seemed to do the trick*. She studied the hall a little closer and saw that between the portraits were decorations that looked like framed medals. Above her head were banners and swords. She wondered what it all meant.

After her flush of new confidence, she suddenly felt nervous again. What if he had just been being polite to invite her to tea? What if she was interrupting him in something terribly important?

But she had no time to leave. As she made to move away, she heard William call, 'Miss Martin. I'm so glad you decided to call on us.'

She turned to see him coming down the stairs. He had tidied up after their meeting on the street, his dark hair smooth and shining again, his tie straight, all cool and businesslike. Yet there was that tiny flash of a dimple.

'Sir William,' she answered with a bright smile. 'So am I!'

Chapter Four

'I'm afraid we are in something of a quandary, Sir William,' said Lord Ellersmere, the head of William's division of the Foreign Office, an hour before he expected Diana Martin to reappear. Lord Ellersmere placed his fingertips against his flowing white moustache and nodded solemnly. 'Indeed we are.'

William turned his attention away from the window and the brightening day outside, abashed to realise he was thinking of Diana, of how flustered she looked on the pavement, and not on the task at hand. 'I thought the Paris arrangements were all in place.'

'So did we,' Lord Ellersmere said with a gruff laugh. 'But you know the Prince. Always changing his mind, dashing off to some spa town or another. He gives this office a headache like no other. But we must do as we must.'

'Because he will one day be our King?'

Lord Ellersmere sighed. 'May that day be a long one away.'

'And he has changed the Paris arrangements again?'

'So it seems. We thought the Queen had persuaded him not to go until the autumn, but he has heard too much about all the excitement and has decided that he must see it for himself directly after the opening.'

'But that's only in a week's time! We would need to arrange for some reconnaissance first.'

'No time for that. H.R.H. says he and the Princess are only going unofficially, for two or three days at the most. They want to go up on the tower and he says the Princess has a yearning to see the Indian jewels. Yet, of course, unofficial only means we must find a way to be invisible and still make sure all the royal niceties are attended to. You are the very best at that sort of thing. Our Bertie likes you. And you know exactly what to watch out for.'

William nodded solemnly. That had indeed been his job in India. Who would have known he would find himself in the same spot at home so soon? If only it all ended in a better state. That was his most important task now. 'I saw in the papers that Maharajah Singh Lep is also on his way to Paris. Does that have something to do with the need to see the Indian jewels?'

Lord Ellersmere's gaze sharpened. 'Yes, I have heard that, as well. We could hope his ship is delayed and he misses the Wales party—and the Wavertons. I understand they will be there, too.'

'Does the Duke still want to display the Star at the Indian Pavilion?'

'The Duke says he is merely the steward of the jewel and it must be shown to the world. But I hear whispers the Wavertons aren't as flush as they would seem.'

William frowned. He had not heard that about his aunt and her husband, who had always been one of the wealthiest ducal couples, always entertaining lavishly. Was that no longer true? Where had Chris heard about that ridiculous Indian investment scheme of Thursby's? Could it be something their uncle was trying, as well? Waverton had always been fascinated by India. If he could couple that with a way to make money quickly...

'And is Singh still unhappy at the sale of the jewel?' William said.

Lord Ellersmere shrugged. 'Who can say? The man is certainly still wealthy enough. But who wouldn't be unhappy about it all?'

'I heard something to the effect that there was an Indian investment scheme floating about in the clubs.'

'A scheme?'

'I don't know the details yet. Probably mining or something of the sort. Silks and gold always seem to be in vogue.'

'Do you think the Prince has heard of it all? Could that be behind the mania to get to Paris soon?'

'I wouldn't be surprised. Bertie seems to enjoy these little schemes as well as the next man.'

'Indeed. It wouldn't be the first time. Her Majesty wouldn't be happy to hear it.' Lord Ellersmere sat back in his chair, looking suddenly weary. William understood the feeling. The job of 'keeping an eye' on the Prince was a constant one. 'Then an even closer eye must be kept on the Prince for now. He is always susceptible to such romantic ideas.'

There was a knock at the office door and a secretary peeked inside past gleaming spectacles. 'I do beg your pardon, Lord Ellersmere, but Sir William has a caller.'

'A caller?' William asked. He was not aware of any appointments. But—could it possibly be Diana? His weariness suddenly faded.

The secretary gave a pinched frown. 'Yes. It's—it's a lady. A rather well-dressed one. She says you invited her to tea.'

Yes, it must be Diana. 'Tell her I will join her in a moment.'

As he left, Lord Ellersmere looked on with bright interest. Anything new or different in their office was a cause of great curiosity, which Will suddenly realised he should have remembered. So much for diplomacy. All his caution seemed to fly out the door when faced with red hair and lively, chocolate-coloured eyes.

'A lady?' Lord Ellersmere said.

'Miss Martin. An old school friend of my cousin Lady Alexandra. I saw her this morning and asked her to tea.' The funniest thing that had ever hit him on the street at such an early hour, surely.

'Martin? A good family. Her father was on the India station once. A good wife, you know, Sir William, can be priceless in our work.'

'I have no thought of marrying soon, Lord Ellersmere,' he said quickly, trying to cut off any gossip in the bud. Not that Ellersmere, or his priceless wife, were gossips. No one would last long in their office if they were. But he had found that men as well as ladies could be great matchmakers. He couldn't tell them he intended never to repeat his own parents' mistakes. Never to burden a woman with his work. 'Our task is an urgent one, after all, and surely secret.'

Lord Ellersmere laughed. 'Too true, my good fellow. But you will need a proper house soon if you want to move ahead and a wife to run it for you.'

William nodded. He knew that was true. But surely Diana Martin had plans of her own. She didn't seem the sort to run a house and sit around waiting for a husband to get back from his 'club'. She was too bumbling, too plunge-ahead-no-matter-the-cost. She needed looking after.

Though, that didn't mean he couldn't enjoy her intriguing company for a cup of tea.

He made his way downstairs and found Diana studying the paintings on the hall wall. She really had grown up since they had met at Miss Grantley's school, he thought, turned into an elegant lady, all glowing happiness. A few of the young secretaries had gathered to gawk at her over the banisters, but she didn't appear to take any notice. Her thoughts were unreadable as she looked at the paintings.

'Miss Martin,' he called. 'I'm so glad you decided to call on us.'

'Oh, Sir William,' she said as she turned to greet him. 'I do hope this isn't an inconvenient time. I just—well, I don't quite want to go home and your office was so near.'

She smiled again and it was as if a ray of sunshine had suddenly pierced the solemn hush of the office. Her cheeks were glowing pink, tendrils of her red-gold hair escaping from beneath her hat, and he felt the energy flow through him from just looking at her. It was—unusual. Amazing, really.

'Not at all, I'm glad you decided to come,' he said, taking her arm. She smelled of those summertime lilacs, soft and sweet. Lord Ellersmere's words, that a man needed a wife, flashed through his mind and made him laugh. He had the feeling that Diana's sort of wife wasn't quite what the man had in mind. 'I was just thinking a cup of tea sounds just the thing.'

He took his hat from the hovering, curious secretary and led Diana out into the pale light of the day. The crowd on the street closed around them, noisy and bustling, always in a hurry, but he was sure she was the only one really there.

She glanced over her shoulder as the heavy door closed behind them. 'It seems like a terribly important place. That sort of quiet doesn't come cheaply and my father always says the calmest places are the ones where the most is happening.'

William laughed. That was another thing he found he liked about Diana Martin—her frankness. No one else talked like her. 'I suppose it doesn't. Come cheap, that is.'

'What do you do there?'

'Oh, a bit of letter writing, a bit of filing. Not much since I got back from India.' He thought of the Prince of Wales and his always-shifting plans, of his aunt and uncle, and the Maharajah. 'Nothing exciting.'

'I don't think I believe you. You've been all the way to India for your work, haven't you? All sorts of interesting and important places.'

'Even interesting places can be dull if you stay there long enough.'

'Can they? I'm not sure I believe you about that, either, though I think I would like to try. Surely if you're bored in Calcutta or Cairo, you can find an elephant to ride at the very least.'

William shook his head, trying not to keep grinning. 'I rarely saw elephants at all, I'm afraid. And surely the same could be said about London. Wasn't it Johnson who said if you're tired of London, you must be tired of life?'

Diana sighed. 'Maybe so, if I was allowed to just wander the city like Dr Johnson. I usually only see the same two or three streets. Today is a great adventure for me.'

William held open the door of the teashop. The smells of vanilla and cinnamon wafted out, along with the hush of quiet conversation, the clink of china, that shut the day outside. 'Then an adventure deserves a cream cake *and* a lemon scone. Or maybe those are just for me, because I am a glutton for sweets.'

Diana laughed as she sat down at a corner table. 'I would also never say no to *two* sweets, Sir William.'

He waited until a maid poured out the tea and took their order before he leaned closer to Diana across the marble-topped table. She smiled, her chocolate-coloured eyes bright as she watched him, and he felt so—light. As if they had both been freed into some wild tearoom adventure, as if they had just escaped the schoolroom. It had been very long since he felt that way, if he ever had. Even when he was a schoolboy, the world had weighed on him. But not now.

'So, Miss Martin,' he said. 'I find I am quite curious about your important errand today.'

She watched him carefully for a moment over the gilded rim of her cup. Finally, she nodded. 'Well, I suppose I know your secret and if you found my notebook you know a bit about mine. I am sure it would be safe with you.'

He sat back in his seat. 'Secrets are always safe with me.'

She smiled that dazzling smile. 'Good, because I absolutely must tell someone. I have procured a job. In Paris!'

So the advertisement tucked in the back of the notebook *had* been hers. He wondered what they taught the young ladies at Miss Grantley's to make them so intrepid. And he found he feared for her, her open brightness and youthful awkwardness set free in the world. Would she be safe? 'A job?'

'Yes. Writing for *Ladies' Weekly* about the fashions at the Exposition.' The cakes arrived on their tiered silver tray, and she took a dainty bite of a violet petit four. 'Oh, this *is* scrumptious, isn't it?'

William nodded, thinking he was quite right— Diana Martin would never be happy being a house-organising, oblivious wife of the sort Ellersmere thought he should have. But she needed help nevertheless, if she was going to run free in Paris. 'So that's what it was.'

Her eyes narrowed. 'It?'

'The clipping that fell from the back of your notebook.'

'Yes, that's it. I've been carrying that job listing around for days and days.'

'And what do your parents think of your new job?'

She bit her lip. 'You don't think I can do it, do you? Because I'm a lady?'

'On the contrary. You seem smart and observant. They would be lucky to have you as their eyes and ears in Paris. I'm sure your articles would sell many papers.'

She gave a tentative smile. 'Do you think so? Really?'

He remembered what he had read in her book, the detailed observations, carefully rendered but with a certain lightness that made it all fun. 'Of course I do. But I have heard that Mr Martin has rather conventional views and you will have to be very careful in such a place.'

Diana sighed. 'Papa. Yes. He has, rather. But I do have a plan. Mademoiselle Leroux, the French teacher from Miss Grantley's, has already agreed to escort me to Paris and Papa does have great respect for Miss Grantley's. And if he and Mama think there will be lots of eligible suitors flocking to Paris...'

William felt a curious tug at his smile, a pang of—could it be jealousy? No, of course not. Just worry for her. As his cousin's friend, surely he should look after her 'And are there? Eligible suitors, I mean.'

She shrugged. 'I have no idea. There will be princes and German dukes and such, but I don't mean to try to marry any of them.'

'No?' he said, feeling rather bemused.

'No. But I'm sure articles about them would sell magazines, don't you think?' She popped a tiny scone into her mouth and smiled. 'Now we know all of each other's secrets. Isn't this terribly cosy?'

He laughed, thinking 'cosy' would surely be the last thing an afternoon with the quicksilver Diana Martin would be. 'Yes, indeed. All our secrets.'

Chapter Five

Secrets. Diana studied Sir William carefully. In his well-cut black suit, his plainly tied cravat, he looked as sombre and respectable as everyone said he was. But his eyes, those unfathomable, night-dark eyes, seemed to see absolutely everything.

She was sure she didn't know all his secrets, not by a mile. But she didn't have the first idea how to discover them, or even if she wanted to. Maybe some adventures were too deep.

She had to admit, though, it felt good to tell him about the *Ladies' Weekly* job and even better to hear that he thought her capable of it. No matter what he said, she knew he had an important job in the expensive hush of that building and his reputation was for hard work and ambition. Surely he would know if she was capable of such hard work, as well. She just wished she could be sure of that herself. But as much as she wanted to shrug off her parents' protectiveness, she found herself the tiniest bit afraid. Scared they were right and she couldn't make her way in the world alone.

She poured out more tea. It was getting rather late and she had a dinner dance to attend that evening, as well as Lord Thursby's promise to call on her that afternoon. But she found herself quite reluctant to leave the wonderfully warm teashop just yet. To give up having William's company all to herself.

'You must have been to Paris,' she said. 'If not for work then for pleasure.' Before she found out about Lady Smythe-Tomas, she wouldn't have thought him capable of going anywhere just for fun. Now she wasn't so sure. Secrets indeed.

'Once or twice.'

'What is it like? I suppose it's not quite as colourful as India.'

'When I was in India, I mostly only saw the inside of a dull, grey office, where it was hot and stuffy and no fun at all,' he said with a laugh. 'Paris has a rare beauty all its own. The shimmer of the river in the moonlight as you look down on it from some ancient bridge. The white stone houses with red geraniums on their terraces. The ladies in their lace gowns, dancing in cafés. The smoky taste of new wine, so much better than what we get here. Coffee and fresh bread.'

Diana gave a surprised laugh. 'Why, Sir William. You are a poet. I must steal that for an article.'

He laughed, too, and to her shock, his cheeks, still a bit bronzed from the Indian sun, turned pink. 'On the contrary. My tutor at Cambridge told me my writing was atrocious. So I stuck to dull desk jobs at the Foreign Office.'

'Well, you make Paris sound wondrous,' she said, pouring out the last of the tea. She spent longer than needed on the small task, trying to cover her own flustered blush. 'I can't wait to see it for myself.'

'Won't you be nervous to be there on your own? Especially with the Exposition crowds. A different city, a different language. You must take care.'

Diana nodded. She had wondered that herself, been nervous and unsure. But the time for that was past. 'I suppose I will be a bit nervous, though I speak French well enough thanks to Miss Grantley's. But nervous in a good way, I think. I've always wanted an adventure, like in the books. How colourless life would be without even one.'

He smiled, a crooked grin that almost revealed his dimple, but not quite. 'I suppose you would call yourself a suffragette, as well.'

Diana straightened her shoulders. 'Why not? I'm sure I could decipher my own thoughts as well as any man. I'm educated, I have an imagination. If I am to figure out how to decide who to sit next to whom at a big dinner party for a prince or an archbishop or something, I can decide how to vote.'

William laughed and he sounded quite delighted. 'I am very sure you could. When I was in India, the Vicereine went back to England for a time and her husband was left utterly baffled by all the social arrangements he had to make. I confess we all were. She had made it all look so very easy.'

'Yes. Men never realise all we have to do *and* we have to make it look simple. Make the world a prettier place.' She gazed down into her half-empty cup. 'I admit I wouldn't want to run India, though, or even the embassy in Paris. I just want to see it all for a while, on my own. Not just a quick sightseeing jaunt like my mother. She bought some gowns and saw the Venus de Milo, and now says she knows everything about Paris.'

'Don't you want to see the Venus de Milo? It's really quite stunning.'

'Of course I do! I told you—I want to see everything.' The door opened, the bell jingling, and everyone glanced up from their tables to look. Curious, Diana turned to see who had caught such attention.

To her shock, it was Lady Smythe-Tomas, dressed as usual in the height of fashion, a purple and cream-striped walking suit and matching hat with towering feathers. Diana suddenly remembered what she had forgotten in the golden glow of the afternoon, of her new job and the pleasure of William's company—that she had first seen William in Lady Smythe-Tomas's clinging arms.

She felt just the same as she had in that moment, embarrassed, a bit jealous, not sure where to look or how to escape. The golden afternoon cracked and she wished she was anywhere else. But they were in the corner of the small shop and there was nowhere to go.

The lady's companion stepped closer to touch her arm, whisper to her beneath the brim of her Gainsborough hat before he left her to go to the counter. And Diana got another shock, for the man was Lord Thursby.

She glanced away, not sure where to look, and turned to William. He was watching Lady Smythe-Tomas and Lord Thursby with narrowed eyes, having suddenly gone very still.

'Should we go?' Diana asked quietly. Yet it was too late. Lady Smythe-Tomas had glimpsed them.

Her catlike eyes glittered. 'Will! My dear, what a surprise to see you here. I would have thought you were far too busy for tea and cakes.' She saw Diana, despite the way she was trying to fit tighter into the corner, and those eyes turned into an inferno. Her reddened lips tightened. 'And—Miss Martin, is it? How sweet of you, Will, to give one of your cousin's school friends a little treat.'

Diana suddenly realised she could be in more trouble than her own moment of embarrassment, if her parents found out about her little tea *à deux* before she knew how to tell them herself. 'Indeed it was kind of him. He is such a good friend to my father. India and all that, such compatriots,' she said quickly. She cringed, realising that William was nowhere near her father's age, but still— needs must. 'I really must be going.'

'You haven't finished your tea,' William said softly. She dared to glance up at him and found him watching her steadily, all inscrutable again.

She wondered what he thought of the whole situation, so like a stage play, and suddenly wished fervently she could tear away his veil and know what was really, *really* happening. 'I am sure Lady Smythe-Tomas and her companion have some place to be.'

At that moment, Lord Thursby returned, his golden hair gleaming in the faint light. He looked shocked, a flash of anger, and then he was all smiles again. 'Miss Martin. Such a surprise. I had called on you earlier, yet you weren't home. I do hope your headache is better today.'

Diana looked down to nudge her cup into its saucer. 'I am quite well, thank you, Lord Thursby. I was just leaving, in fact.'

'Then do allow me to escort you home,' Lord Thursby said. 'A lady can be sadly waylaid in so many places in this city.'

Diana shook her head, beginning to feel a bit frantic. Her lovely afternoon had gone sour so quickly! It was like being shaken awake out of a blissful dream. 'That is kind of you, Lord Thursby,' she said, slowly folding her napkin, 'but I have an errand to attend to first.'

And she had to get to her mother before anyone else did.

'Miss Martin...' William began, standing as she did.

'No, no,' Diana said. 'You must stay here with your friends. Friends of your *own* age.' She couldn't help but tease him just a bit, even with the reminder of just how beyond her he really was. It was so fun to pierce that sombre mien, no matter how briefly. 'Thank you for the tea.'

She rushed out of the shop before anyone could follow her. The pavement outside was more crowded as the day slid into afternoon and she let the tide of people carry her with the flow to the corner. It all felt so much, the sunlight and the people, the new job, the lovely tea, the abrupt ending to it all. She felt quite overwhelmed.

As she turned the corner, hoping she was free, she heard Lord Thursby call after her. 'Miss Martin! Do wait!'

'Blast,' she whispered. Too slow. But she couldn't start running now. He had seen her and her skirts were too narrow anyway. She pasted a smile on her face and glanced back at him.

'Lord Thursby,' she said. 'I really must be finishing my errands.'

'Of course,' he said with a cool, careful smile.

'I only felt I should warn you, my dear—as your true friend.'

'Warn me, Lord Thursby?'

'Yes. About Blakely. He is—well, not as entirely respectable as he might appear. His cousin should have told you, I am sure, but perhaps as another young debutante, new in the world, she could not know. He and Lady Smythe-Tomas…'

Diana felt her cheeks burn and she turned away. She didn't want to be told what she already knew, what she had managed to forget for a while. That she could never compete on the level of a lady like Lady Smythe-Tomas. 'That is kind of you. But I assure you, I never listen to gossip and I have no thoughts of Sir William Blakely at all. He merely treated me to tea. I have—well, other interests right now.'

He smiled, as satisfied as a cat with cream, and Diana suddenly realised with horror that he thought she meant *him*. 'I am glad to hear it. I know you are a most sensible lady. Yet some times the advice of someone more worldly-wise is needed.'

'I shall keep that in mind, Lord Thursby. But now I really must be going.' Diana spun around to hurry away, holding her breath.

'I hope I will see you at the Perkinses' dinner dance tonight,' he called.

'Of course,' she answered. Only because she couldn't figure a way out yet.

Only once she turned on to her own square did she let out her breath. The house looked quiet. Hopefully her mother was still out paying calls and Diana would have time to change her clothes and compose her story, to persuade her parents that Paris was the right place to be.

And to forget her hour with Sir William. He had other interests in life. She needed to do the same.

'Well, my dear, how surprising you are,' Laura Smythe-Tomas said. She tugged off her purple kid gloves, smiling softly at Will as if they shared some secret. 'I didn't realise you knew Miss Martin.'

He watched her warily, suddenly realising he should have been more careful. He had become reckless. 'I knew her father and she is friends with my cousin.'

Her smile turned sharper. 'Of course. It could only be that with a young lady like her, couldn't it? Debs are so dull.'

'I did not realise that *you* knew Lord Thursby.'

She laughed. 'Oh, I've known him for ages. He's advising me on my investments.'

Will remembered what Chris had said, about Thursby and his 'Indian investment scheme', and he felt a jolt of alarm. 'You should be very careful.'

'Darling—are you worried about me? How sweet of you. I can handle a man like Thursby.' She leaned closer and her voice lowered to a purr. 'Are you quite sure you won't have tea with me one day?'

He leaned back and shook his head. 'I am being sent to Paris.'

'Paris! How utterly lovely. It seems as if everyone is trekking across the Channel these days. I should think about joining all of you. Wouldn't want to miss the fun.'

Lord Thursby came back into the shop, his face reddened, his hair windblown. 'Joining everyone where, my dear Lady Smythe-Tomas?'

'Paris, of course. Blakely here says he is going. And aren't you, as well?'

Thursby gave Will a frowning glance. 'Of course. One must go where the brightest lights glow all night. You belong there, my dear.'

'Then I shall!' Laura snatched one of the cakes left on the tray and popped it into her mouth. 'Thursby, dear, do you know Sir William Blakely? He has just returned from India.'

'I believe you know my brother, Christopher Blakely,' Will said, watching the man carefully.

'Of course! Charming man, great cricket player. I don't suppose he plans to follow in your footsteps to the India station?'

'I think he has his own career goals. If you will excuse me, Lady Smythe-Tomas, Lord Thursby, I must be returning to the office.'

'Of course!' Laura answered brightly. 'Don't forget. Call on me before you leave for France. We have so much to discuss.'

Will waved and gave her a polite smile, but he knew as well as she did that they had nothing more to discuss. Their one night at that party at Sandringham was all there was to it, they had known it then and knew it now.

But Diana Martin. He remembered her smile, the bright enthusiasm in her voice that drew him to her like a warm fire on a bleak winter's night. He feared for her, running out into the world with her awkward charm, not knowing what waited for her. He felt a certain responsibility for her.

Now, that connection, he feared, was going to be far more complicated.

Chapter Six

'Diana? Is that you? Where on earth have you been?'

Diana, in the process of handing her gloves and hat to the butler, froze at the sound of her mother's voice from the sitting room. She had hoped to have a little time to tidy herself and think of a good, persuasive speech. But maybe it was better to get it all over with.

'Just back from the dressmaker, Mama. I saw a few friends while I was out,' she answered. She thought of William, his interested smile as he listened to her talk about her new job, those wonderful night-dark eyes. She pushed the thought away, squared her shoulders, stiffened her spine and marched into the sitting room.

Her mother sat near the window, the sun shining on her silver hair, the grey satin of her afternoon gown. She didn't look up from her embroidery, but she waved Diana closer.

As she tiptoed across the thick needlepoint carpet, she saw two large bouquets of white roses, still wrapped in the florist's ribbons.

'I hope you had a good time, dear,' her mother said. 'Did you perchance see Lady Alexandra?'

'No, but I sent her a note this morning telling her how lovely the ball was.'

Her mother sighed. 'The Wavertons do know how to plan a fine party. It's too bad Lady Alexandra's brother is still too young to think of marriage. They would be such kind in-laws.'

Diana thought of Alex's family troubles, which she seldom talked about at school until the sadness overwhelmed her and she turned to her friends. Diana's own parents were exasperating at times, and much too protective, but at least they weren't dukes. 'Yes. Too bad.'

'These came from Lord Thursby while you were out,' her mother said, smiling brightly as she gestured to the flowers. 'So thoughtful. Said that he hopes to have the honour of waltzing with you at the Perkinses' dinner dance tonight. You should hurry up and change, or we'll never be ready in time.'

'Yes, of course.' Diana thought of Thursby, of how he chased her out of the teashop. She wanted, *needed*, to escape that sort of life. She sat down carefully on the sofa opposite her mother, trying to keep her courage up. 'There is something I need to talk to you about for just a moment, Mama.'

Her mother at last glanced up from her sewing. 'What is it, Diana dear? Are you ill?'

'Oh, no. Far from it.' She sat up straighter, gathering all her courage. 'I secured a—well, a job. A rather nice one, writing about fashion for *Ladies' Weekly*. Your favourite magazine!'

'A *job*?' The sewing fell to the floor. 'Diana, have you quite gone mad? Did you hit your head? How did you even come to know of such a thing?'

Diana had practised this moment for so long, but now that it was upon her, the words she had rehearsed rushed around in a tumble in her head. 'It's quite the fashion for young ladies to do a bit of writing these days, you know, Mama. Lady Jones-Rhees even does some typewriting in an office! She says it's very amusing.'

'Typewriting!' her mother gasped.

'Oh, but I won't be doing that,' Diana hastened to add. '*Ladies' Weekly* is sending me to Paris to write about the fashions at the Exposition. It's only temporary, and there will be many important people there. Alexandra and her family are going and they are sure to meet with all sorts of nobility. Royalty even.'

Her mother's lips pursed and Diana began to feel a bit cornered, as she always did with her parents. 'You cannot go to Paris.'

'Mademoiselle Leroux from Miss Grantley's has agreed to go with me as a chaperon. You liked her when you visited the school, remember? She is very sensible and knows the city well. We can take a small apartment from her relatives in the Eighth *arrondissement*, very respectable.'

Her mother didn't need to know that Mademoiselle Leroux was then going on to Cannes. Not yet. This was Diana's one chance for a small adventure and her stomach ached with how much she longed for it.

She thought of William, his encouraging words. He had seen much of the world and he thought she could do this task. Surely he was right.

'She did seem a practical sort,' her mother said slowly. She stared out the window, but she didn't seem to see the familiar London scene. 'You say it's quite the fashion to do some writing these days?'

'Oh, yes,' Diana said eagerly. 'Like—music or watercolours. An accomplishment that adds to the conversation among stylish people.'

'And Lady Alexandra would be there. It might be nice if you found a wider circle of suitors than we see here...' Her mother glanced at the flowers. 'And you would not be gone long.'

'Only a few weeks.' Weeks she knew she had to make count.

'It *is* Paris, I suppose. I did always want to spend more time there when I was a girl. The Venus de Milo was so lovely.' For a moment, she looked quite wistful, as if that girl was closer than ever. Then she sat straighter and gave Diana a stern glance. 'We will have to talk to your father, of course. After the dance tonight.'

A rush of warm relief flowed over Diana and she kissed her mother's powdered cheek. 'Oh, Mama! Truly?'

'No promises, Diana. It is all so terribly *modern*. But if other ladies are going—well, we shall see.'

The Perkinses' dance was not as grand as the Wavertons' ball, but their large drawing room was cleared and ready for dancing, the air sweet with the scent of pale pink roses and hydrangeas in tall alabaster vases. The crowd was younger, full of laughter, and greetings cried out over the sound of the small orchestra tuning up.

Diana bounced up on her toes, trying to see if Emily or Alex were there already. She felt so light, as if she floated on a cloud made of her pale blue ruffled taffeta and lace gown, her slippers tapping at her eagerness to tell her friends what had happened. Her father hadn't yet given his consent for the Paris trip, but her mother was won over and that was more than half the battle.

She tucked the reticule containing her precious retrieved notebook under her arm and plunged into the crowd.

'Only a few dances tonight, Diana,' her mother called. 'We must be bright and fresh for breakfast with your father tomorrow.'

'Of course!' Diana answered. She quickly found Emily standing by the refreshment table, sipping rosebud-pink punch with some of their other school friends.

'Em!' she cried. 'You will never guess. I am going to Paris! Well—hopefully I am.'

'Di, how wonderful!' Emily answered, her eyes

shining with enthusiasm as she hugged Diana. 'Maybe I will see you there. Papa says he is sending me to look at some new things for the stores. He wants to expand the business. You will be the perfect person to help me!'

They chatted for several minutes about all they wanted to see in Paris, before Emily waltzed away with a waiting partner. As Diana turned to reach for a glass of punch, she caught a glimpse of a group that had just entered the drawing room.

One of them was William Blakely.

In his evening suit, he looked elegant and distinguished, quite different from the laughing man she nearly ran down in the street, or the intent friend she found in the teashop who listened so closely to her hopes for Paris. Now he looked so remote, so perfect, so immaculately handsome. She had the strangest, strongest urge to run towards him—and to flee at the same time.

He saw her, too, as his party drew closer to the refreshment table. He smiled and her tea partner was there again, lurking just beneath the austere nobleman. 'Miss Martin. How very nice to see you again so soon. How are your Paris plans coming along?'

Diana laughed. 'Very well, I think! That is, my

mother has agreed. I think she longs to see Paris herself, or maybe she just has hopes for all the European princes she hears will be at the Exposition. We just have to persuade my father.'

'How could he refuse? The Exposition is the chance of a lifetime. No one should miss it.'

'I certainly agree. If only Papa will. I do long for adventure! But Paris must seem like such a small thing to you, not far or very exotic.'

'All travel is an adventure.' The music swelled as dancers took their places for the next set. 'And so is dancing. Would you do me the honour?'

Diana glanced past his shoulder at the dance floor. A lively polka had just started and the thought of twirling around in Sir William's arms was rather intriguing. She nodded and took his arm to let him lead her to their place in the set, just as the music began. It was a wonderful, quick, sprightly tune that made her toes tap in her satin slippers.

She knew she wasn't the finest dancer of the Season, but ever since the lessons at Miss Grantley's she had loved the music, the movement, the swirl and life of the other dancers around her as they made up the patterns of the dance. The story of it all. Usually, it lifted her out of herself for a few moments, into another world.

Tonight, though, she found she didn't lose herself at all. Not when Sir William was her partner. He took her hand and smiled down at her, a small, quizzical smile, as if they shared some delicious secret. It made her feel like giggling and all at once the old magic of the dance came over her again. His other hand touched her waist lightly and they spun on to the floor.

He was a good dancer, light and graceful, his guidance barely visible as he led her in the whirling steps. They seemed to move easily, lightly, as one.

'You are a very fine dancer, Miss Martin,' he said, not even out of breath after an intricate series of small leaps and quick turns.

Diana glanced up into his eyes and almost lost herself in their darkness. 'I could say the same about you. Did you learn on your travels?'

'Yes, here and there. I am a man of many hidden talents, Miss Martin,' he said with a laugh. They spun around again and for an instant were pressed close by the other dancers around them. Diana leaned giddily against his shoulder.

'Yes,' she said. She was beginning to suspect he was certainly a man of many talents.

As the dance shifted again, she became aware of a murmur near the doors. Someone next to them said, 'It's the Duchess of Waverton and her daughter. My, she's becoming a beauty, isn't she?'

'Oh,' Diana said. 'Alex must be here at last.'

But they had whirled again and she wasn't facing the door. 'Why on earth would they let her wear that?' William said quietly, a small frown flickering on his lips. 'It will bring so much attention.'

Surprised, Diana peered closer and saw that Alex was wearing the Eastern Star sapphire, set in a diadem in her pale hair. It matched perfectly the blue-velvet trim of her white-satin gown. She was, as usual, the best-dressed young lady in the room, but Alex looked as if she would rather be anywhere else. She fidgeted with the diadem and her mother the Duchess tugged her hand away.

'I doubt Alex is enjoying the attention much at all,' Diana said.

'No. She's been a quiet thing ever since we were children,' he said thoughtfully. 'Which makes it all even stranger.'

'It does look lovely on her. But she looks as if she would rather hide in the library.'

William smiled down at her as they spun around, making her giggle. 'Like her friend?'

'There is a time for hiding in the library, and a time for dancing.'

'Adventure, eh?' He twirled her in a wide, dizzying circle, making her laugh even more. She wished they could stay there for ever, spinning and spinning until they flew into the sky.

'Always adventure!' she gasped happily.

He spun her gracefully through the growing crowd of dancers, deftly sidestepping other tapping feet and tulle-trimmed hems, until Diana suddenly found herself in a new, silent space. The space of a solarium, just off the ballroom, the doors open for people who needed a respite from the crush.

The air was warm there, slightly damp, and smelled deliciously of flowers. She could hear the echo of music, a few murmured voices and laughter, and she loved the newness of it all.

They swirled to a stop beside a tinkling marble fountain. Diana stared up at him in the faint light, dazzled by his eyes, his smile.

'Is this adventure, then?' she whispered.

For an instant, it was as if a veil dropped on his gaze and he stared at her as if he was hungry for the sight of her. As if he longed for something ephemeral, just out of reach, just as she did. And then his shield was up again and he gave her a wry smile. 'I think it might be. A very foolish adventure.'

'Yes,' she whispered. 'So foolish.' She studied him in the glowing moonlight from the glass dome high over their heads. How beautiful he truly was, she mused, with his sharply carved face that looked like some classical alabaster statue, his glossy waves of dark hair, those fathomless eyes. She reached up to trace her gloved fingertips over the sharp, chiselled lines of his jaw and his lips tightened under her touch. But he didn't move away.

His hands tightened on her waist, tugging her even closer. She went unresisting, overcome with curiosity and some heady, hazy emotion she couldn't yet name. It felt like drinking too much champagne, dizzy and fizzy, and she clutched at his shoulders to hold herself still.

It felt as if they were still dancing, tipping and spinning into space.

As if in a dream, far away yet so wonderfully urgent, his head tilted down to hers and he kissed her.

The touch of his lips was soft at first, warm

as velvet, pressing, teasing, once and then twice. When she edged closer, tightening her clasp on him, that kiss deepened. Grew even more urgent.

She felt so awkward, so unsure of what she should do, yet also so full of excitement. She had never felt so very alive before. She moaned, parting her lips until she felt the tip of his tongue against hers. Shocking and wonderful. The world utterly vanished and she knew only *him*. Only this one perfect moment.

A moment that was shattered all too soon by a burst of laughter near their fountain.

She stumbled back a step and a cold wind seemed to sweep over her as she remembered where they were. What was happening.

'I—I should go,' she whispered, taking a step away, even as all she wanted to do was run back into his arms again. She took a deep, chilly breath of the flower-scented air.

'Diana, wait…' he said, holding out a hand, his face shadowed. 'I am so very sorry, believe me.'

'No, I—I must go,' she said, feeling utterly foolish. Of course he was sorry! She was such an utter silly goose. 'Please, I can't bear it if you were sorry. Not for *that*.' It had been too wonderful and she wanted more than anything to believe he thought that, too. It was like a glowing, iridescent bubble she couldn't stand to see shattered. Yet it was shattered and she felt cold.

She spun around and dashed away, not daring to look back at him. She didn't go back to the dance, but rather found a back staircase and hurried to the ladies' withdrawing room. It was quiet there and she could sit behind a screen, hold his kiss close to her and smile like a fool for as long as she liked.

Until her mother began to miss her, that was.

Chapter Seven

'Oh, Alex! Just smell that sea air. Isn't it delicious?' Diana cried, leaning over the railing of the yacht and waving the felt travel hat, which matched her new, smart blue-tweed suit, in the breeze. Once she had the job at *Ladies' Weekly*, and her mother on board with the scheme, it had been easy enough to get her father to agree. He even gave her a nice clothing allowance, after her mother told him about all the fine young European noblemen who would be in Paris.

But the yacht voyage was all thanks to Alex's father, who leased it for the Channel journey and invited Alex's friend to go with them. She had been fairly vibrating with excitement for days, but whether it was the journey or the memory of kissing William Blakely at the ball, she wasn't sure.

Not that Alex herself seemed to be enjoying it

tremendously. She sat on a deckchair, bundled in a fur, her face pale with seasickness. Though Diana could not completely blame her. It *was* a cold, blustery day, the waves steel grey and lashing against the prow.

'I can smell it well enough from here,' Alexandra murmured.

'Oh, poor Alex,' Diana cried and went to sit in the deckchair across from her friend. 'Is it too awful? Shall I send for your parents?'

'No!' Alex cried. 'They'll only make it all worse.' The Duke was in the smoking salon, while the Duchess and Mademoiselle Leroux sipped tea in the small drawing room. Two guards with stern faces and muscled shoulders guarded the strong box containing the Eastern Star at the end of the deck. 'Besides, we'll be in France soon. See, you can almost glimpse the shore!'

Diana squinted into the grey glare of the sky and sea, and she could indeed see a faint, solid line emerging from the clouds. Was it Calais already?

Diana's heart beat a little faster at having her goal so close at last, almost within her grasp.

'What shall we do once we get there? To Paris?' Diana asked, trying to distract her friend.

Alex drew her coat closer about her throat. 'The ambassador will be there to meet our train and be sure we get the Star safely to the Exposition. So I'm sure there will be speeches, ugh. But after that...'

'Then Paris will be ours!' Diana cried. 'Eiffel's tower. Shops and cafés. Art galleries, dances.' She remembered William would also be in Paris and thought of their dance again. Maybe, just maybe, they would meet in Paris? But she couldn't bear it if he said he was sorry once more and she would feel like a fool all over again.

Alex laughed. 'Lots of dull balls at the embassy.'

'How else will you find your prince?'

Alex leaned back against the striped cushions of her chair, her pale face dreamy. 'I suppose I could meet him strolling along the Seine. I'll lose my glove, he'll pick it up. He won't know who I am, I won't know who he is, but we will just— know each other's souls. If I could only write my own story.'

Diana sighed. 'How romantic.'

Alex turned her head and smiled at Diana. 'I saw you dancing with my cousin.'

Diana felt her cheeks turn warm, even in the cold sea breeze. 'Yes. He is a very good waltzer.'

'And handsome. My mother says he takes after her own father, who was so stunning they say the Queen's cousin wanted to elope with him. But Will works much too hard. He needs someone to help him have fun.'

He seemed quite good enough at having fun, Diana thought with a secret little smile. 'I doubt I could do that.'

'Of course you could! You are the most fun lady I know. You made the days at Miss Grantley's fly by with all the merriment! And then we would be cousins.'

'I don't have time for getting married now, Alex. This *Ladies' Weekly* job is just the beginning.' The beginning of more adventures, she hoped. 'But you're right. He is very handsome.'

Alexandra laughed. 'So you do like him! Admit it.'

Diana shook her head, thinking of Lady Smythe-Tomas and how desperate she had seemed to gain his attention. He didn't need a fashion-writing deb when he had sophisticated ladies like that. 'I just said he was good-looking. Not that I *like* him.'

'Just as you say, then. Look—we're almost there.'

Diana sat up and watched as the shore lurched

closer. More vessels were crowding in on them, all heaving towards the docks. Fishing boats, sailing ships, other fine yachts.

One of them was quite the largest vessel she had ever seen outside liners, at least twice as long as the Wavertons' yacht. It was painted all glossy dark green and red, banners flapping in the breeze. She shielded her eyes from the glare of the sun and made out the letters on the side— the *Filthy Lucre*.

'That is quite the impressive vessel,' Diana commented. 'One of your princes?'

Alex craned her neck for a look. She frowned. 'Hardly. That's Malcolm Gordston's yacht. His *new* yacht—they say he has three. The last won the Silver Cup in America, at Newport, last year.'

'The department-store owner?' Diana said, remembering what she had heard of the man, his good looks, his drive and energy, his ruthlessness. It was all fascinating.

'Yes. We have an invitation to the opening of his new store on the Champs-Élysées. Just in time for the Exposition.'

'I told the editors that I could tell their readers all about it. Maybe I could even find a way to interview Mr Gordston!'

'My mother says he's terribly vulgar.'

Diana laughed. 'Even better.'

As their yacht slowed towards its mooring, the guards drew closer around the strong box and servants scurried around with luggage and baskets.

'Why are your parents bringing the Eastern Star with them like this?' Diana asked. 'I would have thought it was safer in the care of Lloyd's. And the Wavertons surely don't need the publicity?'

Alex shrugged. 'Just to show off, I suppose. My mother couldn't bear to be just one more duchess in a sea of them at the Exposition.'

'Is that why they got you to wear it to the Perkinses' dance?'

'I didn't want to.' Alex stared at the locked box, her eyes narrowed, but Diana wasn't sure that was really what she saw. 'Debutantes wear pearls. Isn't that what Miss Grantley always said? But Mama says I should be more fashion-forward.'

'Well, I can help you with that.' As their yacht tied up at the dock, Diana noticed that Mr Gordston's vessel was in the berth next to theirs. Up close, it was even more elaborate, with striped awnings, gilded window fittings, and carved shutters. The deckchairs were all covered in silk cushions and tasselled rugs.

A gangway was lowered and a gentleman appeared on the deck to disembark. He was quite the finest dressed specimen Diana had ever seen, very tall and slim, elegantly draped in a sable-trimmed coat and tall hat, a carved walking stick in his gloved hand. He tipped his hat to the waiting, gawking crowd on shore, and amber-gold hair, worn unfashionably long, gleamed in the grey light. His features were as perfectly cut as a cameo, except for a slightly crooked nose, and even from that distance she could see his eyes were the palest, purest icy blue.

'Blimey,' Diana whispered, her awe making her a bit vulgar herself. 'Is that Mr Gordston? He looks like Apollo or something.'

Alex laughed. Unlike all the other ladies in the crowd, she watched him with a narrow-eyed, dismissive humour. 'I'm quite sure he knows it, too. Look at how everyone is watching him. They probably do that everywhere he goes.'

Diana looked around and saw that Alex was quite right. Everyone was frozen in the same sort of awe as they watched him walk past, but he just tipped his hat to them, a cool smile on his lips.

'But is he as handsome as William, do you think?' Alexandra whispered and Diana felt her cheeks turn hot again. No—the department-store owner, as amazing as he was, was not nearly as handsome as William Blakely. And she wished she could stop thinking about him, but the memory of their dance wouldn't be banished. It still made her smile like a fool at the oddest moments.

Luckily, she was saved by the appearance of the Duchess, drawing on her gloves as her maid draped her velvet cape over her shoulders. 'Alexandra, Diana, are you girls quite ready? We need to go ashore.'

Alex sighed, and gathered up her valise of books. 'We're just coming, Mother...'

Chapter Eight

'And this, *mademoiselle*, will be your apartment.'

Diana, a bit out of breath after following the stern, rustling black-taffeta-clad landlady up the stairs while trying not to drop her hatboxes and new typewriter case, gasped as the door swung open and she found herself in her new abode.

The building itself was perfectly respectable outside, but quite nondescript, one of the Haussmannian cream-stone constructions with a grey mansard roof and neat rows of shuttered windows all looking down on a quiet little street in the Eighth *arrondissement*. But once inside, there was a lovely little courtyard bright with pots of red and pink flowers, dotted with iron benches in the shade of the yew trees.

Diana's own small apartment, at the top of the house, was papered in pale blue on the walls, soaring up to a floral plasterwork ceiling that gave it all a tall, airy feeling, despite its tiny size. The chairs and sofas were blue-and-white striped, gilded, and the window curtains were blue silk. A few floral paintings gave it a splash of colour. It was quite lovely, very different from her parents' stuffy, darkened, fashionably cluttered rooms in the English style. It made her feel like Marie Antoinette. And it was all hers.

The landlady handed over the keys, gave strict instructions about breakfast times and then Diana was alone. After the noise and bustle of the train ride, the desperate search for enough carriages for the Waverton entourage once they arrived in the city, it was delicious.

She pushed open the window and stared out over the rooftops of the city. It felt like her little eyrie was high above it all, a wondrous sea of grey rooflines and brick chimneys, flowing in an elegant stream towards the silvery ribbon of the river in the distance.

'I am in Paris,' she whispered, still only half-believing it was happening. Unable to stop herself, she danced around in a circle, twirling and spinning.

As her feet moved in a swooping waltz, she remembered her dance with William, the way it felt to be in his arms, their steps moving perfectly together. Suddenly, she wished she was *not* alone, that he was with her. What would he say about the city beyond the window? What would it be like to share all this with him?

'Don't be silly,' she told herself sternly as she spun to a stop. William had only been friendly towards her, surely, despite what had happened in the conservatory—those delicious moments in the conservatory. He was probably already with someone sophisticated and beautiful, like Lady Smythe-Tomas or another of her sort. And Diana had work to do.

She quickly busied herself laying out her precious new typewriter and her notebooks on the little *secretaire*, unpacked her change of clothes from her valise, and put her hats away in the armoire in the tiny bedroom. Since her trunks hadn't yet been delivered, that was all the housework she could accomplish.

She glanced at the little Meissen porcelain clock next to the bed. She had hours before she was to meet the Wavertons for dinner at their hotel. And she was surely in the very best city in the world for wasting a little time!

* * *

'We are strictly unofficial, don't forget,' the Prince of Wales said. He blew out a cloud of cherry-scented cigar smoke on to the Paris street below the open window of the royal suite at the Grand Hôtel du Louvre.

'Yes, Your High—sir,' William murmured. He had been busy that morning in the advance of the royal party's arrival, making sure all the arrangements were in place—and that his office had people to watch the proceedings from discreet distances. Not that the Prince could know about that.

Bertie laughed. 'Good man, Blakely. I knew you would be a fine one to have here in Paris. Lansdowne says he was most sorry to see you leave India. That you always got the job finished, with utmost discretion.'

William nodded. 'I'm grateful Lansdowne considered me useful.'

'I need men like you, Blakely, both now and in the future. Men who know the world and the people in it. The world will only grow smaller and smaller as the time goes on and men such as you and I know that. We welcome it. My mother, though…' The Prince shook his head. His face, florid beneath the luxuriant blond and grey whiskers, was uncharacteristically serious. 'She won't see it. If only she had come with us here, to see how the world does gather together.'

'I would indeed like to learn about the people of the world, sir, how they think and see matters. What we can learn from them.' William thought of Diana Martin, her eagerness to come to Paris, to see new things, find who she was. He had once been like that, too. Longing to see the world, for adventure and excitement. Could he find that again? Be like Diana? The memory of her shining spirit made him smile.

'I knew you would understand! India's loss was surely my gain.' He gestured at the opulently furnished drawing room behind them, at the crowd of 'unofficial' men still in their stiff black suits pinned with the bright press of orders on the lapels. They had been watching them carefully, though pretending not to be trying to eavesdrop, ever since the Prince had led William to the window and offered him a cigar.

'My wife says you are cousin to her goddaughter, Lady Alexandra, the Duke of Waverton's daughter.'

William glanced at the Princess of Wales, who sat on a velvet sofa with two of her ladies in the corner. At forty-five, the mother of five grown children, she was still tall, wand-slim, and ethereally beautiful, her dark hair piled in intricate curls atop her delicate head. Her ladies laughed together, but she merely sipped at her tea as she smiled serenely out at the room. Her increasing deafness only made her seem more dignified, eternally a fairy queen.

William suddenly noticed that the Princess was dressed in the height of fashion, even in her more informal afternoon wear. Her suit was sky-blue silk, with puffed sleeves and a high collar, embroidered with elaborate silver whirligigs. Surely Diana would know what they were called, those pretty silvery bits.

He had to remember to tell her all about it when he next saw her. The way that felt so important startled him. He had never been so eager to talk to a lady before, to say something that would make her smile. And Diana was only someone he needed to protect, as his cousin's friend, an innocent in the city.

An innocent he had been cad enough to kiss. The memory of it pained him now.

The Prince was looking at him with narrowed eyes and William suddenly realised he hadn't answered. Would he continue to think William was 'useful' if he was always distracted? And yet he knew Bertie would be the first one to understand he was daydreaming about a lady.

But that would never suit his austere reputation.

William had to laugh at himself. He had a task to think about in Paris and the advancement of his career. That was all. He couldn't be distracted, as the Prince was so often. He couldn't forget himself again. He couldn't put a lady through what his own parents had endured.

'Yes, sir, Lady Alexandra is my cousin. She always speaks so glowingly of the Princess and her godmotherly kindness.'

'Yes, always so polite. A very pretty girl she is, too, very pretty indeed,' the Prince said. 'We had thought about her for one of my nephews, but she seems so quiet. How can a man know what a lady like that is thinking? Disconcerting.'

'Lady Alexandra is a bit shy, sir. I think she wants to put off considering marriage for a year or so.'

'That would be a waste.' Bertie squinted through the smoke, his small, pale blue eyes shrewd. 'You haven't considered marrying your cousin yourself, then, Blakely?'

'I doubt we would suit each other in that way, sir,' William said carefully.

'Very sensible. My own parents were cousins, y'know. My father often used to say we needed new, strong, dark-eyed blood in our family.' He shook his head as he studied his lovely, long-suffering wife. 'Something in that, I suppose.'

William had a flashing vision of Diana Martin's chocolate-coloured eyes. 'I just haven't found the right one yet, sir.'

Bertie gave a hearty laugh. 'Quite right. Never give in on that point. When I was a young man, my sister was forever pushing long-nosed German princesses my way. But I only wanted the best, so I waited until my pretty Alicky came along. I've never been sorry. Don't wait too long, though, my boy! You need a good wife to organise your household, give you children. Ours are maddening sometimes, I admit, but I love them. Especially now they are growing up.'

'My household needs are simple, sir. A wife would be bored.' Or simmering with unhappiness, like his poor mother.

The Prince laughed. 'Mine were simple, too, long ago. Yours won't stay that way, Blakely, not if what Lansdowne says is true. We'll need your services for a long time.'

'I hope I can be of some use, sir,' William said cautiously.

'Maybe my wife could find you a fine, pretty girl who knows what she's doing in the diplomatic world,' the Prince said. 'She and her sisters are always playing matchmaker to some poor blighter or another. Unless you have a candidate or two in mind already?'

William thought again of Diana, her laughing face as he spun her in the dance, the sweetness of her lips beneath his. 'Not yet, sir.'

'Just as you please.' Bertie stepped closer and said quietly, 'I need you to take a look at something for me, Blakely, before our dinner tonight with the Wavertons.'

'Of course, sir.'

'The pavilion where they are to set out the Eastern Star for display. I've asked for a few modifications before the Maharajah sees it.' He took a slip of paper from his coat pocket and handed it to William. 'So many people have no idea of aesthetics *or* security.'

William glanced over the plans, the layout of the octagonal pavilion chamber. 'I'll see to it at once.'

'Good man.' The Prince clapped him on the shoulder before he went to talk to his wife and her ladies, and William slipped out of the crowded, oppressive, rose-scented room, glad of a breath of fresh air.

Outside, the day was still warm, the sun beaming high overhead in a pale blue sky, gleaming off the half-open windows high in the grey roofs. But the heat didn't keep the crowds away. They streamed past the hotel on the Palais Royal, towards the Exposition grounds on the Champ de Mars, laughing and shrieking with excitement.

William joined them, diving into their ever-moving stream, the air scented with ginger cakes from food carts and expensive French perfumes from the ladies' silk gowns. The words were a tangle of English, French, German, and more, just as the crowd was a blend of fine silks and feathers and plain woollens and cottons, everything and everyone mixed together.

The Prince was right, he thought. The world was coming together, right there in front of them.

Suddenly, he glimpsed a figure near the gates on the Trocadero. Someone small and slender, standing on tiptoes as she paid her fare at the window. Though she was dressed much like the other ladies, in a pale lilac summer frock and straw hat decorated with feathers and fluttering ribbons, the vivid red-gold of her hair beneath that hat immediately caught his attention. It seemed he had been thinking of Diana Martin far too much lately, and now he imagined she was in front of him.

As the lady turned away from the gate, opening up a lacy parasol, he saw he wasn't imagining things after all. It *was* Diana. The face beneath her hat was glowing with excitement. He hurried towards her, finding that he felt ridiculously excited to see her again. He told himself it was only worry for her safety, but he feared he was lying to himself.

'Miss Martin,' he called, making his way towards her through the crowd.

A smile touched her lips and she waved merrily with a lace-gloved hand. 'Sir William! What a wonder you should find me in such a press. The world is small, isn't it?'

He wondered if she had had been talking to the Prince. But it seemed as though when he looked at her the world was wide and full of wonder. 'It does seem so. Have you been in Paris long?'

'I've only just arrived, but I couldn't wait to catch a glimpse of it all. Nor, I see, could you!'

They stood there for a moment, just smiling at each other, and it seemed like the crowd around them faded to an indistinct murmur, a blur flowing past. He just couldn't seem to stop grinning at her like a young fool.

'Are you working on an article already, Miss Martin?' he asked.

'Oh, always. But at the moment I'm just getting my bearings.'

'I have an errand, yet I think a few bearings beforehand wouldn't come amiss.'

'Walk with me, then?' she said, her smile widening, but it seemed a bit tentative in the corners. 'I was just going to look at Monsieur Eiffel's tower, study some of the ladies' hats.'

'Maybe I could help you,' William said—the afternoon suddenly even brighter than before. 'I think I would very much enjoy that, Miss Martin. Thank you.'

Chapter Nine

Diana was sure she had never felt such a wonderful, fizzy sense of excitement in her life. The day seemed to get brighter and brighter all around her, bubbling with a sense of freedom and possibility, of beauty. The world that had always seemed to close in on her beforehand burst open and now she could run free.

And she had William Blakely to share it all with her. She glanced up at him, marvelling at how very handsome he was, his face like a Renaissance painting, all sharply sculpted angles, his dark hair glossy, his smile full of a happiness that seemed as startled and hopeful as her own.

She held his arm as they made their way across the bridge from the Trocadero, towards the famous new tower. It soared up ahead of them, all lacy delicacy that also seemed to be somehow the most solid thing she had ever seen. It flew up into the sky, beautiful and confident, pointing the way to the future.

They passed under the arches of the tower and Diana glanced up to find she could see straight up the centre of the structure. All of its intricate detail, so airy and elegant, rising up into the sky. She wondered if it went straight up into the clouds, where she was sure she was walking herself on such an extraordinary day. If she ran up all those steps, would she find herself jumping into space itself?

And would William be with her, holding her hand among the stars?

Diana laughed with sheer glee at her fanciful thoughts, at the lovely day, and he smiled down at her quizzically.

'It's just all so amazing,' she said.

'Is it what you expected?'

'Better. How could anyone have imagined such a place? Yet someone must have, because here we are. They thought it up and made it real.'

They emerged from beneath the tower on to the Champ de Mars, from shadow into sunlight. The wide, grassy lawns had been turned into avenues leading to fanciful pavilions, surrounded

by flocks of ladies who looked like fluttering but-
terflies in their pale summer gowns and wide-
brimmed hats. The distant trees were in bloom, all
frothy pink just like the women's dresses. Rows
of marble statues—gods, goddesses, heroes of
French history—were interspersed with colourful,
snapping flags and streamers. A series of large
fountains stretched ahead, the waters dancing and
sparkling in the sunlight.

Diana hardly knew where to look first. Straight
ahead rose a great blue dome, crusted with fac-
eted tiles that made it gleam, bursting with bright
colour against the grey of the tower. To the other
side stretched more buildings, hung with banners
that proclaimed their uses—art, commerce, the
machines of modernity.

And everywhere there were small stalls selling fried oysters and dishes of ice cream, cups of
cider, souvenirs of scarves and tiny Eiffel Tower
models, pavement cafés, newspaper sellers. She
could hardly believe she was a part of it all.

'Up ahead is the Galerie des Machines,' William
said, gesturing to the giant blue dome. 'If you'd
like to see a demonstration of Mr Edison's electric
light. And over there are the buildings for paint-

ings and sculptures, the liberal arts with books and manuscripts. I know you would enjoy that.'

'Very much! And what's that way?' she asked, pointing towards the more shadowy lanes that led back down towards the river.

'The pavilions of other nations. Russia, Turkey, Mexico, Egypt. I hear you can visit a Cairo souk, see Balinese dancers, have luncheon in St Petersburg with caviar and vodka...'

'All with one short walk!' Diana said happily. 'Truly, we are living in a wondrous world, Sir William, aren't we?'

He laughed and it sounded to Diana as if laughing was something he didn't do very often. She wanted to hear it again and again. 'I am beginning to think so.'

'But surely you've seen some of those places for real, in your work?'

'I haven't seen them with you, though. It makes it all seem—new, somehow.' He looked surprised and even pleased.

Diana felt herself start to blush and she glanced away before he could see her pink cheeks. She didn't know what to say, where to look. She only knew what she wanted to do and that was stare into his dark eyes. And keep on staring into them all day.

'Where do you want to go first?' he asked lightly and she was glad of the diversion. 'Buy a scarf with the Eiffel Tower embroidered on it? Look at some of the art? Maybe ride the train?'

'I—well, all of it, of course,' Diana said with a laugh. 'But don't you have to be somewhere? If you are meant to be working, I shouldn't be selfish enough to delay you.'

He smiled at her, a smile so open and sunny she wondered if William Blakely had suddenly been replaced by a bon vivant imposter. The different facets of his character were so intriguing. She wanted to see all of them. 'I can't think of anywhere else I'd rather be. I do need to take a look at the India Pavilion. Maybe we could start there? Unless you have work of your own to be doing, of course.'

'I think the Indian Pavilion could certainly be my work, too. I read they have some beautiful silk saris on display. I'm sure the *Ladies' Weekly* readers would want to hear about them.'

As they turned on to one of the gravel pathways, the miniature train that carried people from one area of the Exposition to another clacked past, its whistle blowing as it neared the tiny station with its red-tiled roof. 'Shall we ride there?'

'I don't mind walking. It feels as if I can see every little detail that way.'

He offered her his arm again and they strolled past the collection of buildings, the classical Grecian temples that held the artworks, the modern steel bandstands where dance orchestras played, the little Asian teahouses. As they walked, he asked about her articles, what she planned to write about, and she asked about the Princess of Wales and her clothes for her journey to Paris. Readers of fashion magazines always wanted every detail of the beautiful princess's wardrobe.

'I think she wore blue on the yacht,' he said uncertainly. 'Yes, I am quite sure it was blue.'

'Azure blue? Turquoise? Maybe navy?'

'Um... Blue. And white. Or maybe it was more lavender?'

'Lavender?'

William laughed. 'I'm afraid I am no help to you at all, Miss Martin. I can tell you she looked very pretty. And her daughters all wore matching frocks.'

'Really? All three of them?' Diana thought of the Prince of Wales's daughters, the three girls called the 'Whispering Wales' because they were so shy. But she had heard the eldest, Princess Louise, might be engaged to be married. She doubted William would tell her all about that, though, until it was officially announced. 'Were they wearing blue, too?'

'White, I think. I do know the colour white. And they had feathers in their hats. Or maybe flowers?'

Diana laughed so hard she forgot to watch where she was going and tripped on one of the patches of gravel underfoot. She felt herself pitching forward, a rush of cold panic—and then a pair of strong arms around her, catching her and swinging her up high from the ground, safe. He felt so strong, so warm, and he made her feel giddy at the scent of his cologne. At being so near to her.

'I—thank you,' she gasped, staring down into his eyes as he lowered her to the ground, their bodies pressed scandalously close for a moment. She remembered so well what had happened last time they were so close and she could almost feel that kiss once more, taste the smoky flavour of him, the heat and need. She wanted him to kiss her again, but they were crowded in close by far too many people.

She had forgotten that for just a moment. It had felt like they were the only two people in all of Paris.

'So clumsy of me,' she said, stepping back from him a safe few inches until she felt like herself again, calm and in control. She straightened her hat and retrieved her parasol.

He took her arm again and they made their way down a narrow pathway, past small cafés that smelled deliciously of exotic spices, coming to a gleaming white building built to look like a smaller Taj Mahal. Only on peering closer could she see it wasn't marble, but painted wood. Blue and white tiles lined the doorways and benches sat in the shade of trees nearby, giving a feeling of peaceful retreat.

'I think this is it,' William said.

Diana furled her parasol and tipped back her head to study the building. 'It's lovely. Did you see the real one when you were in India? The Taj Mahal?'

'Only once. It didn't seem like a real place, but a dream.'

A dream built of love, Diana remembered reading. She smiled at him and let him lead her into the shady, cool hall just beyond the doors. Inside, there were rooms leading off the corridors, all filled with glimpsed displays of brilliant silks and filmy, pale muslins, the gleam of jewels, the intricate brilliance of mosaics.

As Diana wandered through the glass cases filled with the glorious fabrics, dazzled, William spoke quietly to one of the turbaned ushers and showed him a sheaf of papers. The man nodded and led William and Diana through a series of corridors to a set of gilded doors that had to be unlocked with an intricate set of keys.

'The jewel room,' William told her quietly. 'Not officially open yet.'

'You mean I get to take a preview glimpse?' Diana whispered back, thrilled at the prospect.

William smiled down at her. 'No articles yet, though. Strictly embargoed until the Waleses see it.'

Diana held up her crossed fingers. 'Of course not. But after the grand opening...'

'Then you can write away.'

He led her into the solemn hush of the room, an octagonal space lined with cases. For the moment, it was only lit by a glass dome overhead, but she could see Mr Edison's new light bulbs in sconces along the blue-painted walls. The walls and stone floor were all various shades of blue, from the almost grey of a dove to a bright azure sky, and the effect of the murky light made her feel as if she was swimming underwater. She wondered if *that* was what the Princess wore, the blue William couldn't quite describe.

She spun around, imagining she was really swimming, gliding past such wondrous treasures from a sea god's lagoon. Jade bracelets, ruby necklaces, golden headdresses, all vivid against the blue.

But the display case in the very middle, beneath the dome, was still empty.

'The Eastern Star will go there for the opening party,' William said.

Diana tried to imagine it, the sapphire resting on the raised satin cushion in the case, but it was hard to think of it anywhere but in the Duchess's hair. It was a gem meant to be worn. Yet at least here so many more people could see it, marvel at its beauty.

Two men in sombre charcoal-striped suits appeared and after politely greeting Diana went to speak quietly with William. Realising he had some official duties, she went and studied a case of gold and ruby bangle bracelets to let him conduct his business. There was much nodding over official-looking papers and thorough examinations of the empty case.

As William carried on his quiet conversation, Diana wandered around the rest of the displays, taking notes for her future articles. The wonderfully intricate embroidered lengths of silk that showed off the emerald and gold necklaces formed into leaves and flowers. She had never seen anything like it and wondered if next season's fashions would be 'Indian' inspired, just as last year's had been medieval.

At the end of the room, she turned to see William looking terribly serious as he nodded at what one of the men was saying. He gestured to the lock on the case and the two men seemed to be arguing with him about something to do with the mechanism. Then William glanced up, saw her watching him and smiled. That smile brought out that wonderfully delightful, secret little dimple and he looked completely transformed. Younger. More free.

But it only lasted for one enticing moment.

'Are you hungry?' he asked, coming to take her arm as the other men hurried away. His touch was light, but warm, secure. Safe-feeling, as she had rarely felt before. 'I thought I saw a samosa seller just outside the pavilion.'

'Samosa?' she asked, sure she would go with him to find anything at all.

'I suppose they're rather like Cornish pasties, little pie-crust pockets filled with meats and spices. They're quite delicious, as well as portable, which is why they're sold on every street corner in Calcutta. I ate them every week when I was in India and I've missed them.'

'Then I certainly must try one.' They stepped out of the cool hush of the near-empty pavilion back into the busy, warm spring day, the burst of music and laughter, the crowds pressing close. He purchased two packets of the little fried pies, crisply golden at the edges, and she took a careful nibble of it.

And then tried not to melt at the flavours that flooded through her, the sweetness and heat all at once. Just like when William had kissed her.

'Oh,' she murmured. 'You are right, this is wonderful.'

He laughed. 'I'm glad you think so.'

'See how many adventures I've had already! All in one day.' They strolled along the narrow lanes, taking in the sight of the carousel of painted horses and lions bearing children shrieking with laughter. She knew she had to remember it all, to cherish it when her future life seemed dull and drab, full only of tea parties and country houses. She would have all this colour, all these sounds and smells, to remember.

And she would have the memory of William beside her, sharing it all. He laughed as he pointed out a child chasing after a bouquet of red and blue balloons, a lady in one of the most elaborate hats she had ever seen cooing to her pack of poodles. He seemed to come alive here, too, away from their real lives of London.

'Tell me more about your life in India,' she said.

He shook his head, smiling. 'I told you—I mostly saw the inside of a drab office, much like the one I see in London, though a good deal hotter. It was a bit dull.'

'I can't believe that. Even if you *were* locked away in an office, labouring for your Queen and country, they must have let you out once in a while.'

'Well, in the summers we would travel up to the mountains, to Simla, where it was cooler. I've never seen anything quite so beautiful, the greens richer than any emerald. Every evening there would be tea on the lawn, as the sun set behind the hills, all pink and gold and lavender, and there would be music from the verandas. The heaviness of the air, the colour and laughter of the people—it was like nothing I ever could have imagined before.'

'You see,' Diana said, enthralled by the images his words painted. 'You want to pretend you're a dull old businessman, but really you're a poet. You see different worlds.'

He laughed. 'A poet no publisher would ever take a chance on, I'm afraid. But it's true the real India wasn't much like the one we see here. Except for these samosas.'

'Well, Parisian India is probably the closest I'll ever come to it at all,' she said. 'Except for your stories and what little my father tells us about his time there. I'll just have to enjoy it as I can.'

'And so you should.' He threw away their empty samosa wrappers and led her to one of the wrought-iron benches that lined the pathways. 'What would you like to do now?'

Diana stared around at them, at all the buildings filled with treasures, all the shops and newsstands, the dazzling lights of the carousel. In truth, she wanted to do everything, but… 'I don't want to keep you from your work.'

William smiled and stretched out his long legs in front of him. 'They do sometimes let me out of the office here, too, just as they did in India.'

'Well—I did think I might go up on the tower. Just to the first platform, for a little while.'

'That sounds perfect. Will you let me be your escort? Unless you're tired of my company for the day.'

Diana was sure she would *never* be tired of his company. It was always changing, always fascinating. And she found the thought of how much she liked to be with him very disconcerting.

'That sounds delightful, Sir William,' she said. 'Thank you.'

Diana and William paid their fares and started up towards the first platform of the tower. A sign indicated that the elevators weren't in use yet, but Diana wasn't sure if she would have taken it having heard of how their installation had been delayed. She preferred the stairs anyway, those winding metal steps where she could stop and peek through the lacy ironwork at the city as it grew further and further away.

The platform was crowded, but William managed to find them a spot next to the railing. He rented a pair of opera glasses from one of the tiny shops tucked into every available corner. Diana gasped when she peered through them.

'Interesting, is it?' William said.

Diana laughed. 'Amazing. Who would have ever thought we could see Paris like this?' Without the glasses, everything seemed so far away, the city a melange of green gardens and neat white buildings, the river a sparkling silver ribbon that lined the Exposition pavilions, the people a pale blur that shifted and moved as one. With the glasses, she could see every detail: the flowers in their tall pots lining the walkways, the ladies' elaborate hats, the food sellers and souvenir stands. She saw the miniature railway; the statue of the spirit of France outside the Invalides, a classically draped marble woman leading the way to freedom.

When she turned the glass, she could take in the city beyond. She glimpsed the square towers of Notre Dame, the gleaming roof of the Louvre, a whole city in itself.

'Is it still an adventure?' William asked.

'I would say so,' she answered and was suddenly aware of how very close he was there at the crowded railing. Their bodies pressed together, so warm, so sweet. She could smell the clean sharpness of his cologne and she wanted to lean in even closer.

She dared to peek up at him and for just an instant, she caught him unguarded. He watched her with a startled expression, as if he was as surprised by the sweetness of the moment as she was. Then he smiled and looked away.

'Do I—have a smudge on my face or something?' she said, trying to laugh away the strange instant.

'Not at all,' he answered, smiling at her again. But it was different now, distant, cool. 'It's just— you do look so pretty with the sun on your cheeks and smiling like that. You look so happy. I've wondered sometimes what that's like.'

Diana bit her lip, feeling suddenly shy. 'I do feel happy today. And…' Did she dare to say it aloud? Yes, she *did* dare. It was a day to dare anything. 'And being here with you just makes it all the better.'

She was quite astonished by it all. That being in Paris with Chris's solemn, serious brother would have ever made her feel so—light. Free. It just went to show that you never could tell about people, really.

His lips tightened and she thought she even saw a hint of a blush on his glass-sharp cheekbones. 'I haven't had a day like this, either. Not since— well, ever, that I remember.'

A frown flickered over his brow, a shadow, and Diana wondered what made him look sad suddenly.

'We should celebrate,' he said. 'Maybe a glass of champagne?'

'In the middle of the day? How terribly shocking, Sir William!' she cried dramatically, pressing her hand to her brow. 'But then, how can I say no to champagne in Paris?'

He laughed and that sadness vanished. He took her arm to lead her to one of the little restaurants. There were four on the first platform: a grand one for multi-course suppers, a Russian café, and two smaller, French bistros. They chose a little bar along one of the railings that had a tall wrought-iron table free.

'This is quite wonderful,' she exclaimed. 'Champagne *and* a view. I will become quite spoiled.'

'Surely no one deserves it more for all their hard work.' William ordered the drinks as she studied the crowd around them, the elegant day dresses of the ladies, the new style of sleeves and narrow skirts, the gorgeous hats.

'I saw that the Princess of Wales had silver work just like that on her gown,' William said, gesturing to lady strolling past in a pink-silk dress and striped jacket. 'I was sure you would know what it's called.'

'Oh, yes. *Passementerie.* It's part of the new style inspired by the art of Arabia. Quite appropriate for the Exposition, I think. And Princess Alexandra was wearing it, you say?'

'Yes.' He described the Princess's clothing he had seen in the hotel earlier as Diana quickly scribbled down notes. He seemed to remember more of that silk suit than he had of the princess's yachting costume. She was struck by how serious he was as he gave her details, not as if it was beneath his dignity to help with a ladies' fashion article at all. As if he really wanted to be of use to her. 'Is that at all helpful?'

'Very. Everyone always wants to know what the Princess is wearing. There will be copies of her dresses here in every store soon. I don't suppose you could give me the tiniest idea of their plans here in Paris, could you?'

He laughed, the last traces of that sadness gone. 'I'm sure my cousin Alex could tell you more. The Waleses' visit is very unofficial, you know. Nothing specific to be known about it yet.'

'Yes, but *why* is it so unofficial? He's the Prince of Wales and other royals have been seen here. German princes of all sorts, Italian counts, and Russian grand dukes.' The champagne arrived and Diana took a small sip, letting the bubbles sparkle over her tongue. It was wonderful, like liquid gold.

'The Prince believes his mother is, well, less than enthusiastic about the modern world. Especially about the French modern world, which has cast off their monarchy, as you know. She wanted the ambassador to come home during the Exposition. But the Prince is becoming more independent all the time. He loves France.'

'Fascinating.' Diana took another sip of her wine, feeling the tingle of those bubbles all the way to her toes. 'And what do *you* think of the modern world?'

'I think we're in it and there's no escape. Even for a queen.' He took a sip of his own drink, his expression thoughtful. Diana had noticed he seldom said anything without thinking it over carefully, understandable for a man who worked in the Foreign Office. She wondered whimsically, her head spinning a bit from the wine, what he would be like when he was not being cautious.

'But why should we want to escape?' he continued. 'There's Mr Edison's light bulbs and phonograph, new music and brightness right at our fingertips. There's new art, new dances, new frontiers opening up for us all. And you are here having an adventure that thousands of readers will get to enjoy through your writing. What could be better?'

Diana looked out over the railing at the city beyond, the wonderful, shining place dotted with pavilions full of wonders from all over the world. The intricate ironwork of the very structure they sat atop. The handsome man across from her, who had travelled all over the world and what he had seen had made him one of the most intriguing people she had ever known. He was right. It was a good time to be alive. 'But the Queen doesn't think so, does she? Nor does my father.'

William laughed. 'Nor do my parents, I think. But here it is. The future arrives whether we want it or not.'

She remembered when Christopher would visit

them at Miss Grantley's, the imitations he would perform about his parents and their railing against the new, 'shocking' theatre, and could well imagine what the Blakelys would say about the Exposition.

'Our poor parents,' she said. 'Think of all they are missing. All we get to witness, ourselves and our friends.'

'Our friends,' he murmured. He gave her an inscrutable little smile, one that made her face turn warm.

She sipped at the last of her champagne and studied William in the light and shadows of the tower, and even though he was still sat close beside her at the tiny table, for a moment he looked far away. There was a flicker of something deep in his eyes, a downturn at the corner of his beautiful lips. He looked—could it be *lonely*? She was sure she saw an echo of her own secret longings written on his face, a longing to be free, to find where she truly belonged. Not just where she was told she *should* be, who she should be.

Could Sir William Blakely, well known for his iron self-control, his dedication to his work, really be lonely sometimes, too? Maybe that was what sent him to Lady Smythe-Tomas? Was it possible that his work drove him away from her again? His great sense of duty?

Diana was startled by the thought. That Will could feel as she did, could long for adventures out in the great, amazing, strange world and yet long for someone to share it all with, would never have occurred to her. He seemed a man content in his own world. What if he had been more upset by his lost romance with Lady Smythe-Tomas than anyone could ever have imagined? What if he still was?

But then he smiled again and that small, startling revelation passed. He looked as he always did, slightly removed from the world around him. Handsome and cool-headed, a man at a distance.

'Would you like another glass of champagne?' he asked.

Diana looked down at her glass, surprised to see it was quite empty. Maybe that was the reason for her romantic, maudlin thoughts. Too many bubbles going straight to her head.

'I would *like* one,' she admitted. 'But I'm afraid it would send me straight to sleep.'

'Perhaps a look around, then? We could take some notes on the tower's variety of restaurants for one of your articles. I know a bit of shorthand.'

More surprises from the ever-surprising Sir William. Men seldom knew shorthand; they thought such things as that and typewriting were for women in the offices. 'Do you indeed? You are far more proficient than I am, I'm afraid. I feel terribly unskilled. The magazine lent me a typewriter, but it takes me an hour to hunt and peck out enough letters to make a paragraph. I'm sure they would be sorry they ever hired me if they knew how really ignorant I am.'

'They hired you because they surely know an astute eye when they see it. A good writer.'

'Do you really think so?' she said, daring to hope she *could* do this job after all. If a man like William, a man with a career that took him around the world, thought she could do it, maybe she could.

'Of course. I saw your lost notebook, remember? You have keen powers of observation and a way to see people's characters and sketch them out in just a few words. I'm sure if you ever decided to try your hand at a novel instead of journalism, your cast would bring the world to life.'

'I did once want to be the new Charlotte Brontë,' Diana admitted to the first person she had ever told except Alex and Emily. 'But writing about fashion seemed to be the best way to get my words out into the world. For the moment, anyway.'

'Sometimes we do have to make compromises for our work,' he said. 'Perhaps your *Ladies' Weekly* would take a short story from you after the Exposition articles? A story about Paris, maybe, and the modern world.'

'What a good idea,' Diana exclaimed. She would need something to distract her when her little adventure was over and her parents expected her back home and on the marriage market. Writing fictional stories for the magazines would be a fine consolation, a way to express her thoughts and emotions when she was no longer expected to have any aside from setting the perfect table. She studied him curiously, but as usual his face gave nothing away. 'Is that what you have to do in your work?'

He looked surprised. 'My work?'

'Make compromises. Find new ways of doing things.'

'I suppose I do,' he said slowly, as if he hadn't thought of it that way before. 'Diplomacy is all about finding the middle way. No one can be all happy all the time. The trick is to find a way to make all parties happy enough.'

'Happy enough.' Diana had been taught the same thing all her life. Ladies should be content to be happy enough to run their houses, have their children, and forget anything else that might lurk deep in their minds and hearts. Forget any urge to do anything else.

She was suddenly tired of all that. Seeing Paris, seeing what life could really be—that was what she wanted.

'What would you have done, if you could choose any work in the world at all?' she asked. 'If you didn't have to always be calm and restrained, and find the middle ground for everyone?'

He looked surprised, as if he hadn't contemplated that before. 'I suppose I would choose to do—what I'm doing. I may not be a large cog in the diplomatic machine, but I do my part to maintain peace whenever I can. I think when I was a boy, my parents would have preferred I show an interest in the army or the church. But neither of those would have suited me as the Foreign Office does.'

Diana nodded. She could see that. His calm politeness, his handsome face that hid his true thoughts, his sharp mind, they were all well-suited to being a diplomat, as making sermons or leading charges wouldn't. 'And now that you are *Sir* William, lauded by the Viceroy, helping the Prince of Wales, I'm sure your parents must be happy.'

'They have accepted it.'

Diana sighed. 'How lovely that must be. You do the work you are suited for and your family just accepts it. You make a difference in the world. It must feel so—good.'

William rested his chin on his palm, a frown creasing his brow as if his thoughts were racing. 'I do feel I am where I should be, that's true. I had never thought about it that way before.'

'No. Men do tend to take their work for granted. It's always been there for them.'

'But you have your work, too. We *are* in the modern world now, remember? Look at all the wonders around us.'

Diana laughed. 'You make peace between nations and build the empire. I write about hats.'

'You bring the world to people who can't be here in person. Through your words, you show them beauty and wonder. You give them an escape and probably inspire other girls to write. That is no small thing, Diana. Don't underestimate yourself.'

No one had ever told her that before, that her writing might help others. That what she did could be useful. It felt quite astonishing. 'Do you really think so?'

'Of course I do. Now, shall we put my shorthand to use? The whole of Paris is waiting for us!'

The whole of Paris. *Us.* Suddenly, she couldn't wait to see the whole city, everything in it—with him.

Chapter Ten

The Wavertons' dinner party for the Waleses, though meant to be unofficial and informal, was surely the most elegant thing Diana had ever seen.

Held in the dining room of their suite at the Grand Hôtel du Louvre, the party had been transformed into a summer garden with flowering chestnut trees in silver tubs and by tall vases filled with tumbles of red and white roses and carnations. The long table was draped in white lace and lined with arrangements of more roses, spilling out in an artfully artless fashion between silver bowls of nuts and mints, and silver platters piled high with pyramids of glistening fresh fruit. A string quartet played quietly in the background, hidden by a bank of potted palms.

The light from crystal chandeliers shimmered on the ladies' jewelled tiaras and the necklaces on their shoulders bared by satin and tulle from Worth. Even an informal dinner with the Prince demanded the finest of jewels.

Diana wished she had William's skills with shorthand, so she could take note of all the delicious details and not forget a thing. But the best she could do was remember it all and write her article as soon as she returned to her little apartment. For the moment, she could only enjoy the beautiful spectacle before her as the group assembled in the sitting room before dinner.

She turned away from her peek into the dining room to study the crowd. The Prince's party had not yet arrived, but there was already plenty of sparkle to rival the bright lights of the city beyond the hotel's gardens. The Duchess wore the Eastern Star as a pendant on a string of pearls around her neck before it was to go on display at the Exposition, along with more pearls and diamonds in her hair and scattered across her purple-satin gown like a bejewelled twilight sky. Alex, seated next to her mother on the sofa but looking as if her thoughts were a thousand miles away, also wore pearls with her pale pink watered silk trimmed with striped ruching.

The Duke stood beside the carved marble fireplace, talking and laughing quietly as they passed around the whisky. Aside from a uniform or two, the men all wore the regulation black and white evening clothes, all starched cravats and creamy brocade waistcoats, a backdrop to the ladies' splendour. But the men all wore bright medals and royal orders, as well, making Diana wonder what an 'official' royal visit would look like.

She glanced out the window, past the elaborate swags of the peach-taffeta curtains and the marble terrace to the darkened garden beyond. A few fairy lights were draped in the trees, lighting a path for the people making their way into the hotel's dining room. But those tiny glimmers of white light were mere echoes of the tower in the distance. It sparkled and flashed in the night, a beacon to merriment. She was sure she could even hear the dance music drifting up from the street, the accordion and the singers of love songs.

It made her think of her day with Will and she smiled secretly down into her drink to remember sipping champagne on the tower, wandering the pathways, eating ice cream, marvelling at the artworks. It had been one of her best days ever, with him by her side to share the beauty of it all, to laugh with her, talk to her.

'So deep in thought. Are you plotting a mystery story about a dinner party where everyone is hideously murdered? I would be.'

Diana spun around, startled, to find Christopher Blakely grinning down at her. His dark blond hair gleamed in the light and his smile was open and merry, full of mischief. For an instant, she could glimpse his brother in his eyes, eyes that held secrets concealed behind smiles, but then it was gone. They really looked so little alike and behaved even more differently.

'Chris! You startled me,' she said, pressing her gloved hand to her pounding heart, just above the lace edge of her bodice. 'But a dinner-party murder-mystery novel *does* sound intriguing.'

'Is that what you're working on writing now?'

'Sadly, no. It's much more dull. I am here to observe all the new Paris fashions.'

'How can that be dull? It gives you an excuse to go everywhere in Paris! Alex says you're very excited about your new magazine assignment, as you should be. *Ladies' Weekly* is lucky to have you.'

'And I am lucky to be there. They could have hired anyone. But what are *you* doing in Paris? Part of the Prince's entourage, like William?'

She felt her cheeks turn warm just to mention his name and she felt a little silly, like a giddy schoolgirl with a first crush. It made her want to laugh even more.

Chris scowled. 'Alas, I'm not half as useful as my brother is. I'm sure he's helping the Prince usher the Princess about just now, she is always so notoriously tardy to everything. I'm just here to enjoy the city.'

'And what have you seen so far? I'm always looking for new ideas for my articles.'

'Oh, the usual,' he said carelessly. 'The Louvre, the Tuileries gardens.' He looked away, waving to a footman for another drink, and it made Diana wonder. Chris wasn't a museum type at all. 'Have you seen Emily about since you've been here?'

'Not yet, but I think she is to be here later this evening.'

The doors opened and a uniformed usher announced, 'Their Royal Highnesses, the Prince and Princess of Wales, with Princess Louise, Princess Maud, and Princess Victoria.'

Everyone in the sitting room, who had been so lazily chatting and sipping their aperitifs, jumped up to gather near the royal party and make their curtsies. Diana glanced over her shoulder, but Chris had vanished into the crowd.

The Prince entered first, portly but strangely regal in his evening clothes, the Garter star gleaming on his lapel. His small, bright blue eyes seemed to take in every detail around him in one sweep, and he smiled when he saw Lady Alexandra and kissed her cheek as she curtsied, his short, greying beard brushing her pale skin. The Princess on his arm, smiling serenely in lavender brocade with amethysts and diamonds around her neck and a matching tiara on her curled dark hair, did the same before they turned to greet the Duke and Duchess. The three princesses, all in similar pale blue gowns, followed closely.

A bit awestruck, Diana studied the people gathered behind them, the equerries and ladies-in-waiting, all dressed almost as grandly as Princess Alexandra herself. Then she glimpsed William in the crowd and he came over to her, smiling. She had to force herself not to run to him, not to smile too broadly. Not to feel that flutter of excitement deep inside at the mere sight of him.

'Miss Martin,' he said, bowing over her hand. 'Lovely to see you again so soon. A working dinner, maybe?'

Diana laughed. 'Not as much work as for you, I'm sure. But I know readers *would* be fascinated to know what it's like to dine with a prince. You wouldn't happen to know which couturier made the Princess's gown, would you?'

'The Prince would be disappointed to know I don't pay attention to every detail as he does, but I'm afraid I have no idea. Could it be...er... Worth?'

Diana bit her lip to keep from grinning. 'Is that the only name of a fashion house you know?'

William chuckled ruefully. 'It is.'

Diana studied Princess Alexandra's gown a bit closer. The brocade was embroidered with the same shade of lavender in a pattern of flowers and vines, half-hidden by her diamond and amethyst stomacher. The hem was gathered up with bunches of velvet violets, each glinting with tiny green and purple sequins. 'That trim seems more like Doucet to me. Fascinating.' She turned and pretended to give William's own attire, black suit and regulation white waistcoat, an exaggerated once-over. He did look much too handsome, and it made her smile. 'And I would say your suit was made on Savile Row.'

'A discerning eye, Miss Martin. I'm afraid I've

always gone to the same tailor, where my father also goes.'

'As do half the men in London. An educated guess.'

'What of your own gown? Is it—what was the name? Doucet? If so, he's a talented chap. You look very elegant.'

Diana laughed and waved her lace fan in front of her face to hide her blush at the compliment. 'Not quite. Just my mother's London dressmaker. But I think she did quite a nice job.' And Diana herself had replaced the pink ribbons that once trimmed the white chiffon with bronze-coloured streamers and silver-satin ribbon rosebuds. That, along with a bit of lace at the bodice, seemed more 'Parisian'. She also had no tiara, but had woven a bronze-coloured classical-style wreath into her hair. She thought it went quite well with her dreaded red locks. 'Will I get in trouble for not having a proper tiara? I heard the Prince demands them on ladies at every dinner.'

'Only from married ladies. I'm sure he will be too dazzled to notice anyway.'

Alex hurried to their sides, her pale cheeks pink. 'Have you heard? The Maharajah is on his way up in the hotel lift!'

Diana peeked over at the royal party, who were still talking to the Duke and Duchess. The doors opened again and a group even more dazzling than the Waleses appeared. It was indeed the Maharajah Singh Lep and his wives and attendants. They were dazzling in bright silks and embroidery, gold, jewels, and ribbons. The Maharajah, tall and slim, though older, was still quite handsome and his wives in their brilliant saris were all dark, exotic beauties.

'Ah, the Maharajah, there you are,' the Prince said, seemingly only the tiniest bit put out that he had been out-sparkled. 'Lost in traffic, were you? Paris is so crowded these days. Do come and meet our kind hostess. The Duke, of course, you already know.'

'Your father invited the Maharajah tonight?' Diana whispered to Alex.

'Yes, as a sort of thanks between them for agreeing to display the Star in a show of unity between our kingdoms, or something like that,' Alex whispered back. 'I don't think Mother was very happy about it. It threw off her numbers at the table.'

Indeed, the Duchess did seem a bit out of sorts, the skin around her eyes tight. But she hadn't been a society hostess for decades for nothing and the smile she offered their guests was dazzling.

'I'm surprised Chris isn't here to see them,' Diana said. 'Wasn't he talking about some investment scheme with the Maharajah at your parents' ball in London?'

William frowned. 'Chris was here?'

'Oh, yes. I was just talking to him before you arrived, but then he vanished somewhere.'

William looked as if he wanted to ask her more, but there was no time. The dining-room doors were thrown open and the Duke and Duchess were leading the way into dinner, indicating the place cards for each guest. Even Chris had reappeared, seated next to an elderly countess in black lace at the far end of the table.

Much to Diana's delight, she found herself sitting beside William. 'Oh, thank heavens!' she whispered to him as the footman unfurled the starched sky-blue napkins. 'I was afraid I would have to sit beside one of the frightfully fossilised equerries who are always sent by the Queen to keep an eye on the Prince and I would have no idea what to say to them.' She nodded towards Alex at the other end of the table, next to Lord Mellington, who it was said had once led a charge in the Crimea and now couldn't hear anything above a shout. He usually sat next to the Princess, the two of them happily smiling at each other in silence, but tonight Alex was his partner.

'Just ask them about their time in Cape Town or Sydney or the Punjab,' William said with a grin. 'They'll talk for hours and you can just nod sometimes and think about writing your next article.'

Diana laughed. 'I do appreciate the time to think, of course, but a bit of conversation over the consommé wouldn't go amiss. Like our glorious afternoon at the fair! Wasn't it lovely?'

William leaned back, smiling, as the footman spooned turtle soup into their shallow, gold-rimmed bowls. 'It was indeed. Quite the nicest day I've had for a long while.'

Diana remembered the champagne on the tower, the way his laugh there sparkled as much as the wine and made her feel twice as giddy. 'For me, as well. All those wondrous sights! I can't recall anything like it. When I was a little girl and we lived at my family's country house, my father would sometimes take me to the village fête. I loved it so much, the ribbons for sale, the music, the cinnamon cakes. My father would carry me on his shoulders, so I could see it all. The Exposition is a bit like that, only a hundred times more grand.' She took a sip of the salty soup, suddenly catapulted back into a long-past sunlit day. 'That was the most time I ever spent with my father at all. Even when he wasn't overseas at his posts, he was terribly busy.'

William nodded, watching her closely as if he considered every word. He didn't just look over her when she spoke, as most men did. 'As was my father. Chris and I hardly ever saw him and when he did appear, I admit we were frightened to death of him. That booming voice, just like a cannon. "Well, now, what trouble have you little monsters been in today?" Chris would usually run and hide.'

'And you didn't?'

'I confess I was paralysed with fear.'

Diana had to laugh at the image of little Will gone still as a statue, since that was obviously the reaction he expected from his tale, but inside her heart ached for the poor, frightened little boys. At least her father had always been kind, if distracted, when she saw him. 'Was your father with the Foreign Office, as well?'

William shook his head. 'He was in the army when he was young, until he took some shrapnel in his knee and was consigned to a desk. I don't think he ever got over it. It was the danger he loved so much. He rather wished one of us would follow in his footsteps.'

'But you didn't feel suited for the army,' she said, remembering his earlier words. The church or the army, yet he didn't seem right for either.

The soup bowls were smoothly replaced by the fish course. 'I had thought about it when I was at school. But when I was offered a place at Cambridge, I realised my talents were more—cerebral.'

Diana hid a smile as she remembered their kiss, the way it had made her very toes curl and her mind go blank with pleasure. 'I would say you are *multi*-talented, Sir William.'

He gave her a curious glance, his eyes narrowed as if in speculation. 'Would you indeed? I am flattered. Most chaps would say I'm only good for books and fusty old offices.'

'Well, us ladies certainly know differently.' Then she remembered Lady Smythe-Tomas, the desperate way she had clung to William in the Waverton library, and Diana glanced away. 'So you found the diplomatic service at Cambridge?'

'I studied the classics. But one of my tutors saw

I was very interested in other cultures and not bad with modern languages, so when I graduated...'

'With a first, so your aunt the Duchess says.' And so Mrs Blakely was said to use as a prod to poor Chris, much to poor Chris's despair.

'True enough. My tutor recommended me to his own brother, who was leading a diplomatic party to the India station and needed a secretary. He agreed to take me on.'

'And you found your calling.'

'So I did. I've always loved learning languages. They're the key to whole other worlds. And once you open those doors, see new ways of being and thinking, talk to new people—you can never see in the old way again. It's quite astonishing.'

Diana was fascinated. What he said sounded the way she felt when she wrote. Lost in new worlds. 'I've always loved hiding in my father's library and reading about Africa, India, America. The colours and scents...'

'A glimpse of which we had at the Exposition.'

'Yes, and now I want more and more!' She lowered her voice and whispered, 'Don't you miss India, now that you've been sent here just to corral the Prince? Paris must seem so ordinary after Calcutta.'

William laughed, that deep, rich sound she loved so much. 'On the contrary. Paris, I am coming to realise, is one of the most beautiful places on earth. And the humidity is considerably less.'

'I suppose we had a taste of it all today at the Indian Pavilion. And tonight with the Maharajah,' Diana said, nodding towards where Singh Lep was talking to the Duchess. A plate of duck *à l'orange* was set before her and she took a nibble of the sweet sauce. 'Those samosas we had were perfection. I have never tasted anything like them in England.'

'And that is just the start of the fair. There's still the Wild West Show, the Galerie des Machines, and much more to see. What is on your list next?'

'Oh, the Egyptian souk! Readers will want to know about the fabrics on sale there and what can be made from them. And, of course, Mr Edison's amazing inventions and the Manets at the arts pavilion. And I promised Mama to make time for the Louvre.'

'And you must try the new bicycles!' Princess Louise, the Waleses' eldest daughter, who sat across from them, said brightly. Everyone glanced at her in surprise, for the three Wales daughters were known to be shy. But Louise's enthusiasm for the new sport seemed to overcome even her shyness. Her plain, pale face shone under the crescents of her diamond tiara. 'I rode one today by the river and I never had such fun. I must take one back to Sandringham when we leave.'

'You haven't ever had so much fun riding your horses, my dear?' the Prince said with an indulgent chuckle.

'Oh, Papa,' Princess Louise answered. 'Bicycles are not nearly so smelly as horses! And the clothes are ever so smart and pretty.'

'Split skirts,' her mother murmured with a tsk.

'Mother dear, even Aunt Minnie wears such things for riding now,' Princess Louise said. 'I think they are adorable. Don't you, Miss Martin? You know so much about fashion.'

Diana was startled. She wasn't sure she had ever been addressed by royalty before, except for a murmured 'How d'you do?' from the Queen at her presentation. And a princess even realised she enjoyed clothes and style? She glanced at William, who gave her a little nod. 'I—yes, Your Highness, I do enjoy fashion very much. The bicycling ensembles I've seen are very pretty, but I'm afraid I've only tried riding once or twice and was very awkward.'

Princess Louise giggled, a surprisingly girlish sound for a young lady rumoured to be engaged to be married. 'Oh, my sister Toria rides them all the time, don't you, Toria? And she's the clumsiest creature in the world.'

Princess Victoria, the tallest and plainest of the Princesses, gave a game little nod and a laugh.

'Louise,' their mother said, softly chiding.

'Well, everyone knows it,' Princess Louise insisted.

'Families,' William muttered in Diana's ear with a wry smile that made her want to smile, too. 'They are the same everywhere.'

Diana pressed her napkin to her lips to hide a laugh. She wondered what he meant, what his own family was like. Were they as strict and disapproving as her own parents?

'Well, everyone should try it,' Princess Louise said. 'Such fun. What do you say, Lady Alexandra?'

'I would love to try it, Your Highness, if no one was around to laugh at me,' Alex said softly.

'My dear, really,' the Duchess clucked. 'You will be far too busy to have time to indulge in such novelties.'

Diana was suddenly even more glad her own

mother wasn't around to see what she did, like the Duchess and Princess Alexandra. She rather would like to try a bicycle.

'I am sure my own wives would be most adept at it,' the Maharajah said. 'It must be much easier than riding an elephant!'

The wives giggled into the silken folds of their sari headdresses.

'Did you ever ride an elephant, Sir William?' Diana asked.

William glanced down the table at the Maharajah, their looks unreadable to anyone but themselves, and Diana suddenly remembered William had known the man in India. Yet he clearly hadn't been looking forward to seeing him again in Paris. She wondered what had happened.

'Once,' William answered. 'I didn't exactly cover myself in glory, I confess.'

'Did you fall off?' Alex teased. '*You*, Will, who are always so perfect?'

'Even your cricket-playing Englishmen must learn new things sometimes,' the Maharajah said.

The next course, chocolate ice cream with tiny biscuits in cut-crystal bowls, was brought in.

'Ah, but my brother is no ordinary cricket-playing Englishman, are you, Will?' Chris said from his place at the end of the table. Diana didn't quite like his tone—it was too loud, too strident, not at all like him.

She glanced at his empty wine glass and wondered how many times it had been filled. Will just looked at his brother steadily, expressionlessly.

'He is the *super* Englishman, able to accomplish anything,' Chris said. 'I'm surprised the blasted elephant didn't bow down to him. Nothing about the stink of humanity on you, is there, Will?'

'There are ladies present, Blakely,' the Duke hissed.

'Including my wife and daughters,' said the Prince of Wales. He scowled at Chris. 'You *have* served a very fine wine, Waverton, but maybe a breath of fresh air is in order for some of us?'

'I will see to it, sir,' William said grimly. He pushed his chair back and slid around the table to take his brother by the arm. He pulled Chris gently but firmly from his seat. Chris tried to pull away, but William held on, a small, polite, steady smile on his lips. 'Come on, Christopher. Just a little walk on the terrace.'

They left the dining room and the Duchess for once looked rather flustered. 'Oh—I—should I ring for coffee?'

'Of course not, my dear Duchess,' Princess Alexandra said with her always serene smile. 'This ice cream looks like it should absolutely not be missed. Is it from Berthillon? I've been told their treats here in Paris are a treasure.'

The quiet shock around the table slid back into chatter and laughter, as if Chris's little faux pas hadn't even happened. But Diana wasn't sure what to do or where to look.

'Have you ever been to India yourself, Miss Martin?' one of the Maharajah's wives asked in softly accented English.

Startled at being addressed once more by royalty in one night, Diana studied the lady across the table. She had a gentle smile that went well with her pale green sari edged in gold.

'No, but I should certainly like to one day, Your Highness,' Diana said.

'I thought perhaps you had. The trim on your pretty gown is so unusual. Much like what we see in our own markets.'

Diana glanced down at the bronze ribbons on her white gown. 'I bought them here in Paris, near the Indian Pavilion at the Exposition. But my father was once in India. He sometimes tells stories about his time there.'

'I do hope you will visit the pavilion again,' the lady said.

'Perhaps when the Eastern Star goes on display?' her husband suggested. 'We have arranged for the music and refreshments of our homeland during the festivities. Maybe there will even be an elephant?'

The Maharajah smiled and it was so charming and open Diana had to smile back. It was no wonder, really, that Chris would be drawn into any scheme involving such a man. But then there was Thursby, too. 'I should like the food and music, but I'm not sure about the elephant.'

'Ah, but they are tender creatures, really! Gentle giants. My grandmother used to say no celebration would be complete without the procession of elephants.' A frown flickered over his face. 'It is sad she is not here to share this time with us. She did so love the Star. To see it again would have been her greatest wish.'

'I am so sorry,' Diana said, remembering the strange story of the jewel's sale. 'Has she been gone long, Your Highness?'

'A few years. She served as regent, just as you once had here in England. But she was a kind, soft soul, as ladies should be, and could not hold on to much of our treasure. My homeland, you see, is an ancient one, filled with lovely treasures, much coveted. When I was a young man, I was persuaded that to share the jewel would foster friendship between our homelands and the Duke seemed a very fine caretaker. As he has been.' He gestured at the trim of her gown. 'I see you are a lady of fine taste yourself. That embroidery is in the style of my home. Have you visited much of the Exposition yet?'

Diana was glad of the change of subject. 'I only had the smallest glimpse so far. I'm looking forward to seeing more of the Indian Pavilion at the opening party.'

'Ah, yes. To see the Star among its rightful jewelled companions again,' the Maharajah said with a strange little smile. 'I promise, my dear lady, you will not want to miss it.'

William returned and Princess Alexandra gave him her calm smile. 'I do hope dear Christopher is well,' she said, gesturing to a footman to bring Will more ice cream.

'A touch of the catarrh, ma'am,' William said smoothly, taking his seat again. 'He is in the library, resting.'

'How unfortunate,' the Princess said. 'A bit of

soda water, maybe? I do find that helps stomach troubles.'

'Our family has a sadly weak constitution at times, ma'am,' the Duchess said. 'I fear my nephew is rather delicate.'

Diana pressed her napkin to her lips to keep from laughing. Chris—delicate? He could be described as many things, but not quite that. And William certainly not.

'What did you do with him, really?' she whispered to William. 'Chuck him over the balcony?'

'Locked him in a linen closet until he can learn to behave properly,' he answered. His expression was so strict and cold, she wasn't sure if he was serious or not. Certainly she could believe he could be so stern if needed. Hadn't she once even thought him utterly dour and humourless? But then he smiled at her and she laughed. 'He really is in the library, with a bottle of the Princess's soda water. He's in no shape for a proper talking-to until tomorrow, I'm afraid.'

'He seemed fine when I saw him earlier. Maybe he really is ill?' she said, thinking of his odd behaviour lately.

'He will be fine, once he thinks things through.

He's always been impulsive. He has to realise he's not a child any longer.'

Diana took the last taste of her ice cream and wondered what he meant. How was Chris being a child? The money troubles? And how many times had William been the responsible one, the one who saved his brother, his family?

As Princess Alexandra rose from the table to lead the ladies out with the Duchess, she said, 'I have invited a few people for cards later. If you could not spend long on your cigars, Bertie dear? You wouldn't want to miss a game of bridge.'

'Of course not, my dear,' the Prince said in a fond, indulgent tone.

In the sitting room, over cups of tea and petits fours, there was much giggling over Chris's behaviour.

Alex shook her head sadly. 'Poor Chris. Whatever could have got into him? He has not been at all the same lately.'

'Money troubles, maybe?' Diana said. 'He did mention some investment scheme to do with India.'

Alex looked shocked. 'Oh, I do hope not! That

sounds quite perilous. I'm sure he can't be in such trouble as all that.'

There was no chance to say any more, as Princess Louise came over to talk to them further about bicycling. She had found a place near the river that rented the machines and persuaded them to give it a try. As they talked, there was a sudden loud crack from beyond the windows and the night sky was lit up in flecks of gold for an instant.

'Oh, fireworks!' Princess Louise cried. She ran to the windows, all the other ladies following.

A shooting spray of red and gold raced up high above their heads, illuminating the tower in the distance. Smaller, star-shaped bursts followed, along with spinning, fiery Catherine wheels.

'How beautiful,' Alex gasped, her face even more ethereal in the glow of the fireworks. When she was entranced by beauty, her shyness vanished.

As Diana watched, also entranced, she felt a warm, steady presence at her back. She turned to see that William and the other gentlemen had joined them from the dining room, just in time to watch the show. The Prince had led his wife to the balcony, but William stood with her, so close she could feel the warmth of his lean body, smell the faint spice of his cologne. The moment seemed like a tiny, perfect dream.

'Isn't it gorgeous?' she whispered to him.

He smiled down at her, his face all carved angles in the shadowed light, his eyes dark and fathomless. 'Gorgeous indeed. I knew you would like Paris. It does suit you.'

'So it does.' She looked back to the fireworks, the sea of rooftops and chimneys. The elegance of the city, the old stones and the newness of the Exposition, the sophisticated beauty. She had dreamed of such things in her room at home and now they were hers. Adventure was hers, at least for a while, and William was beside her.

Her gaze followed the arc of the lights into the sky, but she was most aware of him close beside her, his hand brushing hers in the darkness.

Music suddenly burst out from the garden below, Offenbach's *Infernal Galop*, quick and light, just like the city. Just like her heart when she saw William. She leaned out the window to glimpse a small orchestra in the latticed summerhouse among the trees. It only added to the rare, fragile, precious magic of the moment.

'Oh, my favourite song!' Princess Alexandra exclaimed. 'Shall we all go down and dance?'

Her husband gave her an indulgent smile and patted her hand. 'Why not, my dear? It sounds grand.'

Laughing with excitement, everyone trooped out of the drawing room and down the steps, spilling out into the lit-up garden.

William offered Diana his arm. 'What do you say, Miss Martin? I hope I didn't disgrace myself so much at our last dance that I don't deserve another.'

Diana well remembered their last dance, how being in his arms made her feel, and she blushed. She did that far too much in his presence! 'I think one more chance just might be warranted.'

She took his arm, feeling the flex of his muscles under her gloved touch, and they followed the others out into the garden. He put his arms around her, holding her close, and twirled her into the night.

Dancing with him was just as magical as she remembered, their steps moving lightly, perfectly together. As the fireworks exploded overhead in a shower of silvery light, Diana was sure she felt just the same way in her heart, sparkling and bubbly and free.

He felt so warm under her touch, so strong. When they were close like that, she felt she could see him, the *real* him. That some of his usual diplomatic caution dropped away and he laughed as he twirled her among the other dancers. The sound of it was so wonderful, like warm chocolate smooth and dark on a cold night, and she longed to hear it again. To see him smile at her once more.

There were so many things she wanted to say to him. Yet the moment was so magical, his touch on her, the exhilarating movement of the dance as they seemed to sway and turn as one, that she couldn't shatter it with words. Wouldn't make him withdraw from her at any cost. So she just held him as close as she dared and lost herself in the moment with him.

She was bold enough to slide her gloved fingers a little closer along his shoulder, letting them touch the rough silk of his hair above his collar. It curled around her fingertips, and he smiled down at her, that crooked lilt of his lips in the shadows.

'Do you believe in something like fate?' she asked impulsively. 'I mean—that we're meant to find a happiness that waits for us in one certain spot in life?'

His head gave a puzzled tilt. 'Fate?'

'Yes. I read about it in a book Alex loaned me,' she said. She felt her cheeks turn warm. Surely he would think such a question silly! Yet she had found the words in that book intriguing and that moment seemed to illustrate them perfectly. She didn't tell him it had been in a French romantic novel, of course, but surely such stories held much wisdom? 'Fate designs our perfect life for us and we just have to find it. I've thought about that a lot here in Paris. It's so beautiful here, I feel as if I've always been meant to walk these lanes. Dance in this garden.' Dance with him, with the stars overhead and his smile beaming down at her.

'I think we're meant to do our duty,' he answered, his voice soft and deep. 'Maybe your fate designs us to accomplish that.'

Diana shook her head at his seriousness. 'Maybe. But my idea of fate is certainly more fun than that!'

He laughed. 'I can't argue with that. Life should have a measure of fun, certainly.'

'We have to search for our happiness, I suppose, make it ourselves. Fate can only help us a bit. Yet I can see here in Paris that happiness *can* be made. That it just waits for us to snatch it up and run with it!'

His smile turned strangely wistful. 'Oh, my sweet Diana. That is very wise. I only wish…'

His Diana? She felt a tiny, warm touch of hope blossom deep inside, the tingle of a fearful excitement. 'Wish what? That it was true? Surely it can be.'

'For you it is. And you deserve it more than anyone I know.'

'And so do you!' she said eagerly. 'Can we not do our duty and also be happy?'

'Tonight I think that is so,' he said with a laugh. He sent her into a quick, graceful twirl into the night-dark garden, making her giggle.

'Isn't it marvellous?' she gasped, as he spun her into the shadows of the tall trees in the garden.

'Marvellous,' he murmured. He smiled down at her and, as if he was as caught in the magical moment as she was, he leaned closer. The dark glow of his eyes told her he wanted to kiss her, just as he had in that London solarium and she wanted to be kissed. So very much. More than she had ever wanted anything in her life.

But before their lips could touch, a shadow fell

over his face, like a cloud sliding in front of that magical moon, as his glance flashed over her shoulder.

Chilly with disappointment, she whispered, 'What...?'

'Oh, my! We came for cards and found dancing, how delightful.'

Diana spun around to find Lady Smythe-Tomas watching the gathering with an amused smile on her beautiful, catlike face. Her gown, purple and black striped crepe over darker purple satin, edged with jet beads and sequins, matched her headdress of black feathers, making Diana feel dowdy in her debutante pastels. She held on to Lord Thursby's arm, and smiled out on to the crowd as if they had gathered just for her.

The magic of the night suddenly seemed to fizzle, like the fireworks fading overhead and leaving just the scent of smoke. Thursby and Lady Smythe-Tomas made Diana remember the real world, the one that always waited beyond magical dreams.

'Laura, my dear,' the Prince said, going to kiss her cheek with great enthusiasm. Princess Alexandra's laughter had also faded away, leaving her with her usual smiling mask. 'How beautiful you look tonight. You ladies do flower so here in Paris.'

'How can we help it, sir?' She glanced at William, a sidelong look. 'It isn't so terrible for you gentlemen, either. How lovely this all is.'

'And you must have a dance.' The Prince studied the crowd of the party. 'Blakely, you've been a most useful sort lately and working much too hard. You certainly deserve a reward.' He held out Lady Smythe-Tomas's hand to William.

William could hardly decline, even if he wanted to. And Diana was not at all sure he would want to. She studied his face, that face that was so maddeningly expressionless sometimes, and remembered the way Lady Smythe-Tomas had clung to him in the library. 'Thank you, sir,' he said, bowing towards her. 'Would you do me the honour?'

'Of course,' the lady said with a dazzling smile. She and William waltzed away into the garden, so elegantly that it made Diana's heart ache to watch them. She felt as if she was sinking down to the ground from the delightful clouds that had been in her head.

Suddenly feeling very alone, Diana glanced around. Alexandra was dancing with the Maharajah, laughing at something he said, and the Prince and Princess stood together still, but seemed rather far apart.

'Would you care to dance, Miss Martin?' she heard Thursby ask.

She pasted on a polite smile and turned to face him. He was a handsome man, she had to admit, and his smile was kind, almost eager. Perhaps she was wrong about him, as she had been about too many other things lately? And she couldn't think how to politely refuse, to go off and be alone as she suddenly want to do.

'Thank you, Lord Thursby,' she said and slowly took his offered hand. But he tried to hold her rather closer than the figures of the dance called for and she edged away.

'You and Lady Smythe-Tomas must be great friends,' she said, trying to break the uncomfortable feeling that had crept over her again. He looked down at her, a strangely amused half-smile on his face.

'I knew her late husband,' he answered lightly. 'He asked me to look after his wife. I take my friendships most seriously, as you would see if you would just give me a chance.'

Diana glanced at Will and his partner, the two

of them spinning in a smooth arc. 'I—and have you been in Paris long yourself, Lord Thursby?'

'I only arrived today, but I'm looking forward to seeing all the sights this week.' He twirled her lightly. 'Your mother tells me you are here to write about the Exposition. In a professional capacity?'

Diana didn't quite like the way he said the word 'professional', as though it was something to laugh at. 'For *Ladies' Weekly*, for a few weeks. It's all been very exciting.'

'I'm sure. But not what a lady would prefer to be doing, of course.'

Diana edged away again, but his hand on her back held her where she was. 'This lady enjoys it very much. I may want to continue after the Exposition closes.'

'Surely not! Do you not want a home to run, a place in society? As all women in your position prefer.'

'And what would a lady prefer to be doing, except to be in the most beautiful city in the world?' she asked, looking around rather desperately for Alex, or the Duchess, or *anyone* who could come to her rescue. But everyone was too distracted by the fireworks, which had reached their grand finale of wheels and rockets, all red and green and gold.

'Organise her house, of course. Help further her husband's career. Surely you do wish for those things, Miss Martin? They are your birthright, what you've been educated for.'

Diana rather hoped her time at Miss Grantley's prepared her for more than that, but she knew a man like Lord Thursby wouldn't hear that. She gave him a tight smile, and was quite relieved that the music and the fireworks ended and Princess Alexandra called them in for card games.

'Do excuse me, Lord Thursby,' she said, hurriedly turning away. 'I need to find my friends.'

But as she followed the others up the steps and back into the hotel, she glimpsed William and Lady Smythe-Tomas, talking quietly near the edge of the terrace, their heads bent together. They looked most intent and serious together. And some of the magic of the Parisian night faded like the smoke of the fireworks.

'What on earth were you thinking, Chris?' William asked as their carriage bumped over the Parisian cobblestones, bearing them back to their lodgings. His brother sat on the seat opposite, his evening clothes rumpled, his hair standing on end. He held his head in hands. 'You know how the Prince hates a scene.'

Christopher shook his head. 'I don't know. It was all just—so much. My temper got the best of me. You know how I am.'

'Yes.' Will remembered when Chris was a boy, how headlong he would rush into everything. Will sat back on the carriage seat, watching the pale stone of the Parisian buildings as they flashed past. 'But we are adults now. We have to make our ways in the world.'

Chris gave a harsh laugh. 'Are you joining our parents and saying I should marry a good, steady lady?'

'Of course not. You know I'm the last person to urge a marriage that might not be happy. We see that too much in our family.' His parents, always arguing behind their own doors even as they kept up appearances in society; the Duke and Duchess, their uncle and aunt, with nothing in common but their title. Will had never wanted that and he didn't want it for his brother, either. 'But what is amiss with you lately? What have you been doing while I was abroad?'

'I just want to do what's right, Will.'

'As we all do. Why do you think I go into the Foreign Office every day? Our parents are worried about you, as I am. Have you given Thursby money for that investment scheme of his?'

Chris crossed his arms, a mulish look on his face. 'That's none of your business, nor is it that of our parents. They only care when they think a scandal might attach to their precious name. They should look to themselves if they're so worried and so should you. None of us are angels.' He looked out the window. 'Why would any respectable lady take me on, anyway? Or you, for that matter. You're so quiet, so secretive.'

Will had no answer for that. He had to admit Chris was right. He *was* secretive. He had to be. He would be no fit husband for a woman he cared about. A woman of talent and spirit, like—like Diana Martin.

Once he had thought her innocent and somewhat awkward, someone in need of looking after. But now he saw how wrong he had been. She wasn't awkward at all—she was enthusiastic and spirited, she saw the world in fascinating new ways. Ways he wished she would share with him.

He pushed away thoughts of her, but still she was there, at the edges of his mind. As she was too often of late. He laid awake at night, just re-membering how sweet her kiss was under his lips. How her laugh sounded. But she was too spirited indeed for him to put his family's unhappiness on to her. 'I just hope you know I want to help you, Chris, no matter what. We're brothers. We're all we have.'

He turned to Chris, only to find his brother was asleep, his rumpled golden head slumped to his shoulder. Will laughed ruefully and wished he could forget the world beyond the carriage just as easily. But he knew he never could.

Chapter Eleven

'Are you sure it's a department store? It looks like a palace,' Diana said as she stared up at the façade of Gordston's department store on the Champs-Élysées. Even on that fabled street, lined with gilded shops and elegant restaurants, it stood out.

The white stone gleamed, while the gold letters of the sign sparkled in the sunny day. The tall plate-glass windows were filled with the lure of bright silks and satins in all the latest styles. A photo of Princess Alexandra in the hat she had worn only the day before stood beside an array of perfect copies.

Alex laughed. 'Of course it's a shop. You saw the man's yacht. Surely he does nothing by halves. Ooh, look at this!' She pointed at a smaller window, where a pearl and diamond tiara and matching earrings rested on a purple-velvet cushion. 'Isn't it lovely?'

'Perfect for a royal wedding. Or maybe a ducal one?' Diana teased.

Alex made a face. 'Don't let my parents hear you. They're sure I'll meet some dazzling *parti* while we're here. Which reminds me—I promised them we would be back in time to go with the Waleses to Eiffel's tower today.'

'Oh, yes, we should hurry. Emily's waiting.'

They joined the throng of fashionable people flowing up the white-marble steps and through the revolving door into the store, excited to be the first few chosen to experience the store for its grand opening. If Diana had thought the outside dazzling, inside it was quite otherworldly. The polished alabaster floors were lined with glass cases, all filled with the most alluring array of silk scarves, hats on stands, jewellery and cut-crystal bottles of scent that filled the air with the rich smell of summer roses and heady lilies. Mannequins on tall plinths displayed gowns of fluttering chiffon and handmade lace. There were gilded staircases and even elevators operated by girls in sharply tailored red suits.

'I've heard that there's a café on the fourth

floor,' Alex said. 'If we hurry, maybe we could grab a cream cake before we leave!'

'How can you think of food, Alex, when there is so much to see?' Diana asked, as she jotted down a few notes.

'Oh, you know me, I always think about food. I still dream about the lemon tarts at Miss Grantley's tea hour. Look, there's Emily!'

They rushed across the crowded floor to greet their friend, who already carried several wrapped packages.

'What a brilliant idea to meet here,' Emily cried, kissing their cheeks. 'It's absolutely stunning. I'll have to tell Father to come here and meet Mr Gordston. I'm sure we do some business with him. Is he here, do you think? I've heard he's very handsome indeed, as well as having the best of taste.'

Alex's pale cheeks turned pink. 'No time for that today, Em. We are on an errand.'

'Oh, yes,' Diana said, suddenly remembering *why* they were there in that magical place. 'We have to find bicycling suits.'

'Bicycling suits?' Emily said. 'How exciting. I think I did see some ready-made ones on the second floor.'

They climbed the wide, winding stairs, pointing out famous actresses and a princess or two, all of them dressed in beautiful suits and gowns, the flowers on their hats like a summer garden. As they went, they told Emily about the planned biking excursion with Princess Louise, and invited her along.

There were indeed ready-made ones on the second floor, with a roving array of dressmakers in black silk with tape measures looped around their necks, ready to make any alterations. Alex and Emily sorted through an array of muslin day dresses, while Diana examined a heather-coloured tweed suit on a mannequin. A small sign said it could also come with a divided skirt for bicycling or equestrienne sports.

As she studied the cut of the double-breasted jacket with its lapels, she suddenly caught sight of a familiar figure. Lady Smythe-Tomas, clad in an afternoon gown of tawny silk trimmed in white-ribbon roses with a rose-covered hat, stood at the counter. It was certainly no surprise to see the most fashionable lady of London society at the most fashionable department store, but it was a surprise that she looked—angry. Her pretty, catlike face was puckered in a frown and she waved her gloved hands at a saleslady.

'*Non, non,*' the woman said, softly but firmly. 'I am afraid the books say no more credit at this time.'

'That cannot be! I am one of Gordston's best customers. Everyone copies my gowns. Don't you know who I am? I must speak to a manager.'

'I am the floor manager, *madame.*'

'Then I must speak to someone higher up! To Monsieur Gordston himself.'

As Diana watched, astonished, an errand boy was sent off and Lady Smythe-Tomas and the manageress continued to argue in voices too low to be heard. Even though the words were inaudible, Diana could see the lady's taut expression.

Lady Smythe-Tomas turned away from the woman with a huff and Diana instinctively ducked behind the mannequin. She didn't want to be seen watching an embarrassing scene. Soon Alex and Emily wandered back to her and she turned to them in relief.

'What do you two think of this?' she asked, glad to be distracted from the spectacle of Lady Smythe-Tomas arguing with a saleswoman. 'I quite like the colour, but it says it also comes in caramel and carmine. I think I have a hat that would go with it.'

Emily weighed the fabric between her fingers with the ease of expertise. 'It's quite fine, especially for ready to wear. Look at the cut of the lapels and trimmed with velvet, too. Is the new longer-jacket length *au courant*, Di?'

'Everything at Gordston's is absolutely up to the minute and of top quality, I promise,' a deep voice, slightly accented with a Scottish brogue, said behind them.

Startled, Diana whirled around to see the Norse god they had glimpsed on his fine yacht standing behind them. Alex gave a little gasp.

He smiled, as if amused he had surprised them. 'Lady Alexandra. It's an honour to have you in my humble store. I hope you've found something you like.'

Alex pursed her lips. 'Of course. As you say, everything is quite stylish and I would be most surprised to see otherwise. Mr Gordston, may I present my friends, Miss Diana Martin and Miss Emily Fortescue.'

He gave a small bow. 'Miss Fortescue. And Miss Martin. Of *Ladies' Weekly*?'

Diana was surprised to hear he knew of her

job. 'So I am. I'm writing about the Exposition for them.'

'If you'd like a tour of the store, be sure and let us know,' he said. *'Ladies' Weekly* is a fine publication. And, of course, any friend of Lady Alexandra's...'

Delighted, Diana opened her mouth to accept the invitation, but Alexandra startled her by seizing her hand. 'She is very busy this week, Mr Gordston. And I'm sure everyone has heard a great deal about your store already.'

His lips quirked in amusement. 'I do hope so, Lady Alexandra. We strive to be the best, always. Miss Martin, if your busy schedule allows, do let me know if I can be of any assistance. Now, if you will excuse me...'

Mr Gordston bowed again and made his way to the counter where Lady Smythe-Tomas waited, tapping her kid shoe impatiently. He smiled at her and her angry expression melted away.

'Alex, whatever was that about?' Diana whispered. 'Of course I would like a tour of the store! It would make a lovely article.'

Alex shook her head, her cheeks pink. 'I'm sorry, Di. He just—rubs me the wrong way, I think.'

'You?' Diana said, shocked. Alex was the nicest person she knew, always thinking the best of everyone around her. Sweet and shy.

'Certainly you should take the tour,' Alex said. 'Just ignore my silliness.'

'Isn't that Lady Smythe-Tomas?' Emily said, watching the little scene at the counter. 'Whatever do you think could be the problem?'

'Maybe they put the wrong ribbons on her new hat,' Alex said.

'It looks more serious than that,' Emily said. 'Father says there isn't a shop in London that will give her credit now.'

'Really?' Diana gasped. 'I would have thought her photographs alone would pay quite well. And they say Lord Smythe-Tomas was quite flush.'

'Expensive tastes,' Emily said drily. 'You would be surprised how very many people live above their touch. Keeping up with the Waleses is no cheap prospect.'

They watched as Lady Smythe-Tomas put her hand softly on Mr Gordston's fine wool sleeve and smiled up at him from beneath the brim of her hat. Diana remembered that scene in the Waverton library when she had looked at William much like that.

'Perhaps she should marry Mr Gordston, then, and have him settle her bills,' Alexandra said.

Emily laughed. 'A shopkeeper? I've been in the business long enough to know what someone like the famous Lady Smythe-Tomas would say about *that*. Still, I'm sure she'll find someone soon enough. Now, should we order our bicycling togs? I think I rather fancy the carmine tweed myself.'

As they were leaving a half hour later, their new clothes ordered, Diana paused to study a hat on display. It was quite an extravagant affair, with a wide, swooping brim, trimmed in a large striped bow and a sweep of feathers.

'You should try it on,' Emily urged.

Diana laughed. 'I'm sure my mother would never let me wear it. Much too daring, she would say.'

'All the better, then,' Emily said.

Diana rather agreed. Her parents seemed so far away, their rules unimportant. One of the sales assistants took it off the display for her and Diana carefully balanced it on her head. She studied herself in the mirror, turning this way and that, studying the effect of the feathered confection.

She laughingly blew herself a kiss, twirled

around—and found herself looking right at William, who was grinning in amusement. She felt her cheeks turn warm, but had to laugh at her own silliness. Why did she always look like an impulsive schoolgirl in front of him?

'Will,' Alex said, going to give her cousin a quick hug as Diana took off the hat and tried to hide her blush. 'Whatever are you doing here?'

'Very important work indeed,' he answered, still watching Diana. She didn't look at him, but she could feel the sweep of his gaze like a touch on her skin. 'I have to arrange a delivery for your godmother the Princess.'

'Oh, you must tell us what she's ordering!' Emily said. 'Di can put it in one of her articles.'

Will took out a letter and studied it with a puzzled frown that made them all laugh. 'I'm afraid I can't make sense of it. I should just give it to a saleslady and let the professionals handle it, yes?'

'I can probably help you,' Diana said. 'Let me see.'

'Perhaps you could instruct the staff what's needed and I could walk you home after?' he said. 'It would be a tremendous help.'

Diana felt a flutter of excitement at his words, at the thought of spending a little time alone with him, talking to him, seeing his rare smiles. She glanced at Alex and Emily, who looked as if they were about to collapse in giggles. She feared they would make her do the same.

'Of course,' Emily said. 'You must do your duty by your Princess. We will see you this evening, Di.'

She took Alex's arm and they hurried away, whispering together. Diana smiled up at Will and they made their way to the receptionist desk at the front of the store to leave their list. Once that errand was taken care of, with Diana briskly ordering what was required, Will led her out into the bright, sunny Parisian day.

They chatted of light things as they walked, passing the overflowing flower carts, the sweet-smelling candied-almond vendors, the children with their hoops and wagons, and Diana was sure she couldn't remember a lovelier afternoon. Will was beside her, smiling at her, his hand on her arm as he led her across the street, and it made her want to twirl and dance.

She glanced back at the store as they turned a corner and suddenly remembered Lady Smythe-Tomas had been there. She wondered if Will had seen her there, what he thought when he encountered her. But those memories were quickly gone as they made their way through a green, flower-filled park.

A group was having a picnic under a shady grove of trees, their blanket spread with a basket filled with delicacies, the ladies' white skirts like flowers against the grass.

'It reminds me of when we first met,' Will said with a smile. 'At your school, when Chris and I came for tea.'

'And you went swimming in the lake?' Diana blurted, before she could remember she wasn't meant to see that. She clapped her hand over her mouth and Will laughed.

'Now, how could you have known that?' he asked. 'It was very improper of us, I admit, but it was a hot day and your lake looked most inviting.'

Diana nodded, still feeling her cheeks hot with her blush. She couldn't help but wonder what it would have been like if *she* could have jumped into the water with him. Dived through the waves to catch his hand and feel his arms come around her, all weightless and lovely. 'I'm surprised you remembered me there.'

He gave her a surprised glance. 'Of course I remember you there. You were so sweet and kind to an old, work-preoccupied chap like me.'

'I thought it must have been quite dull for you, having to listen to us schoolgirls play the piano and chatter on over the tea things.'

'On the contrary, it was a wonderful respite. I was full of thoughts of going to India, of what might wait for me there, and you all were very welcoming and entertaining. I wish I could have stayed longer.'

Diana studied some of the children playing around the picnic blanket, laughing as they chased each other in a game of exuberant tag. 'Miss Grantley's was always like that, a wonderful haven. I do miss it sometimes, along with my friends there. But I love being here in Paris, too.'

'Paris suits you,' he said quietly. 'As did your school. You have changed since that day.'

Diana was startled by his words, that he had noticed anything like that at all. She glanced up at him from beneath her hat and found that was he smiling down at her, a quirky half-smile that she couldn't quite read. 'Have I? I feel like the same person inside. Longing to see all the world, but afraid of it, too.'

'I hope you never lose that curiosity, that wonderful spirit,' he said. 'I wish I could have held on to the person I was years ago.'

'In what way?' she asked, fascinated.

He shook his head. 'In the way all us old men wish we could be schoolboys for ever, I suppose. Before we see too much of the world.'

Diana felt sad that he felt 'old' when he was nothing of the sort. When surely the world held so many fascinations for him still, wonders she wished he could share with her. 'Maybe we should have a Parisian picnic soon, then. Make you have fun again before you are utterly in your dotage.'

He laughed, that wonderful, warm laugh she loved to hear, but which he found so seldom. 'Yes, I would like that.'

'No swimming in the fountains, though,' she added. 'I do think the Parisians would rather frown upon that, don't you?'

And to her delight, he laughed even harder and gave her a little twirl on the path before they turned towards her lodgings.

Chapter Twelve

As William walked back to the British Embassy along the river after leaving Diana at her door, he didn't see the sunny day, the people laughing as they sipped their wine at outdoor cafés, the children shrieking with pleasure as they ran past. He didn't even think about the work that was waiting on his desk. He could only see Diana as she looked when she took his arm and smiled up at them as they walked.

Her pleasure in every detail of the day was infectious and her laughter made him want to laugh, too. Made him forget everything but talking to her, letting some of her sunny warmth flow into his cold heart and make him feel alive again. That seemed to be her gift, to see the beauty in life around her and make everyone else see it, too. She had blossomed since she left Miss Grantley's, found her own glowing beauty. She seemed to belong in Paris, she and the city sharing the same pleasure in small moments, the same easy elegance. Watching her was like falling under an enchantment.

But Diana, for all her fresh beauty and buoyant enthusiasm that raised his spirits just to watch her, was surely quite dangerous. She distracted him at a moment when he couldn't afford such things, made him want things he had learned long ago couldn't be his. He wouldn't dim her blooming pleasure in the world by dragging her into the murkiness of his work. He couldn't.

He stopped for a moment on an ancient bridge and studied the city around him, The pale stone buildings turned a golden-pink in the sun, the diamond-like ripples on the river gleamed as boats cut through the waves. It was almost as if he was seeing it for the first time, seeing it through Diana's eager eyes. Usually he didn't really study his surroundings. He had too much work to do, too much to think about. Even the strange beauty of India had rarely affected him. But now it was like a new world of light and colour, thanks to Diana. He could almost see what those new-fangled Impressionist artists saw.

Images flashed in his mind of Diana eating her ice cream at the tower, laughing at the picnicking children, preening in the ridiculous hat he longed to buy for her. Diana dancing in his arms, her lips so tempting, her touch so soft and sweet.

He found he wanted to tell her all he saw now, wanted to share it with her, hear what she thought of it all. Watch her changing expressions, her bright smile, as she took in the world around her. He had never been so fascinated by a woman before, or by anyone really. His life had been one of work and responsibility, self-reliance. From his youth, with his parents involved in their own lives, their distant marriage, and with Chris to look after and keep out of trouble, Will had known he had to be responsible solely for himself. To work hard and protect himself. It had gone well enough for him.

But now—now he felt the tug of something different. Something utterly new for him. Thanks to Diana Martin, he saw the world with fresh eyes. Fresh possibilities.

Yes, he realised with a sharp tug. He was beginning to like her. Maybe more than like her. Yet what could that even mean? His work, his circumstances, had not changed and never would. He had his job, his family, his future to think about. And she had hers. How could he make such a woman of light and fancy happy?

Everyone said he should marry and one day he would, but Diana didn't seem like the sort they probably had in mind. She was independent, curious, a lady who enjoyed her own work as he enjoyed his. He would never want to see her change, to watch her lose that bright spirit she was growing into and thus become unhappy, as his own mother so often was. He couldn't bear that.

And what did he know of love and marriage anyway? What could he offer her?

He thought of the marriages he knew. His parents, who spent as much time apart as possible. His aunt and her husband, the Duke and Duchess, who had only their position in common. The Prince with his many mistresses, the Princess with her serene smile and wounded blue eyes. He was very sure that Diana deserved better than that.

But he couldn't make himself stop thinking about her, even at the most inopportune moments. At his desk, he seemed to hear her laughter. In meetings, he wondered what she was doing. His hard-won iron control was slipping and he had to stop it. He just wasn't sure how. Diana was seeing the world anew, but it seemed that he was, as well. Encountering thoughts he had never had before.

'Blakely!' he heard someone shout and was glad of the distraction. He turned to see a group of the young undersecretaries from the Embassy hurrying towards him. 'What are you doing out here? We were just on our way back to work.'

'Yes,' Will answered. 'So was I.' And that was where he belonged. Work—not romance. He had to remember that.

Chapter Thirteen

Diana tried to keep her attention on making her notes for the *Ladies' Weekly* readers, but it was proving to be impossible. She couldn't stop thinking about her walk home with William the other day. He had remembered her from Miss Grantley's! He thought about her. As she thought of him?

The reporters were corralled in a grassy space near the Eiffel Tower to await the Waleses' arrival, but even stuck there she had too much to see. It was an ideal morning, as if made for royalty, with a pale blue, cloudless sky stretching overhead and the gilded domes of the Exposition pavilions sparkling in the distance. A light breeze blew, fluttering all the bright flags, and carrying the scent of the chestnut trees and the rose bushes.

Word had spread that the Prince was arriving that day and the crowd had grown steadily at the base of the Tower, a flock of dark suits and pale day dresses, held back by the helmeted *gendarmes*. Monsieur Eiffel was there himself, a dark, bearded figure gesturing to the details of his great creation as he waited for the royals at the foot of the new elevators.

Diana went up on the tips of her kid boots, trying to see everything. She wondered if William would be with the Prince, if she would see him, and then she made herself push those thoughts away. She had to concentrate on her work now, not be distracted by the memory of William's rare smile, by all she longed to ask him, tell him.

'They say the Queen even recalled her ambassador,' the reporter behind her, a man from the *Herald*, said with a laugh. 'Doesn't want to be seen approving a Gallic celebration of getting rid of a king, even if it was a hundred years ago. Wonder what she thinks of this little visit, eh?'

His companions snickered. 'Trust old Bertie to never miss a chance to ogle the *mademoiselles*!'

Diana thought of Lady Smythe-Tomas and the Marlborough House Set she belonged to, the romantic house parties and discreet affairs—and sometimes not so discreet. How deep was William

in with them? And how out of her depth *she* felt.
How young and silly she surely seemed to him.

There was a sudden surge forward as the royal
carriage arrived. The Prince stepped out and
reached back to help his wife. A great cheer went
up at the sight of Princess Alexandra, wearing a
gown to match the day of bright blue-and-white
silk with a black hat trimmed with lilies of the valley. She waved her gloved hand and gave a sweet
smile. Behind her were her daughters and the
Duchess of Waverton serving as lady-in-waiting.
Alex wasn't with them and Diana wondered how
she had escaped the excursion.

But William *was* there, a tall, lean figure in his
dark suit and a tall silk hat, his hair glossy in the
sunlight, just as he was when they walked home
from Gordston's through the park. He surveyed
the crowd with his usual calm watchfulness and
she half-hoped, half-feared he would look her way.
She instinctively waved at him, sure he wouldn't
see her there, yet he did. He smiled and waved
back, his solemn face quite transformed. To her
surprise, he left the royal party as they greeted
Monsieur Eiffel and came to where she stood behind the cordon.

'Why don't you come up with us, Miss Martin?' he said. 'You could write about the elevators. They say this is one of the first times they have been used.'

Diana glanced around uncertainly at the crowd of other reporters, all of them calling questions to the Prince, who ignored them. 'I don't know...' she began, suddenly shy to be with him again.

'Of course you can. Come now, no time to waste.'

She smiled. 'Yes, thank you.'

He took her arm and led her to the royal party, where the Prince was chatting with Monsieur Eiffel and the other officials in French about the wondrous future of technology. The Duchess greeted her with a nod and Princess Louise asked if the bicycling outing was set.

'I do hope so, Your Highness,' Diana answered with a laugh. 'I have already bought a new outfit at Gordston's.'

'Am I included in this excursion?' William asked. 'I feel like I haven't been in the proper outdoors for days.'

Princess Louise giggled at him. 'Of course you are, Sir William. Papa will insist we have a suitable escort, after all. Perhaps your handsome brother would want to come, as well?'

William's smiling expression clouded a bit, but only for an instant. Diana wasn't sure she had even really seen his polite smile flicker. 'I'm afraid I haven't seen him since our little dance party. But I'm sure he would enjoy it very much.'

Diana remembered when they had last seen Chris, after he had imbibed a little too freely at the Wavertons' party, and she wondered if he was quite well. But there was no time to ask about Chris. A path was cleared and they were swept ahead to the waiting elevators.

At first, she felt a little flutter of nervousness at the confined space, yet it was surprisingly large and renovated for the royal visit with a garden bench and footstools, pots of flower arrangements. And William was right next to her, pressed close by the royals and their entourage.

She closed her eyes for a moment, feeling the vibrations of the machine beneath her, the touch of his hand through her glove, and she remembered kissing him. How it felt just like this, soaring up into she knew not what.

At the second platform, everyone was given a tour while the Prince was borne to the very top of the tower. William offered Diana his arm again and together they strolled to the railing, talking and laughing about the sites around them, the crowds, the bands playing in the cafés, the merits of one souvenir miniature tower over another. She was sure she had never seen him quite so light-hearted before, so quick to smile. It made her want to smile, too.

Once again, William supplied Diana with a little pair of opera glasses, through which she studied the crowds below. They looked like trails of ants from that distance, sweeping along the pathways and between the buildings. When she adjusted the lens, she could see them much more clearly, faces and gowns. 'Oh, look,' she cried, glimpsing a familiar figure near the Galerie des Machines. 'There is Christopher. Perhaps he has just been hiding here at the Exposition.'

But then she saw he was not alone. He was with Lord Thursby and they stood outside the doors of the pavilion, talking quite intently.

Before she could stop him, Will took the glasses and caught a glimpse of his brother's companion. His lips tightened.

'And here I thought he was safely at his hotel,' he said. 'Not meeting with Thursby.'

'Is he still involved in that investment-scheme idea?' she blurted out.

He glanced at her curiously. 'You know about that?'

'I—not really,' she said. 'That is, I don't know anything of the details. I did warn Chris he shouldn't have dealings with Lord Thursby, but he won't listen to me. I'm sure he thinks a lady is just ignorant of such matters and that can't be changed.'

'A lady who goes out and finds her own work as a reporter can't be ignorant of the world,' he muttered, still watching his brother through the glass. 'But foolish young men can certainly be.'

'Has Chris been foolish lately?' she asked, worried about her friend.

'He has always been impulsive, not always thinking before he acts,' Will said with a tight smile. 'I fear my mother rather indulged him. He was her baby and her comfort when she and my father were not getting along well.'

'Your parents are unhappy?' she asked softly, shocked by the sudden glimpse into his family, his past. She knew little of the older Blakelys, except that Alex said her aunt was often travelling to spas and watering places, her health delicate, while Mr Blakely stayed in the country and hunted and collected stamps.

He gave her an unreadable glance. 'They married before they knew each other well enough, I'm afraid. My mother tended to cling to Chris and it was not easy for him.'

'And you?'

'I had to see that duties were done,' he said shortly.

'Sir William, do come and look at this,' Princess Alexandra called. 'It's all quite fascinating.'

William gave Diana a quick, tight smile and went to the Princess's side. Diana glanced back to Chris and Lord Thursby. From that distance, it was impossible to see their expressions, but she still longed to call out a warning to Chris. What would she even say if she could do such a thing? Say not to deal with Lord Thursby because she had a 'feeling'?

But once again she was distracted by the sight of William. She wanted to know so much more about his family, about the troubles he had while growing up. She wanted to hold him, comfort him, banish that cold distance in his eyes. But she feared he would never let her help him at all.

Chapter Fourteen

It was a warm, sunny day, perfect for a bicycle ride as their little party set off along the Seine. The sunlight, brilliant and clear, shimmered on the rooftops of Paris and made the river sparkle like a string of diamonds. The crowds on the bridges waved and called out greetings to the *bateaux* that splashed through the waters. Paris seemed to have put on her very best attire for the day, magical and almost unreal.

Diana steered her rented bicycle carefully over the cobblestones, trying not to take a tumble and make a fool of herself. She had only ridden a few times and it seemed the saying was correct—you never forgot how. But she did try to stay at the back of the group, so they wouldn't see quite how much she wobbled.

Princess Louise led them, flying confidently

along. Away from her mother and sisters, she no longer seemed so shy, but like a confident young lady having a bit of fun. Her plain face shone under the brim of her tweed hat. Diana could certainly sympathise with her. Emily and Chris, clearly recovered from whatever had ailed him, rode just behind the Princess, the two of them shouting out challenges to race each other. Neither of them seemed to get too far ahead, though. Alex was in front of Diana, peddling carefully as if she wanted to concentrate, or was deep in thoughts of somewhere else.

Diana gave a quick glance over her shoulder to see Will behind her. He also looked deep in concentration, a fierce frown on his face that was really quite adorable. She had dressed so carefully that morning in her new caramel bicycling suit, made sure her hair fell in pretty curls from beneath her felt hat. She had even rather fancied she did a nice enough job of looking modern, jaunty, and *sportif.* She had even dared hope he might give her an admiring glance, a smile. Maybe flirt just a bit?

Yet, beyond a polite greeting when they had all met at the bicycle stand at the quay, he had said nothing at all to her. He seemed quiet that day, preoccupied as they rode onward. Had that tiny confidence, that glimpse of his past at the tower when he confided in her about his family, caused him to draw away again? The few times she did find him looking at her, his eyes seemed shadowed. The man who had laughed with her on the tower, who had kissed her, was nowhere to be found. Now the sad, solemn Will was back. She longed to know what he was thinking.

When she remembered that kiss now, her cheeks burned and she felt utterly foolish. When William kissed her, everything else had vanished. It was like—like soaring up into the sky, floating in the clouds.

Yet now he seemed like a stranger, or at best a distant acquaintance. It made her wonder if she had just been a silly, naive fool to ever even begin to dream about a man like William Blakely. He had travelled the world, built a career, served royalty, while she was a debutante who wanted to scribble tales. Why *would* he be truly interested in her?

And then there was Lady Smythe-Tomas. Diana knew she should never have forgotten about that, about the scene in the Waverton library when Lady Smythe-Tomas begged William to 'give her another chance'. If a woman such as she was in love with him, a renowned beauty, sophisticated and elegant, knowledgeable in the ways of modern romance, how could Diana compete with that?

She sighed, bumping over a particularly large stone in the lane. Romance was nothing like in those novels they had read so secretly at Miss Grantley's. She couldn't even fathom it at all. And yet—how lovely it had felt when she laughed with Will, kissed him, saw the magic of Paris all laid out before them. Now, when he was so close to her and yet so far away, she felt as if she was sinking. Her heart slowly deflating.

'You must race us, too, Diana!' Emily called out. 'We can see which of us can reach the Gare d'Orsay first.'

Diana laughed. She didn't want her friends to see how confused and sad she suddenly felt, didn't want them to guess she had ever begun to dream about a man like William at all. 'I'm quite sure it wouldn't be me! You're all much too fast for my poor cycling skills.'

'You would certainly defeat me,' Alex said, giving a little shriek as she hit a bump and her hat was knocked askew.

Diana glanced back at Will. He gave her a quick,

tight smile before he looked down at the path again. Her instinct told her she had to protect herself, to draw back like a turtle into its shell and forget she had ever had romantic daydreams. Yet something about the look in his eyes before he turned away, some sadness, some distance, urged her to reach out again. To try to find that man she had glimpsed on the tower.

'What do you think, Sir William?' she called. 'Could we outride them?'

She was finally rewarded with a smile, a real one, the one that brought out his dimples and made him look ten years younger again. Maybe he was simply preoccupied with his work, or Chris's problems. Or with Lady Smythe-Tomas.

'I am a slow, creaky old man,' he said. 'Chris would beat me handily, then he would never let me forget it. Like with our first ponies when we were children.'

'I can't help it if I'm a natural sportsman,' Chris answered teasingly.

'At least try!' said Emily. 'The winner can buy us lunch at the café.'

'Then doesn't that make losing more of a prize?' Alex asked. 'Us dawdlers would be the ones to keep our francs!' But she did pedal faster.

They all rode along as swiftly as they could until the shining glass dome of the Gare d'Orsay came into view. Princess Louise won, of course, being by far the fastest of them all along, and they found a lively café just beyond the bustle of the station. A table was set up for them on the pavement, under the shade of the green awning, and carafes of sweet red wine appeared on the table.

Diana hoped William would sit next to her, but he ended up across the table, between Princess Louise and Alex. They laughed together across him and he smiled bemusedly at their chatter. Emily and Chris, next to Diana, challenged each other to another ride and she tried to laugh and chatter with them, tried not to stare too much at Will.

As plates of fragrant mushroom tarts and escargot, along with baskets of fresh bread, were brought out, the talk turned to the events planned before the royal party returned home to England.

'They say there's to be a ball at the embassy before we leave,' Princess Louise said. 'But I'm not at all happy with the gown I brought. Papa said it would all be quite informal, so I only have a dinner dress.'

'You should visit Gordston's, ma'am,' Emily

said. 'We were just there and they have a wonderful selection. Their seamstresses are very quick with any alterations, as well. They had these bicycling costumes finished in no time!'

The Princess looked a bit doubtful. 'Readymade?'

'You needn't fear about the quality,' Alex said. 'We even saw the stylish Lady Smythe-Tomas shopping there and they say she only wears the best.'

Diana glanced at Will to see how he reacted to the woman's name. But he wasn't in the diplomatic service for nothing. His polite smile never wavered. Sometimes he was so maddening that way.

'Did you buy a new gown at Gordston's, then, Emily?' Chris asked.

Emily laughed. 'Me? Heavens, no. I'd spend far more there than I really should on Father's account, but I doubt an embassy ball is in my Paris future.'

'Of course you have to come!' Chris insisted. 'It will all be too dull without you. I hate the blasted things. Surely having a brother at the Foreign Office has to be good for something, like getting invitations to "dos" for one's friends?'

William looked speculatively at his brother. 'I'm sure there will be room for everyone,' he said.

'My father would never say no to even more pretty faces at a party!' Princess Louise said, making everyone laugh. More wine arrived at the table and talk turned to the sights of the fair, the art displays and marvellous new machines.

As they left the café, Diana paused to examine a display of posters plastered to a street lamp: the Wild West Show, with the tiny Annie Oakley and her guns; Turkish dancers; the Russian ballet. And one with a sketch that looked familiar—the Eastern Star that Alex's family wore so often. There was also a rather incongruous tiger behind the jewel and the minarets of the Taj Mahal.

See the unveiling of the famous Eastern Star sapphire, on display for Days Only at the Indian Pavilion! Meet the Maharajah Singh Lep and the Duke of Waverton! In person! Paid invitation only!

The date was for the next day, which meant Diana had to procure her invitation and plan her article.

'I do hope my parents don't see that,' she heard Alex say and turned to see her friend laughing at the poster. 'So vulgar. I think I may have to steal one to take home with me.'

'Along with one of those Eiffel Tower music boxes?' Diana said.

'Of course. Souvenirs of Paris. Until we can return and have *no* official events to worry about.' Alex linked her arm with Diana's and sighed as they studied the buildings around them, the glass dome of the station, the river beyond. 'It's all so beautiful, isn't it? So beautiful I think I'll start crying. Don't you wish we never had to go back to real life at all?'

Diana gave Alex a worried glance, wondering at her melancholy tone. 'Maybe we don't, Alex. Not really. Not when we're all together like this.'

Alex smiled, but even that looked sad. 'Of course not. You and Emily always make things more fun.'

'See? We never have to go beyond this life together at all,' Diana said with a laugh. She just wished she could believe it herself.

On the way home, she came to a shop she had only seen in the drawings of glossy fashion magazines. 'M. Worth—Rue de la Paix,' the discreet, dull-gilt letters said. Diana stared at it in wonder, as it was quite the loveliest place she had ever seen. Quieter than the bustle of Gordston's, dark stone with red-velvet curtains at the windows, ladies in velvet and satin swirling through the doors.

She glimpsed a gown in the window, an exquisite creation of pale blue *peau de soie* overlaid with spotted tulle, trimmed simply with a vine of grape leaves that trailed over the draped, narrow skirt in the newest style. It had a deep V-neckline, framed in more frilled tulle, and small cap sleeves that would look lovely with long white gloves.

She couldn't help but wonder how she would look in such a creation. What Will would think of her.

She straightened her shoulders, tilted her hat just so, reminded herself that she was not just any tourist on the street, that she worked for *Ladies' Weekly*—and she marched into the shop.

Chapter Fifteen

After two astonishing hours, Diana tumbled back out on to the pavement, blinking to find herself in the real world again.

Monsieur Worth's salon had been all she ever imagined and more. The velvet sofas, the salesladies in their crisp black and white uniforms offering champagne as bolts of silks and velvets were spread before her, sketches displayed. Duchesses and princesses and famous courtesans gliding past on their way to fittings. It was all so magical. And she was promised a new gown, to be delivered before the next ball! She couldn't help but fantasise a bit about how much William might like it, might notice her once more if she appeared like an exotic Worth peacock before him, dazzling in her new sophistication. It was all like a dream.

The clatter of a passing trolley pulled her back

down to the real earth, the real city, and she re-alised she had to be practical or she would be run over before she could even wear the gown. She hurried off down the street, afraid she was grinning like a mad person. She had to resist waving to every passer-by, stopping to gawk at the pale pink light on the buildings, buy every flower from every cart.

She swung around the corner—and was startled to see Will coming across the street, like one of her dream visions brought suddenly to life. His sharply tailored coat was dark against the diamond sparkle of the city, his eyes shadowed beneath his hat as he hurried along. He looked distracted, as he had during their bicycle ride.

'Will!' she called before she could stop herself. He turned to look at her, his expression startled, and she waved.

He smiled back, a sight she felt a small thrill to see, and crossed the street to her side. 'Miss Martin—Diana. You're looking happy this afternoon. Working?' He gestured to the row of shops, the Worth sign.

'Oh, yes, though it doesn't feel very much like work. It's all so fascinating.'

His smile widened. 'Are you returning to your lodgings now? Can I walk with you?'

'Oh, yes, thank you,' she answered, trying not to feel too excited at his offer, which she feared was merely politeness. She noticed the leather portfolio under his arm. 'Do you not have to be at your own work?'

'It can wait for a while. It's a lovely day in Paris, how often do we have that? And I confess I would love to hear your thoughts on this Monsieur Worth, who has all the city buzzing.'

Diana laughed. 'I would love to have your company, then, though you may be sorry you asked my opinion on Worth. I could talk about it all day.'

Will offered his arm and she slipped her gloved hand into the crook of his elbow. He felt so warm under her touch. He led her along the narrow, cobblestone back lanes, between the lacy wrought-iron balconies and gates leading to hidden courtyards, and asked her questions about the business structure at the salon and her thoughts on its effectiveness. No one had ever taken her so seriously before, listened so closely to her, and the distant Will from their bicycle ride seemed quite vanished. She wished their walk would never end.

They emerged on to the river, across from the

Île Saint-Louis, and Diana gasped at the sight of Notre Dame across the water, the late-afternoon light turning the towers golden and sparkling. 'I don't think I could ever be tired of seeing such beauty, do you?'

He stared down at her, his expression hidden under the shadows of his hat, and she wondered if he thought her enthusiasm silly. 'Will you be sorry to return to London?'

Diana laughed nervously. 'I don't know yet. I will be sorry not to walk out my door and see Paris every morning. And I'm not sure what will happen once I'm at home. But I suppose I will be interested to find out.'

'What do you think you would like to do?'

She thought about it for a moment. 'I know what my mother would like. For me to consider this time a little adventure before I settle down to marriage and keeping house.'

'But you don't want that?'

'I wouldn't mind marriage, I think, if it was right. But I would also like to keep writing. Keep seeing new things. Meeting new people.' New, fascinating people—like him. She was sure she could never be tired of discovering new things about him, just like seeing the sights of Paris anew every moment. 'What of you? Will you travel to India again?'

'Maybe not India, but some place. Wherever my work sends me.'

'And where do you *want* to go?'

He laughed. 'I never thought about it like that. Wherever I can do some good, I suppose. Maybe I will even stay in London for a while.'

'London has its own pleasures, I'm sure. But I fear there will be nothing like this at home!' she said, gesturing to the boats on the river, with their beautifully dressed passengers sipping champagne even in the middle of the day. Their laughter echoed over the water, like the drifting ribbons of a beautiful dream. 'Just look at that hat...'

She gestured too hard in her enthusiasm and suddenly felt her feet slip out from under her on the damp stones. Her stomach lurched as she started to fall, but she had no time to be afraid. Will reached out and caught her, lifting her back up safely, his arms strong and warm around her. She wound her arms around his neck and held on to him as tightly as she dared. She found she never wanted to let go.

He stared down at her, his eyes so dark, so fathomless. It was like diving into the water and falling deeper and deeper, sinking into an enchantment she didn't want to be free of. His head tilted towards hers and she thought for one breathless moment he was going to kiss her. She longed for that caress more than she had ever wanted anything.

But he only gave her a crooked smile and slowly set her back on her feet. 'You should be careful on these stones,' he said. 'They're slippery.'

'Y-yes,' she murmured, swallowing the bitter bite of disappointment. 'I do need to remember to take care.'

He took her hand in his and she took some comfort in the feel of his fingers curled around hers. She would have to find contentment in what she had from him, in these moments she could store up and take out of her memory once she was at home and Paris, and William, were only a distant dream.

Chapter Sixteen

The Indian Pavilion sparkled in the evening twilight like something out of a fairy story, standing out even among all the beautiful wonders of the Champ de Mars. The white wood, painted to look like the marble of the Taj Mahal, was lit up in gold, red, and blue by paper lanterns strung in the groves of trees all around the building.

The lights shimmered on the ladies' satin and silk gowns and their brilliant jewels as they made their way up walkways lined with servants in white turbans and long tunics with gold sashes. They offered trays of silver goblets filled with wine.

Diana followed Alex and her parents as they joined the long line waiting to enter the pavilion. She was very glad of Monsieur Worth and his wonderful help, for all the ladies were clad in their finest for the evening, each one hoping to catch the royal eye and maybe even a coveted Marlborough House invitation. The Duchess of Waverton wore pale grey Doucet with a blue-marabou trim, while Alex had her own new Worth of pale pink embroidered with silver stars.

Trying to remember it all for her article, Diana studied everyone around her, German princesses, French *comtesses*. There was even the famous Buffalo Bill Cody himself, fresh from his Wild West Show in cream-coloured buckskins beaded in blue and red, his hair and moustache long, topped with the most astonishing hat, accompanied by Annie Oakley and her husband. She was a tiny, pretty, dark-haired woman, disappointingly dressed in a most demure and conventional dress of green brocade and white lace.

What she didn't see, though, was William. She hadn't seen him since she had almost fallen into the river and they had almost kissed. She had thought of that moment so many times, thought of all the different ways it might have ended aside from what actually happened. She wondered if he thought about it, too, or if he was embarrassed to have been there with her at all.

As they stepped into the foyer, caught in the

bottleneck of people trying to move to the main octagonal display room, she moved to the side to avoid treading on all the fur and braid-edged trains around her. She caught a quick glimpse of herself in one of the mosaic-framed mirrors and smoothed the cap sleeves of her new blue-satin gown. It was quite nice, she thought; if only William could see her in it.

But what would he *think*? Would he think she even looked rather—pretty? Would he think she was stylish, elegant? Maybe even a proper diplomat's lady?

'Don't be so silly,' she whispered to herself. Of course Will wouldn't think of her as a *wife*. And she had never worried if a man thought her pretty enough. With her red hair, she had no hope of too much in that area. She was just meant to look respectable enough, to blend into the walls and observe everyone around her, try to guess their stories. She had never thought so much about her own story.

Now she suddenly found she wanted to be at the centre of her very own tale. To be thought pretty, at least by one man. For just a while, when they had taken tea at the shop together in London, strolled the Exposition, when he kissed her so wonderfully that the whole world shifted, she had begun to imagine that it might be possible.

But then there was the way he behaved towards her later, quiet and distant. Had he suspected she might be becoming infatuated with him and tried to put her off? Or worse, had she done something wrong? Had almost falling into the river been too much? Too awkward and embarrassing for him?

'No,' she said. No, she refused to be that girl. Maybe she was not at sophisticated as Lady Smythe-Tomas, but she *was* learning. She was in Paris, by herself. And she had a new Worth gown. Surely that was enough to celebrate? She had glimpsed herself for a moment through William's eyes, when he encouraged her to follow her dreams of writing, and she had liked what she saw. She had to remember only that, not her doubts.

She held her head up high and smiled. She spun around and hurried into the main display room.

It had been beautiful, mysterious, when she saw it with William, but now it was quite magical. Moonlight shone down through the glass dome and Mr Edison's lights were shaded with pink and blue silk covers. The great man himself personally explained them, a stout, grey-haired man, with his pretty, dainty wife on his arm. Her pink dress perfectly matched the shades and Diana made a note to ask her who had made them both later.

In the corner she glimpsed Lady Smythe-Tomas, in dark green satin beaded in sea-coloured sequins, whispering with Lord Thursby, but they quickly vanished in the crowd.

The royal party hadn't yet arrived, but the Maharajah and his wives and attendants were there, waiting near the display case, which was draped in a blue-velvet cover. His gold-brocade tunic shimmered and flashed, brighter than anyone ease's garb, and he seemed quite animated as he talked to the people around him about the history of the Star in his homeland.

Alex took Diana's arm, her face pale. 'Oh, Di, you must stay with me during the unveiling. Mother says I have to stay on the dais with the royal family, where everyone can see me!'

'You mustn't worry about that, Alex,' Diana said soothingly. 'You look beautiful. Quite the loveliest lady here.'

And so Alex was, as usual, with her fairy-princess blond hair and wide blue eyes. Yet she never seemed to believe that.

Before Alex could answer, Emily pushed her

way towards them through the throngs, drawing a man along with her. And not just any man—one who towered above everyone else, handsome in a golden, Viking god-like way, dressed in stylish black and white evening clothes. Mr Gordston.

Alexandra seemed to turn even paler and Diana remembered her puzzling statement that Mr Gordston 'rubbed her the wrong way'.

'Look who I found!' Emily said merrily. 'Mr Gordston himself. I had to tell him how very much we admired his lovely store.'

He bowed, his gaze lingering for a moment on Alex. 'I am gratified to hear it, ladies. I do hope the bicycling costumes were most satisfactory.'

'Perfect,' Emily said. 'I should very much like to hear more about your business soon, Mr Gordston. Where you find your merchandisers, things of that sort.'

He laughed, and reached for one of the silver goblets on the footmen's trays. 'Now, Miss Fortescue, I can't give away all my secrets, can I? Especially to such a shrewd and worthy rival as your father.' He gestured to the glass cases all around them, the sparkling array of gold and jewels. 'Now, if I could find a source for such glorious merchandise as this…'

They all made their way around the displays, exclaiming over the necklaces and bangles, the curtains of embroidered silk. As Diana took her own goblet of wine, she noticed that Alex had vanished. What was even stranger, it seemed that Mr Gordston had noticed that, as well. He looked around them with a small frown on his sculpted face.

Diana turned to ask Emily if she had seen her, when suddenly she felt a gentle hand on her arm. *William,* she thought with a tiny thrill.

She spun around, smiling with ridiculous excitement, only to feel her heart sink when she saw it was not Will who stood there, but Christopher.

'Chris, I think—' she said and broke off with a gasp. Her friend didn't look at all like himself, his face pale and pasty, his eyes shadowed with purple. 'Are you ill? What's amiss?'

'Di, I think I've made a hash of something. I meant so well, but—now it's all gone rather south.'

Diana wondered if it had something to do with Thursby and his investments. 'Surely William could help you? Or Emily, even? They're far more sensible than me. They would know what to do. Oh, Chris. I am quite sure whatever it is, they'll know what must be done.'

'No!' Chris practically shouted, making the people closest to them give them startled glances. Chris took a deep breath, stiffened his shoulders, and visibly gathered himself up again. He took her arm and led her to a quieter spot along the wall. 'Will and Emily are the last two people I would want knowing.'

'Chris, please,' she said, very worried. 'Is it money? That investment scheme you mentioned, maybe? Or—or even a woman, something like that? Whatever it is, it can be fixed.'

He gave her a sad little smile. 'Di. You are a good friend. You always see the best in people, don't you?'

'Not all people,' she muttered, thinking of Thursby and his schemes. 'But you, Chris, of course. Please, do tell me.'

The doors opened and the royal party appeared. The Prince wore his blue Garter sash and jewelled star over his evening suit and the Princess wore matching midnight-blue with a cut-steel tiara. Will was just behind them and Diana felt her stomach give an excited little lurch to see him again, felt her cheeks turn warm even though he hadn't looked at her yet.

While she watched them, Chris vanished.

Diana glanced towards the dais beside the centre display case, where Alex stood with her parents and the Maharajah to greet the Waleses. Alex gave her a desperate glance and Diana remembered her promise to stay with her, but now she was desperately worried about both Alex and Chris. She had never seen him like he had been in the last few days.

She pushed her way past everyone to the foot of the dais. She caught a quick glimpse of William standing behind the Prince, so tall and reassuring. She desperately wished she could talk to him, tell him about his brother, but he was too far away.

'Let us waste no more time in revealing this beautiful treasure Waverton has so graciously agreed to share with the Exposition, and thus the world,' the Prince said, drawing her attention to the dais.

He gestured to his wife and Princess Alexandra stepped forward to tug at a gold cord and sweep the blue-velvet curtains away from the display case.

The Princess screamed and fell back a step, tumbling into her husband's arms. Everyone else pressed closer, a great cry rising up.

The display case was utterly empty. The Eastern Star was gone.

* * *

The Indian Pavilion, previously so serene and calm, descended into a sea of pandemonium. The French *gendarmes* in their dark blue uniforms swarmed the octagonal display room, questioning confused guests, poking through the empty case as if the sapphire might magically appear.

The Waleses and the Wavertons, along with the Maharajah, had been hastened quickly into another chamber, a small one at the back of the building where there were no windows and the doors could be secured. William watched as the Prince paced and fumed, putting an unlit cigar in his mouth and then snatching it out again, as his wife disapproved of smoking among ladies in even trying circumstances. Princess Alexandra sat calmly in the corner, while the Duchess sobbed hysterically. Alex tried to press smelling salts on her mother, but the Duchess kept pushing the bottle in her daughter's hand away.

'What good will that do?' the Duchess snapped.

'This is outrageous!' the Duke shouted, his face purple-red. 'We trusted the Exposition, trusted you people, and look what happened! We've lost the jewel, an irreplaceable, precious jewel that was entrusted to me years ago. What's going to be done about it? I demand this place be turned upside down until it's found.'

'We are doing everything possible, your Grace,' the head *gendarme* said. 'My men are questioning every guest.'

William knew from long experience in the Foreign Office just how well *that* would go over. A party filled with the cream of English and French society, royalty, marquises, dukes, and especially the Maharajah, whose kingdom was so important to the British policy in India at the moment. All of them being questioned by the police, being put squarely at the centre of what was sure to be a sensational scandal. Heads would certainly roll.

It definitely had the potential to be the biggest challenge of William's career thus far. Yet somehow all he could think about, all that made him frantic with worry, was Diana.

Where *was* she? The last glimpse he had of her was as Chris led her and Emily Fortescue to a safer corner of the display room. She had looked as shocked as everyone else had, but at least his brother had managed to step up to the occasion, looking after the ladies. She wasn't alone, but Will wanted to see her for himself, tell her there was nothing to worry about. To hold her, look into her eyes, reassure her that she was safe. He would always keep her safe.

And was Chris really the safest guard at the moment? He remembered how strangely his brother had been behaving lately, his dishevelled state when Will glimpsed him earlier. Something had been going on with his brother, something worrisome, and Will suddenly wondered if it had something to do with the Eastern Star.

The *gendarme* approached him, his bearded face stern beneath his helmet. 'Monsieur William Blakely?' he said briskly.

'Oui,' he answered.

'I have a few questions for you. It should not take long. His Royal Highness says you are most needed by him now.'

Will quickly told him all he knew, which wasn't much. The journey from the hotel to the pavilion had been most uneventful except for Princess Louise losing her fan. The tense greetings with the Maharajah and his party. The arrival at the pavilion. He hadn't seen the Eastern Star at all since the Duchess last wore it and the Duke's own security officers, along with the Foreign Office, had been in charge of the transfer earlier that day.

'And you work for your English Foreign Office, do you not?' the *gendarme* asked.

'I do. But my job here in Paris is merely as equerry to the Prince. I have had nothing to do with the handling of the jewel.' Unfortunately. He would have been far more cautious.

'But you know who has?'

Will gave him the name of the Prince's own head of security, who was no doubt being most strenuously questioned even at that moment. He decided to say nothing about Chris, about his 'Indian investment' and mysterious behaviour lately. Not until he could question his brother himself.

'Is that all, *monsieur*?' Will asked.

'For now, *merci*.' The *gendarme* turned away to talk to the Duke and Will made his way back to the Prince. Bertie still looked irritated and very much in need of his cigar, but he had calmed down. His royal storms, though turbulent, ended quickly.

'Infernal police,' Bertie muttered. 'Wasting all our time, when it's clear it must have been an outside operation! The piece is probably far away by now. They should be combing the city, not pestering us.'

'I'm sure they do have men out in the streets

now, sir,' Will said quietly. 'They must cover every eventuality, just as our London police would.'

The Prince sighed and tossed his unlit cigar aside. 'As if this would have happened in London! But I'm sure you are right, Blakely. We must co-operate. An international incident would do us no good and only prove my mother right that I shouldn't have come to Paris. It must all be resolved and discreetly.'

Will glanced at the Maharajah, who was frowning but quiet. 'If you don't mind me asking, sir, how was it decided the Star would be displayed here at all?'

The Prince hesitated for a moment, but then he answered. 'You know that Singh Lep's kingdom is the centre of a—a plan for our Indian holdings at the moment?'

Will nodded.

'The jewel was sold willingly enough to Waverton all those years ago, everyone knows that,' Bertie went on. 'But there have been a few—questions since then. Nothing worth giving credence, of course. Displaying the jewel here as a show of unity was the idea. Everyone seemed happy with the plan. Until now.'

The Duke approached them. He, too, had grown

calmer, but his cheeks still burned red and Will worried about his aunt's husband's temper. 'Do excuse me, sir, but would it be possible for Sir William to see his cousin, my daughter Alexandra, back to the hotel? She is not feeling well and they say they still must question the Duchess and myself. The nerve of them!'

'Of course, of course,' Bertie said, waving Will off. 'Poor Lady Alexandra, to be exposed to such matters! It should never have happened. Ladies and their tender hearts.' As Will bowed and turned away, the Prince caught his arm. 'It must all be hushed up, Blakely, as much as possible. We have to get the Star back.'

Will nodded and went to take Alex's hand. She did indeed look rather pale and weary.

'Are you quite all right?' he asked.

She gave a brave, bright smile and nodded. 'Much better than Mother, I think. I haven't seen so much excitement in ages! We should find Emily and Diana, make sure they get home.'

Will wanted nothing more. In the main gallery, they found the two ladies standing near one of the cases in the corner. Chris had gone again, but they were supporting each other, talking quietly together. Diana looked curious, a bit worried, but not frightened, and Will felt he could breathe easier just looking at her.

'I am to see Alex home,' he said. 'Let me accompany you both, as well. I don't think any of us need to be alone now.'

'Oh, yes, thank you, Sir William,' Emily answered.

Diana looked hesitant for a moment, glancing quickly around the room, and he wondered what she was looking for. But she nodded and smiled as he led them out of the pavilion, out of the stuffy air of shock and fear and into the clear night. The rest of the fair went on as if nothing had happened, all sparkling lights and merriment, the faint sound of music.

Will glimpsed Thursby helping Laura into a carriage and for an instant, he glimpsed another face in the depths of the vehicle—Chris. His brother, with Thursby, and the jewel gone.

But he couldn't call out, couldn't make a scene, not with the ladies with him and the Prince's warnings of discretion. He would have to find Chris later and he wouldn't go easy on him when he did.

The ride through the streets of Paris was quiet, Will lost in his thoughts, Alex and her friends whispering once in a while, then falling back into silence. Beyond the window there were cafés and music halls, as if there was another world out there.

The carriage went to Diana's lodgings first and he took her arm to see her to the door. She leaned against him, looking quite concerned about something.

As he took her hand and quickly kissed it, he sought for words that would reassure her. 'Whatever it is, Diana, there is no need to worry. The jewel will be found and everything set right.'

'Yes,' she murmured. 'I do hope you're right.'

Chapter Seventeen

Diana stared down at the pages she had just finished so painstakingly typewriting. *Ladies' Weekly* would expect at least one or two pieces to arrive that week and she was rather happy with these articles. An account of the wonders to be seen at the Exposition, the tower and the pavilions, the variety of the crowds, and one about the new styles of gowns in Paris, especially what Princess Alexandra wore. She was halfway through one about Gordston's department store, to be completed after she had her promised tour. She was sure readers would enjoy that, a vicarious voyage to Paris.

Yet she had no idea what to write about the dramatic events of the night before and she could think of little else. She'd been awake all night, watching the Parisian moon rising beyond her bedroom window, going over every detail she could remember about the night's ill-fated party. Where everyone stood—the Prince of Wales and his entourage, the Maharajah, the Duke and Duchess, the other guests. The footmen who moved about with their trays. It had been so crowded, so full of noise and colour, that small details seemed to blur in her mind.

None of the other displays were tampered with and many of them had to be just as priceless as the Star. But only that one piece was gone.

She sat back in her chair and remembered Christopher, how worried he had been that he might have messed something up. Was it possible that the 'Indian investment' had something to do with the Star? She couldn't believe Chris would be involved in such a crime, he was too nice, too open-hearted—or at least he used to be.

But what about the Maharajah himself? What were the real circumstances of the transfer of the Star all those years ago? She thought of the Koh-i-Noor, the enormous diamond Queen Victoria herself had extracted from another Indian prince. Maybe the Maharajah wanted the Star back? And he had looked rather odd when the name of her father was mentioned. Papa had been in India when the Duke was—she made a note to write to him.

And then there was William. He had seemed so concerned last night, as well he would do. Should she bother him with her worries about Chris? She definitely couldn't, *wouldn't,* believe *William* would have something to do with the theft. His whole career was built on service to Queen and country; his reputation was impeccable.

Yet she remembered the mysterious hush of his London office. So innocuous, so like thousands of other places of work all over town. But façades could hide so much and she might be unworldly, but she knew how many quiet operations had to go on every day to keep Victoria's kingdom safe. Weren't they in so many of the novels she loved, the history classes at Miss Grantley's—spies and traitors, secret operatives of all sorts?

What was Will really doing in that office of his? What had he done in India? She was very puzzled. The mystery of him was so intriguing, so much a part of him, but also so maddening!

She reached for her box of stationery and started writing that letter to her father. Maybe he would remember the Maharajah from his time in India. She said nothing to him of the theft, only that she had visited the display of the Star and was curious. She tried to keep her missive light and fun, emphasising the meeting of royalty. It would never do to alarm them and be summoned home right when things were getting most interesting.

Above all, she had to discover how William and his brother were involved. She had to find out what her feelings really meant.

She sealed up the letter to her father and added it to the manuscript packages before she pinned on her hat and headed out into the day. It was a bit cloudy, the sun hidden behind grey skies, but that hadn't deterred the crowds. In fact, the streets seemed even more full of people.

Despite her concern, she couldn't help her own curiosity. She hurried through the gates of the Exposition and made her way towards the Indian Pavilion. It was closed, of course, two turbaned guards at the doors turning people away, but otherwise there was no hint of trouble. No swarms of *gendarmes*, no English royal bodyguards.

She bought a couple of the newspapers printed daily with Exposition news, but there was nothing there, either. Only an account of the Waleses' visit to the Eiffel Tower.

She quickly mailed off her packages and de-

cided to see some of the shops along the Champs-
Élysées. But before she could leave the grounds
of the fair, she caught a glimpse of Chris. And he
wasn't alone. He sat on one of the iron benches,
tucked behind a statue of Apollo in his sun char-
iot. He was with Thursby again.

Diana ducked behind one of the stands selling
ice cream, and studied the men carefully from
where they could not see her.

She couldn't hear their words, but their expressions were easy enough to read, filled with anger.
As if they argued. Chris had been with Thursby
too often of late for it to mean nothing. Perhaps
their investment was going badly now.

'What on earth are you doing there, Diana?'
she heard someone say behind her and she spun
around, her heart pounding. She would surely
make a terrible spy, if she could so easily lose
sight of her surroundings!

It was Emily, impeccably dressed in a pale blue
suit and boater hat, watching her with a frown.

'Stealing an ice cream, of course,' Diana said.
She beckoned Em closer; she knew she could trust
her friend. 'I just came here to mail some packages and saw them on that bench. Chris Blakely

with Lord Thursby and they don't seem happy about their conversation at all.'

Emily frowned. 'Chris with someone like Thursby? They don't seem like they would be friends at all. Let me see.'

Diana pointed them out and Emily joined her in studying the quarrel. After a few minutes, the two men departed and went their separate ways.

'That fool,' Emily said, but she didn't look angry—she looked worried. 'He should know better. What if Thursby's ridiculous scheme has something to do with what happened last night?'

That was exactly what Diana herself was worried about. What if Chris was involved in what had happened at the pavilion? His actions would cost not only himself, but his brother and his career. She couldn't let that happen.

Diana was so distracted as she turned the corner of the street towards her lodgings that at first she didn't see the figure on the doorstep. There were too many people flowing past on their everyday business, too many cobblestones to avoid underfoot and too many thoughts crowding in her own head. But as she came closer, the figure stood out, like a flash of clear, pure sunlight in the cloudy blur. His suit was dark against the white stone of the steps and he held on to the narrow brim of his hat against the breeze as he studied the street.

It seemed incredible that he should appear just when he was in her thoughts like that. She hurried towards him, then suddenly slowed, unsure what to tell him. What did he already know about Chris and Thursby? What could be going on behind the bright scenes of the Exposition? Why was he there, at her lodgings?

But he had seen her and waved—there was no more time to hesitate. She smiled and dashed the last few steps. 'Sir William! What a surprise.'

He smiled back and she dared hope he was glad to see her. That he had sought her out especially for some happy reason. 'Miss Martin—Diana. I wanted to see how you were doing after—well, after the rather interesting events last night.'

'Interesting?' she said with a laugh. 'It was more fascinating than an evening at Drury Lane. I'm doing quite well, despite a rather sleepless night. I've just been to deliver a few parcels to be mailed.'

'Articles for *Ladies' Weekly*?' He peered at her closely. 'Not one about the theft, I hope?'

Diana felt a pang that he did not trust her. He

had asked for discretion, for the sake of the Prince. She had promised it. Surely he remembered that? 'Of course not. You did warn me it shouldn't be known yet, if it can be helped.'

He smiled ruefully. 'I'm sorry. I know you wouldn't gossip about it. You are the most kind and trusting of people.'

He thought her 'kind and trusting'? It wasn't as wildly passionate as 'fiery and beautiful' would have been, like heroines in novels, but it gave her a tiny, glowing touch of happiness anyway. She *wanted* him to think well of her, to trust her, just as she longed to trust him.

'They were just articles about Princess Alexandra's wardrobe and a letter to my parents.' She remembered Chris in the park with Thursby, and shook her head. 'How are *you* faring? I'm surprised you aren't with the Prince.'

'I was. They questioned us all morning, much to His Highness's fury, but nothing has yet been found. Waverton is most unhappy, of course, and the Maharajah says he will break off all relations with the British now that his trust has been so violated.' William rubbed his hand over his face in a weary gesture and Diana saw that, handsome as he always was, today there were shadows under his eyes.

'Won't you come upstairs for a moment?' she said. 'It's very quiet there, no irate royalty at all, and I could make us some tea.'

He laughed and she was glad of the sound. '*You* will make the tea?'

She held up her head haughtily. 'I *am* of some use in some ways, I promise. I can make us a cup of tea, even though I can't find lost jewels.'

He glanced up at the house. 'Are you sure your landlady won't mind?'

'Not if we are very quiet,' she whispered.

He laughed again and she led him into the building and up the narrow, winding stairs to her flat at the top of the house. It was quite empty at that time of day, everyone off at their work or enjoying the Exposition, and they made it to her rooms with no interruptions.

She was quite glad she had tidied up that morning, putting away unmentionables like stockings and corset covers, and tucking away the far too many pairs of shoes she had brought to France. The only mess was around her typewriter. She urged him to sit down while she made the tea and hoped he wouldn't see that she *did* fumble around a bit before she could find the tin of tea leaves and set the water to boil.

'Have there been no clues at all?' she asked, arranging a tray with cups and plates of biscuits from the patisserie next door.

'None, I'm afraid. The gallery had been closed and locked until the party and none of the guards say they saw anyone go near the place. It's watched night and day, even after the Exposition closes, and the *gendarmes* also make their rounds every hour.'

'Could it have been one of the guards themselves, then?'

'They all swear not and the Maharajah declares he hand-picked each of them himself. He is quite furious. He claims the jewel was only sold to the Duke after Waverton promised it would be safer in England and that his trust has been broken.'

Diana nodded as she put down the tray on the table beside his chair and poured out the tea. It all felt so wonderfully, cosily domestic. She knew the jewel theft was a most serious matter and it had been worrying her all night, especially after seeing Chris. Yet she couldn't help but feel a strange little twinge of—of contentment. It felt so oddly *right* to be sitting there with Will, taking tea, talking together, as any couple would at their home.

She pushed the thought of 'home' away. There was no time for it now, no place for such hazy dreams.

'Is that really the only reason the jewel was sold? To keep it safe in the Duke's hands?' she asked.

He took a deep drink of his tea, frowning down into the cup. 'This is really quite good,' he said.

Diana laughed. 'You needn't look so surprised.'

'I don't think anything you chose to do well could surprise me, Diana,' he said with a smile. 'And as for the Star—who knows. Waverton *is* a duke and accustomed to getting what he wants. And they say the Maharajah's kingdom has long been short of funds. When I was in the India Office, he was always negotiating new terms of friendship with the British, always demanding loans and changing things at the last moment. I had hoped my dealings with him were done.'

'Then he showed up here. But is he really so in need of funds? He was covered in diamonds and pearls at the parties.'

William frowned thoughtfully. 'We all have to keep up appearances, one way or another.'

Diana studied him carefully, wondering what

he was hiding under his calm smiles. His careful, expressionless watchfulness. 'Very true. I suppose it would explain all the sudden enthusiasm for Indian investments so many people have.'

'People like my brother,' he said quietly. 'Yes. It is a concern.'

Diana struggled with the fact that she needed to tell Will that Chris had asked for her help, that she had seen him arguing with Thursby at the park. But he looked so tired, so worried, she also wanted to distract him for a moment. Make him smile again.

'Oh, look!' she said and hurried to the window. The large portal looked out into the branches of one of the tall chestnut trees that lined the street. She had been watching a bird building its nest there ever since she had arrived and today there were tiny birds peeping out at her. 'Isn't it quite adorable? Tiny little bits of life, right outside my own window.'

She suddenly realised he stood very near her side, so close she could feel his warmth, smell the clean, sharp scent of his cologne. She glanced up at him, and found he watched her very closely. 'Adorable indeed,' he said.

Then she was in his arms, their bodies so close

nothing could come between them in that moment, and he was kissing her. And it was the most wonderful thing she had ever known, ever dreamed of knowing. It was all she had wanted since their first, too-soon-interrupted kiss, and now it was happening again. Really, truly happening.

She went up on tiptoe and wound her arms around his neck, holding on to him as tightly as she could. Unlike the first time, when she had felt so awkward, so girlish, now she knew exactly what to do. Exactly what she wanted.

Her lips parted beneath his, his tongue touched hers, lightly at first, tasting, testing. But when she met him with her own flare of passion, it deepened, grew hotter, frantic, full of a need too long held back.

Her world, the whole proper world of family and writing she thought was organised so well, tipped completely off its axis and whirled off towards the moon.

He drew her even closer, his arms so safe around her, and she felt that wonderful, fizzy, champagne-like excitement grow and expand, drawing her onwards deeper and deeper. She didn't want to let it go, ever. She didn't want to lose that fragile, beautiful spell.

She went up on her toes to kiss him again, pressing one swift touch to his lips, then another and another, daring him to fall into that spell with her. He groaned and pulled her even closer, until there wasn't even a breath between them. She was lost in it, in him, until she was sure they were one being.

But it couldn't last for ever. He drew back slowly, pressing tiny, fleeting kisses to her cheek, to the soft, sensitive spot just below her ear that made her giggle.

'Oh, Diana,' he whispered hoarsely. 'I don't ever want to leave, but I'm afraid I must.'

She nodded and went back down off tiptoe to hide her face against his shoulder, letting the soft wool of his coat block out the light. He smelled of some sharp, citrus soap, of clean wool, of that delicious heat that was only him. 'I know. Duty does call.'

'Would you meet me tomorrow? At the Louvre, maybe?'

She smiled. 'The Venus de Milo? That sounds perfect.'

And so it did. The perfect Parisian rendezvous for her little Parisian romance. But, oh, how she didn't want to let go now! If it was so hard to do now, how much harder it would surely be later.

He should not have done that. It was surely the most impulsive thing he had ever done in his life. It was against every ounce of iron control he had perfected in his work, his life. Everything always calm, cool, in its place. Until Diana. Until she changed it all.

It was also, beyond a doubt, the most wonderful thing he had ever done. And the most foolish. It couldn't happen again.

William made his way down the narrow Paris lane, not even seeing the flower stalls, the shops, the laughing crowds. All he could see in his mind was *her*. Her wide, shining dark eyes, her lips parted as she stared up at him.

When he had looked down at her, those chocolate-coloured eyes, her brilliant hair shining in the sunlight, when he took a deep breath of her lilac perfume and felt the warmth of her body pressed so close to his—it was as if some primitive urge he usually kept caged up deep inside of him broke free. Before he could lock it away again, he was reaching for her, holding her close, breathing her deep into his heart.

And how glorious it was. She was so warm, so soft, her small sounds of desire so deliciously sweet. No force on earth could have stopped them.

What had he been thinking? The few times he had given in to his urges in the past, as with Laura Smythe-Tomas so long ago, it was just that—a physical urge. And the ladies were all sophisticated, older women of the world who felt the same, or so he had thought until Laura had wanted to revisit their old liaison. Diana wasn't like that at all. Diana made him feel in ways he had never imagined before. She made the world look new. Made him think of things he never had before.

The truth was, he hadn't been thinking at all. Only feeling. Wanting. Being with Diana always felt so right. She made him feel alive. And it was the most astonishing thing.

He found he wanted to be with her all the time and not just to kiss, to touch, as glorious as that felt. He wanted to talk to her, confide in her about his work, hear her opinions, read her articles. Watch her delight in the Eiffel Tower, or a pretty hat, an ice cream or glass of champagne. *Life.*

In his work, he so often saw the worst of things. Battles, injustice, danger. With Diana, he finally saw the best.

Yet she deserved so much. A comfortable, settled home, a family free of conflict, as his could never be. Not a man absorbed in his work, with a brother possibly in trouble, trying to save them all from scandal.

If he truly cared about Diana, and he did, he couldn't ask her to take on his responsibilities. He had to protect himself from being so vulnerable if he was to do his job. Above all, he had to protect *her*. Protect that wondrous, innocent delight in life she had that was so precious.

He had wavered in his resolve when he kissed her. He couldn't do it again.

He hurried up the steps into the Grand Hôtel du Louvre. As he made his way through the lush brocaded lobby and up the stairs towards the royal suite, he was surprised to see Lady Smythe-Tomas come down.

She was tugging on her gloves and her face was tilted downward, half-hidden by her feathered hat. She didn't notice him at first, but he saw she was frowning, her jaw tight. It was very odd. Laura never frowned. She claimed it caused wrinkles.

But keeping company with men like Thursby surely didn't help that.

She looked up and saw him, and her expression changed. Her smile flashed out, as it always did at parties. 'Will, darling. Are you staying here? Of course you must be with the Prince's party, how delightful.'

'In less grand accommodations than the Prince, I'm afraid,' he said. 'Are you staying here?'

'Oh, no. I have my own favourite little place here in Paris, so near the shopping. But I do hope I'll see you at the embassy ball?'

'I'll be there.'

'Do save me a dance.' She pressed his arm and then wafted away down the stairs, leaving the bellboys looking awestruck after her.

William suddenly wondered about the guards at the pavilion, the ones who claimed they saw nothing at all.

When he made his way into the Prince's suite, he found a small meeting in progress with equerries from the embassy. Since the Princess was gone, the Prince smoked one of his cigars as he paced around the table in the small library of the suite. The air was thick with the cherry-smoke scent.

'Ah, there you are, Blakely,' Bertie growled.

'What a mess, eh? It must all be cleared away before my mother hears of it.'

'Of course, sir,' William answered. He had to forget about Diana now, to do his job. 'What do we know so far?' It turned out not very much, but they went over what the *gendarmes* had found out at the pavilion, other crimes at the fair that might be connected.

Just as they were clearing away their papers, Princess Alexandra swept in, her daughters trailing behind her. The Princess was dressed in a steel-grey taffeta suit trimmed with—yes, with black-braid *passementerie*. Despite his worries, Will had to smile at what he had learned from Diana and he knew he had to tell her about it.

Cradled in the royal arms was a tiny white kitten, shivering, its blue eyes wide.

'Oh, Bertie dear,' she said with one of her famous trilling laughs. 'Look what Louise found by the river. Lost and hungry, the poor darling. Shall we keep it?'

Will watched as the Prince gave her an indulgent smile and the royal ladies cooed over the cat. If only lost sapphires, and maybe even lost hearts, could be retrieved so easily. He couldn't help but wonder, as he always did lately, what

Diana would think or say. What her thoughts would be on jewel thefts and family tangles. And if she might like a kitten...

Chapter Eighteen

'I tell you, I want out! I can't do this any longer,' Christopher Blakely shouted. He hadn't been sleeping for a couple of nights and felt the tug of tiredness deep in his mind, giving credence to his words. He ran his hand through his hair, leaving it standing on end, hoping he looked suitably frantic.

But Lord Thursby's face could have been made of stone. He lit a cigar and turned away to stare out the window of his hotel suite. It was an expensive view, past grey-velvet curtains and over the slate roofs of Paris to the iron tower in the distance. A view everyone knew Thursby couldn't afford and that was what had led them to where they were. It was what would catch Thursby in the end, hopefully.

If they were all lucky and if Chris's nerve could

hold. He wasn't sure how Will did such work, all over the world, and yet his brother always looked so cool, so calm. Will had always been the strong one, Chris the daredevil. When they were boys, he had thought his own way was so much more fun and indeed the work had started out gloriously exhilarating. That was why he had agreed to take it up again.

Now, as he watched Thursby, as time slowed down and then seemed to speed up again at a most alarming rate, he thought Will had always been right. Steady and cool won the race.

Chris *did* want out. But not until everything was finished. Not until he had shown himself he could do it. Show…

Well, show *her*, he supposed, even if she never knew.

'It is much too late for that,' Thursby said. 'You were at the pavilion. You saw how far things have gone.'

Chris felt everything go very still in that second. He didn't know if it was the sleeplessness, or the moment of not turning back that made it feel so strange. 'There is a buyer?'

Thursby laughed. 'Of course there is. I'm not so foolish as to go to so much risk with no assurance of reward. You can't just take something like that to a pawnshop in Spitalfields.'

Chris held his breath. 'Who?'

Thursby stared down at his cigar with narrowed eyes. 'That's not your concern. Not yet, anyway. I'll have one more small errand for you, very soon. Then we will be clear and our investments will pay off handsomely.'

Errand? Such as what he had been doing lately, getting new investors for the 'Indian mines' and such. He didn't much care for looking like such a fool. 'I doubt the Duke sees it that way.'

Thursby laughed again, a most unpleasantly metallic sound. 'The Duke? Oh, I'm sure he won't mind at all once the insurance money comes in. He can buy his wife a bauble much better suited to her porridge face and the Star will have its own home again.'

'Is it going back to India?'

'That's not our concern, either, once the money comes.'

'And the new job in India you have been angling for all over London?'

Thursby gave him a sharp glance and Chris wondered if he had gone too far. 'I admit I wouldn't mind a change of scene soon. I suppose you heard

that from your officious brother behind his Foreign Office desk?'

'You've been calling on the father of my cousin's friend Miss Martin, asking about his Indian
days. Or so I hear.'

Thursby's frown turned even sharper, like
a knife blade. 'The lovely Miss Martin. Yes. It
doesn't hurt to cultivate connections, as I'm sure
you know. A pretty wife never hurts a man's pros-
pects, does it? You should look into it yourself.
Once we're done here, you'll be able to afford it.'

'Pretty young wives bought and paid for?' Chris
heard a woman say at the door and he turned to
see Lady Smythe-Tomas standing there. Unlike
Chris, she looked as if she was not feigning the
strain. Her cheeks were pale beneath a layer of
rouge, her eyes hollow, despite her fashionable
gown, her distracting hat.

She threw her velvet muff and kid gloves on
to a table and spun back around to face them. 'Is
that what you're going to do with your loot, then,
Christopher Blakely?'

'I'm hardly old enough to get married, am I?'
he said lightly.

She gave a harsh laugh. 'Then maybe you'll buy
one for your brother? He does seem fond of this

Miss Martin you all like so much. Maybe he and Thursby could have a bidding war.'

Chris didn't want Diana involved in such ugliness at all. Not her or any of her friends. 'He doesn't want to marry, either. I'm sure you've heard that about him.'

She gave him a venomous look. She reached for a decanter of port on a side table and poured herself a generous measure. 'Well, we can all buy what we want when we're done, can't we? Whatever our black little hearts desire.'

Chris left soon after, choking on the thick atmosphere of that hotel sitting room, and hurried through the streets and over one of the ancient bridges to the Île Saint-Louis. First he stopped at a café, to be sure he wasn't followed from the hotel, and he was glad of the quick glass of wine to steady his nerves again.

Did Thursby really think to sell the Star back to the Maharajah, or to some other Indian buyer? Or was India merely a feint? Chris had to find out and soon. They had to move fast now.

He paid for his wine and made his way back out to the street. It was much quieter there on the island than it was near the Exposition, the passersby very different. Men in suits going to their work, nuns from nearby Notre Dame.

He studied the street carefully as he put on his hat and couldn't see anyone who looked out of place or suspicious. Still, he knew he had to be careful. One false step and the Star would be truly gone. He put his hands casually in his coat pockets and strolled on, whistling a music-hall tune and trying to act a bit foxed.

But when he turned the corner, he saw the very last person he would ever want to encounter acting in such a way—Emily. And she was hurrying towards his direction so quickly, so tall and brisk and lovely in her tailored blue suit and boater hat, that there was no avoiding her.

'Chris!' she called out, smiling as she waved. 'Whatever are you doing in this part of town?'

'Oh—there's just this nice little café over there,' he said, trying to keep up his 'drunk fool' act. It was so very hard to do with her. 'A good Bordeaux, very cheap.'

She wrinkled her nose. 'Well, it must be very nice *and* very cheap, to bring you so far from all the Exposition fun.'

'*You* are all the way out here. But I suppose fun has never been your first priority.'

She frowned as she looked at him and he wanted more than anything to grab her hand, to tell her it was all an act, to beg her not to see him that way. But he couldn't. 'Indeed not. I'm meeting with a silk distributor.' She tucked a package closer into her elbow. 'I'm surprised you're not calling on your aunt. Alex says the Duchess is quite upset after what happened at the pavilion.'

'I can't think why she would be. It was a hideous trinket, really. And how could I be of help to her?'

'Quite right.' She gave him a quick, flickering look, up and down. 'I must be on my way. I suppose I will see you at the embassy ball, if it's still on.'

'I suppose you will. Save me a waltz?'

Emily just laughed and hurried on her way. Chris stared after her until she turned the corner out of sight, feeling that terrible tug of longing that pierced him whenever she was nearby.

She can never know, he told himself again. Yet he couldn't help but wish she was still there, standing in front of him.

Only once she was gone did he hurry up the back steps of a quiet brick building near the church. 'Lord Ellersmere is here and waiting for you,' a secretary said.

Chris nodded and followed the sound of voices along a corridor. One was low, desperate, persuasive. One was booming, gravel-rough, very distinct.

'...of course the ball will go on,' the Prince of Wales growled. 'I'm not slinking home now, just when things are getting really interesting here, no matter what my mother says. And that is final.'

The office door slammed open and the Prince appeared, his long wool coat swirling around him, equerries hurrying behind. Chris ducked behind a cupboard and waited until Bertie was gone before he knocked on the office door. Maybe he *would* waltz with Emily at the embassy, after all.

Lord Ellersmere sat behind the desk, his head resting wearily in his hands, as so many heads did after an encounter with the stubborn prince. 'Ah, Blakely. I hope *you* have some good news for me, at least...'

Chapter Nineteen

The marble halls of the Louvre were crowded, but strangely hushed as Diana made her way slowly through them, trying to take it all in. The vivid paintings, the artists making copies at their easels, the sculptures, the grand frescoed ceiling over her head. It was all quite fascinating and not a little overwhelming.

She made her way to the sculpture hall, the long, narrow space lined with the glowing, pale marble of gods and goddesses, forest nymphs and warriors.

She glimpsed William by the Venus de Milo at the far end of the hall, where they had agreed to meet. He hadn't yet seen her and was gazing up at the lady's serene stone face. Diana took the moment to study him. He was handsome, as he always was, but alone, thinking himself unobserved, he looked younger, more relaxed. A small smile on his lips. It made Diana feel ridiculously as if she would melt with pleasure.

'Sir William,' she called. He turned and his smile widened, his dimples flashing. She hurried to his side.

'Miss Martin—Diana,' he said and in his deep, soft voice she remembered their kiss. He took her hand and bowed over it, all very proper, but so warm and sweet. She tucked her hand into the crook of his elbow as they turned to Venus.

Diana tilted back her head and examined the statue from under her hat. Venus seemed to look down at her, a half-smile carved on her lips, as if she understood Diana's emotions even over the centuries. 'She is certainly beautiful. I see why my mother remembers her so fondly. But doesn't she make you wonder what she's really thinking?'

William looked up at her, as well. 'She doesn't give up many of her thoughts, does she?'

'She is rather like *you*, then,' Diana said, wishing he would let her in. 'Kindred spirits.'

He glanced back down at her, his expression quizzical. 'Do you really think I'm so mysterious?'

Diana watched him for a moment, then finally

nodded. Surely she could be honest with him now, after all they had seen together? 'Of course you are. It's terribly maddening sometimes. But I suppose you must be that way, for your work.'

'My work,' he said softly. 'Yes.' He pressed his hand over hers on his arm and they strolled along the black and white marble floors of the gallery, to the furthest end. There weren't as many famous pieces of art there, thus not as many tourists, and they could be quiet together.

'I did not mean it is a *bad* way to be,' Diana said, eagerly trying to explain her words. Longing for them to fully see, fully understand, each other at last. 'I just want you to know that I—I understand. I know how easy it is to keep one's thoughts to oneself. I always did that, too, until I found Alex and Emily and had real friends at last.'

'I know,' he said. Quietly, simply, yet there was so much in those two words, in the glance he gave her. 'Oh, Diana. There is so much I want *you* to know. I want to hear your thoughts on so many things. Yet we are all caught in matters beyond ourselves at the moment.' They stopped in the shadow of an alabaster goddess and he nodded at her with a smile. 'Ah. It's your namesake.'

Baffled, she turned to the statue. It was Diana

the Huntress, holding her bow high with one hand and reaching for an arrow from the quiver on her back in the other. She had such a fierceness of purpose that Diana envied her. 'So it is. She doesn't hide her purpose behind a smile as Venus does, does she?'

William laughed. 'No. Diana is determined to reach her goal. Just as you are. It has been nice to watch you here in Paris.'

'Really?' Diana said, astonished. But she saw only openness, honesty in his dark eyes.

'You seem to have come alive here. Found yourself, as we all should be so lucky to do.'

'I think I have, yes.' She was surprised to realise how true that was. She loved the city, loved writing about all she saw around her. Above all, she loved sharing it with William. Their kisses, the walks by the river, the moments high in the clouds atop Eiffel's Tower—it had all been quite wondrous, like something in a book.

'You help me see things in new ways here,' she said.

He shook his head. 'I wish I could watch you all the time, that I could just—'

He broke off and Diana impulsively took his hand. Even through their gloves, it felt warm, safe.

She dared to hope and studied his handsome face carefully for any hint of it. But he was still too much the de Milo.

'You are right,' she said. 'We do have our work to do here. So much is beyond us. You don't need to tell me anything, not yet certainly.'

He raised her hand to his lips and pressed a kiss to her gloved fingers. For just an instant, time seemed to stand perfectly still, narrowing only to the point of that kiss. To the two of them, all alone in the crowded museum.

'Shall we walk a bit?' she said, the spell still shimmering around her. 'Unless you have to return to work?'

He shook his head, a small smile on his lips. 'Not yet. We can stay here in this enchanted palace a little longer.'

She took his arm again and they strolled together in easy companionship through the galleries, past the panorama of Napoleon's coronation, Liberty and her people, portraits and landscapes and scenes of mythology. Yet Diana hardly saw them. It was difficult to see anything but the man who walked beside her. He seemed lighter there, laughing with her, wrapped with her in that new, warm intimacy.

They talked lightly of the sights of the city, the embassy ball the Prince insisted on attending, of what they would do once they left Paris. They didn't talk of the theft of the Star, of what might happen to the two of them, together, once they were back in the everyday world of London.

'Will you keep writing?' he asked.

'Oh, yes. I've found myself quite addicted to it. I don't know if *Ladies' Weekly* would want me to stay on, or if I would have to turn to fiction, but I will keep it up in some way.' She hesitated, wondering if she should even ask. 'And—and your work? Do you know, yet, if they plan to send you back to India, or if you will stay in London from now on?'

He stopped to examine a scene of an Italian Renaissance city, its gleaming white buildings strung out over a green hill. 'I won't know for some time yet where I'm bound next. There has been some talk of Vienna, but who really can tell?'

'Vienna?'

'Yes. Not as exotic as India and certainly more etiquette-bound, but interesting.'

'I should think so. The palaces, the clothes. The parties! All that waltzing. They do say it's very beautiful.' She studied the city in the painting, too, and tried to imagine it all. Will, in Vienna. 'I think I—well, that is, everyone would miss you.'

He glanced down at her, a glint in his eyes like stars in the night sky. 'Would *you* miss me, Diana?'

'Of course I would. No one speaks to me as you do, except for my Miss Grantley's friends.'

'And how is that?'

'As if I was a person, not a silly girl who must not know her own mind.'

'Diana the huntress,' he said with a laugh. 'No, you are far from not knowing your own mind. And I would miss you, too. Very much.'

She swallowed hard past the sudden hard knot of hope in her throat. 'Well, you are not at the Schönbrunn yet. We're still here in Paris. What should we do next?'

'A cup of tea?' he asked hopefully.

She laughed. 'Is that all?'

'I admit my feet are rather aching. This is an astonishingly large place, isn't it?'

'So it is. Very well, a cup of tea it is. I saw a rather cosy-looking café at the entrance, if we can find it again.' She paused to examine the Italian cityscape once more. It couldn't be more of a wondrous, distant fantasy than the moment she was in right there. She would do anything to hold on to it. 'I know you can't really talk very much about your work right now, but—have you had a chance to talk to Chris yet?'

'My brother?'

'Yes. Since the Star went missing, I've been rather worried, you know. I think you have, too.'

'Yes.' A frown flickered over his face. 'Chris has always been rather too impulsive, I'm afraid. And secretive since we got to Paris. But I promise I can keep an eye on him. I always have.'

Diana nodded, remembering what he had said about his family, his parents' distant marriage, Chris always falling into trouble, Will keeping control of it all. It made her heart ache for him. 'Of course you have.'

He pressed his hand over hers and she glanced up to find him watching her intently. She felt her lips part, wondering if he would kiss her again. But he just drew back with a small, sad smile and said, 'Now, what about that tea?'

Chapter Twenty

As Diana laid out her gown for the embassy ball that evening, waiting for Emily to arrive to help her fasten the buttons at the back, she couldn't help but sing and twirl, just a tiny bit. Because surely she would soon be dancing again with William?

Perhaps they would even kiss, as they had when dancing before. The glow of those memories had kept her up too many nights since then and she couldn't help but giggle a little with excitement to think it might happen again. Very soon.

She picked up her gown and twirled around with it, imagining his arms around her again, his smile. She had thought he might kiss her at the Louvre, might let her in at last, only he drew away again. She wanted to be a part of his life so much, too much. But she would settle even for a dance.

There was a knock at the door and, thinking it

was Emily, she quickly laid down the dress and drew her dressing gown close before she answered it. It was not Emily, but her landlady, with a handful of mail.

'Do you have company, *mademoiselle*?' she said suspiciously. 'I heard music.'

'Not at all, *madame*,' Diana assured her, hoping she hadn't heard about Will's earlier visit. 'I was merely singing a little, getting ready for the evening.'

'Hmmph.' Madame sniffed. 'Rent is due tomorrow.'

After she left, still suspiciously peering into the apartment, Diana sorted through the letters. There was one from her parents, which she opened right away, hoping for news of the Maharajah.

Her mother wrote first, gossip from London, descriptions of the country house she had rented for the autumn, shooting parties they were already invited to when Diana returned.

At the bottom was a brief message from her father, expressing surprise that she should be interested in his 'dull' days in India.

Just heat and flies...lucky to be out of it all.
But it is funny you should mention the

Maharajah. I remember meeting him once or twice, when his grandmother's entourage would come to see the Viceroy.

He had a sapphire he was very proud of, always wore it in his turban, as such young men always seem to do nowadays. The Viceroy wanted to purchase it on behalf of the Queen, but the young Maharajah never would part with it.

Until suddenly Waverton had it. No one knows how he persuaded the grandmother to give it up. W. must have spent a great sum on it. But I don't know much else about it all.

There were whispers that the royal kingdom wasn't as wealthy as it once was, but thus it is everywhere these days. I wondered what had happened to him. Fancy you meeting him in Paris.

Don't stay too long. Your mother frets about you. Say if you need money.
Love, Papa

Diana lowered the letter with a thoughtful frown. The Maharajah hadn't wanted to part with the sapphire, until the Duke somehow found a way to procure the jewel from his grandmother as acting regent. What could it have been?

There was another knock at the door and this time it *was* Emily, dressed in a sea-blue-silk ball gown, a fashionable hairpiece of diamond and pearls formed into waves in her dark hair.

'Oh, Di, you're not half-ready,' she cried. 'We'll surely be late.'

'Fashionably late, as one must be in a place like the Faubourg Saint-Honoré,' Diana said, tucking the letters away. 'My hair is quite done and my gown only needs fastening.'

'So I see.' Emily picked up the dress and studied the sleeves. It was the Worth again, but Diana hoped no one would notice. It was too beautiful not to use again, especially in its Parisian home. 'What news from London?' she said, gesturing to the letters.

'Oh, the usual. My parents are talking about the autumn shooting,' Diana said as she stepped into her frothy petticoats.

'Any news of that Indian-investment scheme everyone is talking about?'

'I don't think so. Why would there be?'

Emily frowned as she studied the fastenings of the gown. 'I don't know. I thought maybe your father would know something of it, having been in India once and still belonging to those sorts of clubs.' She gave the tulle and silk a little shake. 'I—well, I am a bit worried about Christopher Blakely.'

Diana was startled to realise she hadn't been the only one to notice Chris's strange behaviour lately. 'Chris? Really?'

'Yes. I saw him on the Île Saint-Louis, which seems a strange place for him to be. And he was behaving oddly.'

'Oddly?'

'He said he had been drinking, which wouldn't be at all a surprise, even though it was morning. But he didn't smell of wine. And I am sure he was lying to me. I can see it in someone's eyes when they are.'

'I admit I've been rather worried, too. He didn't seem at all like himself that night at the Indian Pavilion and we've both seen him with some rather—unfortunate friends. Even his brother says he's concerned.'

Emily gave her a sharp glance and slid the layers of the gown over her head. 'William Blakely? You've been spending a bit of time with him lately, haven't you?'

Diana tried to look careless. 'Just a little bit. He *is* Alex's cousin, after all. We can't escape the friendship.'

'Is that all?' Emily said with a grin, pulling the fastenings together at Diana's back. 'Someone I know says they saw you together at the Louvre, talking most quietly.'

Diana felt her cheeks turn hot and she wondered if very many people had seen them together, when she was too wrapped up in Will to notice anything else. There couldn't be any gossip, not if she wanted to keep her job, or to keep her parents at bay. Yet she so wished she could confide in someone about her confusion, her hopes and fears! 'He is very amiable.'

Emily laughed teasingly. 'Is he indeed? He must have changed since that visit he made to Miss Grantley's, then. He was so sombre there, so stiff and serious.'

'He isn't really like that at all,' Diana cried. 'He is most kind, and—and amusing.'

'Amusing, is he?' Emily said, still smiling that infuriatingly all-knowing smile. 'Shall I have my father look to the refurbishment of an embassy soon? I'm sure Lady Blakely would go nowhere else than Fortescue's.'

'It's not like that,' Diana said weakly, feeling her face turn even hotter. It *wasn't* like that. But did she want it to be, deep down inside? 'He is just, well, nice.' Nice. Such a pale, insufficient word for what William was.

Emily's smile turned gentle. 'I am sure he must be if you're befriending him. Well, shall we finish up your toilette, Madame L'Ambassadeur? I know you will want to look very *nice* for the evening.'

Diana tossed a hairbrush at her, but it just made them burst into laughter, and they couldn't stop giggling as Diana's gown was straightened around her, the feathers pinned into her hair, her earrings found, and slippers dug out from under the bed. They were still teasing each other as their carriage jounced across the city, coming up with more and more elaborate decorating schemes for mythological ambassador's residences.

But the sight of the British embassy at the Hôtel de Charost made even Emily quiet. It was a grand dwelling indeed, fit for a pre-Revolution *duc* or *comte*, all pure white stone and soaring wrought-iron balconies, light gleaming from every window. A red carpet stretched from the drive up the steps and through the gilded doors.

As a liveried footman, complete with powdered

hair, helped her alight from the carriage, Diana smoothed her own hair self-consciously. Even though it had been teasing, she couldn't help but remember Emily's words. This was William's world, his career. Would she fit into such a place? Did she want to?

Would *he* want her to?

'Come on, stop daydreaming,' Emily called as she sailed through the doors and Diana hurried behind her.

Luckily, even though they were a bit late, they could not outdo the famously unpunctual Princess of Wales for timeliness. The royal party had not yet arrived and everyone was arrayed in the hall of the ballroom to wait for them.

Diana couldn't imagine what the grand ballroom would look like, if that was just the hall. The walls of pale green silk were lined with portraits of ambassadors and their wives, with the Queen scowling down on all of them from her own gilt frame. Marble and ebony tables lined the edges of the green and gold carpet, displaying rare *objets d'art*. Tall glass windows looked down on to the large garden below, lit softly with Chinese lanterns in the trees, outlining neat flowerbeds, topiary hedges, and an iron and glass summerhouse.

Diana studied the crowd there, seeing so many of the royal and aristocratic faces that had graced all the Paris parties. Russian grand duchesses, German princes, American millionaires. But she couldn't see William anywhere, though she told herself sternly she was *not* looking for him. No doubt he was with the Prince and attending to his work, as she should be. She took a glass of champagne from a footman's tray and sipped at it as she studied the ladies' gowns for her next article.

'Oh, how glad I am to see you both!' Alex said as she broke through the crowd to hurry to their sides. She wore pale pink and white tulle and silk, like a sunset cloud, yet she looked rather strained and anxious. 'Mother won't stop fussing at me about how "peaked" I am looking. She will never be persuaded this paleness is just my natural colour! I haven't had a moment to myself all day.'

'You aren't looking pale at all, Alex,' Emily said. 'In fact, I would say you are looking quite robust today. Is it a new coiffure?'

'Indeed, you do look splendid,' Diana agreed. Alex did look quite lively, her sky-blue eyes shining.

'Perhaps you've found a handsome swain, like Diana,' Emily teased.

Alex looked at Diana with wide eyes. 'Have you got a swain, Di? Oh, do tell!'

Diana looked away, feeling that horrid blush creeping back on her. She wished she had some of Alex's 'paleness'. 'Indeed I have not. You two do like to tease.'

'What else are almost-sisters for, Di?' Emily said with a laugh. 'To tease and be teased in turn.'

'Does that mean you'll be the next one with a swain, Emily?' Alex said.

Emily laughed even harder. 'Who knows? There are so many interesting gentlemen here in Paris, aren't there? Such—modern attitudes everywhere. A lady could get quite used to it all, I think.'

Diana rather agreed with her. It *would* be easy to get used to the elegantly informal Parisian life. Too easy.

The doors opened at last to admit the royal party. The Prince was first, Princess Alexandra on his arm, dripping with her diamonds and pearls, her mink-trimmed cream-coloured train sweeping behind her. Everyone immediately formed two lines and dropped into bows and curtsies as they greeted their hosts.

While Bertie was busy flirting with the hostess, Diana glimpsed William standing behind him. He looked handsome as always in his black and white evening suit, a small smile on his lips as Princess Louise said something to him. Diana was sure her blush was flaring again and she waved her fan in front of her, hoping he wouldn't notice.

'Ah, Lady Alexandra,' the Prince boomed. 'How lovely you're looking tonight. Perhaps you would honour me with the first dance?'

Alex looked absolutely petrified at the idea, but Diana knew she had no choice. 'I—thank you, Your Highness.'

He took her arm and led her into the ballroom, chatting with her about the differences between French and English racehorses. He didn't even seem to notice she was too frozen in fear to answer. The Duke took in the Princess and Emily was claimed by one of the German archdukes.

'And perhaps I could beg your hand for this dance, Diana?' she heard William say behind her and she whirled around to face him.

She was afraid she must look rather like a simpleton, staring at him through a sudden haze of delight, but she just couldn't seem to help herself. It was such a sunny, delightful feeling that came over her when he was near. 'Thank you, Sir William. I would be most pleased.'

'My poor cousin,' he said, nodding towards Alex where the Prince had led her to the head of the dance. 'She seems quite terrified.'

'Who wouldn't be?' Diana said. 'Someone as shy as Alex, having to dance with the Prince while everyone watches her? No wonder she looks like a rabbit in the crosshairs.' She noticed that Alex was going up on her toes, trying to scan the crowd in the ballroom, and Diana wondered if her friend *did* have a swain somewhere.

'I'm sure you would be most equal to the task,' he said, smiling down at her.

Diana laughed, ridiculously pleased he thought her so. 'I'm not so sure. It does look like rather an intimidating experience. I'd much rather be here dancing with you.'

His smile widened and his dark eyes glittered. 'Are you sure? A lowly Foreign Office desk man?'

'Quite sure—if you are allowed to dance when you're on duty like this.'

'I think one waltz can be spared.' He gave her a low bow and she went into his arms to be swept into the dance.

As always, he was a wonderful dancer and led her so perfectly through the steps that it felt as if she was floating. They whirled and turned, past a sea of satin trains all swishing in time to the music. It was quite magical.

'I feel as if I'm in a fairy tale!' She laughed and leaned against his shoulder as they rounded a corner. She could feel how strong he was, how lean, deceptively powerful beneath his fine evening coat. She wished the dance would never stop.

Yet it did, of course, swirling to a halt. She bounded once more on her toes, making Will laugh. 'Would you care for a glass of punch, or maybe some of the ambassador's best champagne? I think we deserve a little rest before the next set.'

'So do I,' Diana said. Or maybe she just wanted to sip champagne next to him, laughing about how ridiculously lovely the evening was. How wonderful it felt to be close to him. He pressed her hand warmly and she almost laughed at the delight of it.

As he left to fetch the drinks, she wandered through the tall, open glass doors on to the stone terrace that overlooked the Hôtel du Charost's famous gardens. They were indeed beautiful, towering old trees lining white walkways, perfectly kept flowerbeds that shimmered red and yellow and purple under the night sky. A few Chinese lanterns hung in the trees and around the glass summerhouse. It was quite enchanted.

But it was not empty. Diana heard the echo of rough, angry voices, speaking in French. She went up on tiptoe, trying to peer into the darkness, wondering who dared bring such fury into such hallowed beauty.

She heard one English word, 'Stop!', and thought with a fearful jolt that it sounded rather like Christopher Blakely. Was Will's brother in trouble again?

Worried, Diana glanced over her shoulder, but William hadn't yet returned and no one else was nearby at all. She could hear music from the ballroom, along with laughter and the clink of fine crystal, and she was afraid Will would be stopped several times before he could come back. She peered out into the garden again, trying to tell shadows from people.

She took a deep breath and rushed down the marble steps into the garden. Her heeled shoes sank into the soft green grass, but she plunged ahead. She had to help if she could, if her friend was really in trouble.

She could hear the echoes of angry voices from behind the summerhouse and tried to peer through the mist of the Parisian evening, which had descended over the embassy like a curtain of silvery tulle. She thought she saw someone on the ground, heard the dull thud of a blow, an angry voice.

She gasped and ran up the slope into the summerhouse. She couldn't quite tell where the noises were coming from, but they seemed louder here. She ran to the far end, where the tall windows looked out to the garden.

Aside from a few lanterns strung in the trees, the large, sweeping lawn was in darkness and she saw only shadows. Wishing for some of the glasses from the Eiffel Tower, which had made the details of the whole city so clear, she narrowed her eyes and tried to decipher what was happening.

She thought she saw something pale flash in the gloom, maybe white shirt fronts. She heard the angry hum of voices, too low to distinguish any words. But there was no mistaking that dull thud of yet another blow.

Her heart pounding with fear and cold uncertainty, she let out a low cry—even as she knew there was no one close enough to hear her. She had to get help, to find Will.

She dashed back to the door of the summerhouse and down the steps to the garden. The embassy, all alight with music, seemed so close, yet so far away. She turned towards it and suddenly thought she heard a sound behind her, a swish like a footfall in the grass.

She half-turned to see what it was and something hard hit her between her shoulder blades. She felt the ground shift beneath her, her feet sliding out from under her, and she desperately tried to regain her balance. Just as she thought she had righted herself, another hard blow landed on her shoulder and there was no mistaking it this time. Someone pushed her.

She tried to twist around, but she fell forward, the air rushing past her ears, her heart pounding so hard she could hear nothing else. She tumbled to the ground, her knee and hip landing hard with a flash of pain. She thought she heard the thud of running footsteps coming from a long way away, and then for long, indecipherable moments, there was nothing at all but a ringing noise, a shifting blackness in front of her eyes.

Diana lay there for lord knew how long until she heard the sound of her name being called. She pried her eyes open as pain exploded in her head. Her whole body felt sore, but she knew she had to get up, to find help.

She forced herself slowly to her feet and turned

towards the beckoning lights of the party. Her ankle turned under her, sending shooting pains up her leg, and yet she had to move forward. She had to be like the heroines in the novels.

With one careful step after another, her teeth gritted against the pain, she found her way to the foot of the terrace steps. There her leg refused to go on, to carry her up the hard stone steps.

Yet she could see William, standing at the balustrade with their champagne, staring out into the garden as he called her name hoarsely.

'Will,' she called, cursing the way her voice came out so low and rough. 'Will! I'm here.'

'Diana? What's happened?' He ran down the steps to her side and reached out for her as she swayed, seeming to forget the glasses he held.

She caught one of the glasses before it could fall and gulped down the contents. The bubbly liquid was blessedly numbing and gave her strength.

'I thought I saw Chris in the garden, having a fight of some sort,' she said as Will helped her sit down, his hands gentle on her back, his face creased in concern. He held her close and she felt suddenly warm, safe. Not so terribly alone at all.

'A fight?'

'Yes, but I couldn't see very well at all. I tried to get a closer look...'

His expression shifted into fury and—and was that fear? 'You got in the middle of a fight?'

'Yes—no. Not at all.' Diana shook her head, trying to clear her thoughts. The chase, the pain and the wine all combined to make things very fuzzy. 'I couldn't see them, only hear them. I was coming back to find you when I...'

'You fell?' He knelt down beside her and quickly examined her foot and ankle.

'I think I was pushed,' she said, suddenly very sure of the truth of her words. She *had* felt a hand on her back, shoving her forward. But then who-ever it was had vanished.

'Who was it?' he demanded, his voice full of suppressed anger. His eyes glittered in the night.

'I couldn't see.' She looked down and saw her skirt had a tear in the tulle and silk. 'My Worth gown!'

'Never mind that. I'll get you another Worth gown. Or ten, or twenty.' He suddenly pressed a fierce kiss to her brow and his arms came around her to hold her close. The frightening night seemed to vanish and she felt warm and safe. 'You're here now, that's all that matters.'

Diana dragged in a ragged breath. She *did* feel safe there, with William, but she was still afraid for Christopher, out there in the darkness with who knew what kind of people. 'But what if it was Chris out there?'

William frowned. 'My foolish brother will just have to fend for himself for the moment. I'm going to fetch you a doctor. I saw the Prince's physician dancing in the ballroom.'

Diana grabbed his hand, scared he was going to leave her alone. 'No! I'm sure I don't need a doctor. I just need to go home and clean this up a bit.'

'Of course you need a doctor! You can't even stand up.'

'What's happened?' a woman's voice asked, worried but not panicked.

Diana twisted around to see it was Lady Smythe-Tomas at the top of the steps. Surely the very last person she wanted to find her in such a condition! In the shadows, she looked solemn, watchful, her face half-concealed by the feathers of her deep mauve headdress.

William glanced at her, then back to Diana. 'I'm afraid Miss Martin has had a bit of a fall.'

Lady Smythe-Tomas came down the steps, her satin skirts swishing, and knelt down beside them.

There was no hint of the careless, laughing Professional Beauty as she examined Diana's foot,
her torn dress. 'So I see. Poor Miss Martin. We
should be most careful, champagne and marble
steps don't always mix. I can see her to the ladies'
withdrawing room, Sir William, if you want to
fetch the doctor? We can clean this up, but I rather
think this scrape might need a bandage.'

William gave Diana a reassuring smile, and
squeezed her hand before he helped her to her
feet. 'I think that would be best, thank you, Lady
Smythe-Tomas. I'll only be a moment,' he said
and hurried into the embassy.

'Here, Miss Martin, lean on me, I'm stronger
than I look. I do think there's a back staircase
here some place.'

She was indeed stronger than she looked, Diana
thought as Lady Smythe-Tomas helped her to the
terrace, past astonished maids and footmen, and
up a winding back staircase to the ladies' room
on the top floor. She was surprisingly practical,
easing Diana up the steep stairs with a minimum
of fuss.

Then Diana remembered that she was good
friends with Thursby, who somehow had Chris
under his power. For just an instant, she wondered

wildly if the lady was carrying her into more danger. But it was only a comfortable chamber with sofas, dressing tables, and *chinoiserie* screens, with ladies' maids waiting to fix hems and offer face powder.

Lady Smythe-Tomas sent one of them to fetch soap and water, and she helped Diana sit down in a cushioned chair. She examined the scrapes carefully, her face calm and kind. Diana suddenly wondered if, far from being wary of Lady Smythe-Tomas, she should warn her about Lord Thursby. If he was indeed out there, fighting with Chris, couldn't she be in danger, too?

Yet something held her back. She didn't yet know *who* had pushed her, let alone how the lady and Thursby were connected. And then there was her connection with William...

'Yes, we should always be very careful,' Lady Smythe-Tomas said softly. She took the basin the maid gave her and dabbed at the scrapes on Diana's leg, careful and professional. 'What made you go out to the dark garden? Besides William's handsome eyes, of course. *That* I understand.'

Diana felt herself stiffen at those words, faintly teasing. 'He went to fetch some champagne. I thought I saw someone I knew in the garden.'

Lady Smythe-Tomas glanced up at her, her eyes hooded. 'Someone you knew?'

'Yes. Then I…fell. So silly.'

'Then you didn't really see anything?'

Diana shook her head. It was surely better if the lady thought her a silly girl, seeing things that weren't really there, getting hysterical about nothing.

The doctor came in then, his leather valise in his hand, his cheeks still pink from the dancing. 'Well, I hear someone is in need of medical assistance! A fall, Miss Martin? Tsk, tsk. Let me just take a look.'

'I cleaned the worst of the blood, Doctor,' Lady Smythe-Tomas said. 'I think this scrape is worryingly deep, though.'

Diana glimpsed William behind the doctor. He hovered in the doorway, his face very serious again with concern. She half-held out her hand, longing for him to come to her side, yet he turned and left.

Suddenly cold and rather lonely, as well as confused about the whole strange night, she turned back to the doctor and watched him as he clucked over the scrapes. The maids fluttered around, offering more soap, some bandages.

Lady Smythe-Tomas gave her a steady smile and said, 'Let me just fetch Miss Fortescue. You arrived with her, did you not? I'm sure she will want to see you home safely. No more garden adventures.'

'Thank you,' Diana said. 'You've been very kind and most helpful.'

Lady Smythe-Tomas laughed. 'That's me. A new Florence Nightingale.'

Only once she was gone did Diana think to wonder how she knew Emily had escorted Diana to the party in the first place.

Chapter Twenty-One

William's head was full of whirling thoughts as he made his way to the building on the Île Saint-Louis early the next day. He knew Diana was safely at the hotel with Miss Fortescue, recovering from her attack at the party. He also knew Chris had not returned to his lodgings after the ball—and Diana said she thought she had seen him in the garden, in some kind of danger, which led to her chasing after them and being pushed.

She was fortunate that time. He knew very well she might not make such an escape again. He had known all along it would be wrong to let her get too close to his work and now he had been proven hideously right. He couldn't forget that again.

The thought of her in danger made him feel infuriated and also scared. They weren't emotions he was familiar with and he hated having them about her. His beautiful, brave Diana. He knew he had to do something about it, as he was more accustomed to action.

He found his way to the discreet, old brick building tucked away on a quiet lane near the cathedral. The morning bells were tolling the hour, still too early for the secretary to be at his place in the hall. Indeed there were very few at their posts yet, which was why William was there. To have a quiet look at something that might tell him what was going on. How he might keep Diana safe.

He made his way into the file room, a small, windowless chamber tucked behind the main offices. Cabinets covered one wall, notes about all the various tasks the office was taking on. He found the folder for Paris and sorted through all the carefully accounted details for the security of the Wales party. He found his own dossier, which detailed his work in India. The details there weren't a surprise.

But another document was. It had information about the other people working quietly in Paris and included two people he had only half-suspected, or never suspected at all. Christopher Blakely and Lady Smythe-Tomas. They both worked for the London office.

'Chris, you fool,' he muttered, scanning the neatly printed lines. He had known his brother had done work for the office before, but Chris had declared he no longer did. Yet here he was, mixed up in the complicated business of the Star and Indian-investment schemes. No wonder he had been in such trouble lately.

His brother really should be on the stage, William thought wryly. He was wasting his natural talents. And surely on the stage he couldn't get into such trouble, fighting at embassy balls for the sake of his job. Surely, once this was all over, he could persuade Chris to take on a more official, open job with the office. One where he didn't have to associate with people like Thursby.

Laura was more of surprise. He wasn't aware she had ever done work for them before, she was too busy with parties and gown fittings and photography sessions. But maybe that put her in the perfect position to see and hear things. He felt foolish for not seeing it before. He thought of her with Thursby at the tearoom and dances, and her cool efficiency when she helped Diana at the ball.

He turned to the last page, a summary of what they had heard since the Star was stolen. It seemed his aunt's husband, the supposedly rich Duke, had already filed for insurance payment on the Star, even though the jewel had only been missing a few days.

There had been tails set on Thursby, notes of who he had been seen meeting, where he had gone.

It seemed he had been a very busy man in Paris, and one with an impressive array of criminal associates. They ranged from a supposed Russian count known to run a jewel ring, to a gang of lowly fences in Montmartre.

Impressive—and a great concern. Especially when he saw the hastily scrawled note at the bottom of the page.

Thursby paying court to Miss Diana Martin, whose father is retired from the India station. It is believed he thinks the Martins have valuable information to help him in new investment schemes.

Mr Martin above suspicion, but Miss Martin could be young and naive enough to help him unwittingly.

Young and naive. William gave a doubtful huff. Young Diana might be, naive definitely not. He had once made such a mistake about her himself, but now he knew he was wrong. She was dogged in pursuit of her goals, smart and quick. But Thursby's schemes were obviously complicated and the man was known to be desperate for funds. He would be ruthless in ridding himself of anyone he thought stood in his way. And Diana had spurned him already.

And then there was the nasty incident at the ball.

William also knew that his own office would also not hesitate to get people out of the way as quickly as possible, if they thought such action was needed. Their goal was to find the Star and break apart Thursby's schemes, before they could affect Indian relations or bring scandal to the Prince while he was in Paris. Everything else on the job was secondary.

William read over the report one more time. He had to persuade Diana to return to England immediately. It was the only way to keep her safe.

He saw again her frightened face in the embassy garden, the blood on her leg, and he felt a grim resolve to never see such things again.

Determined, he put the file back in its place and left the hush of the empty room, with its scent of old paper and dust. While he was absorbed in his thoughts in there, the day had begun in earnest.

Secretaries were now at their desks, hurrying past on errands, their arms full of files, typewriters clicking. Yet everyone spoke in hushed voices, force of habit when one's job was keeping secrets.

Lord Ellersmere, who had quietly arrived after the Prince to see to the security of the Paris office, called out to William as he walked by Ellersmere's half-open door.

'Blakely, good that you're here,' Ellersmere called. 'Can I speak with you for a moment?'

Intending to get some answers, William strode into the office. Ellersmere was not alone, though. Chris was with him, giving Will a sheepish smile. Other than that, he looked perfectly calm and ordinary, sipping at a cup of tea.

'Sir William,' Ellersmere said. 'Good to see you again. Mr Blakely here has been filling me in on some things, but we need to speak to you, most urgently. We are rather close to resolving this Thursby business, I think. There is a meeting set up later today at the Indian Pavilion. Now we need the help of yourself. A professional, you might say…'

Half an hour later, William stepped out into the sunny Parisian day, the details of the Indian business strong in his mind. The involvement of his brother, the assistance of the Maharajah, who had agreed to help lay a trap for Thursby in exchange for control of the Star again. And even fiercer was the resolve to get Diana safely out of the way, however he could.

Chris walked beside him, scrambling to keep up with Will's quick stride. 'Are you angry with me, Will? I was going to tell you, just as soon as I could, but Ellersmere thought it was better no one know the details yet. It's been dashed hard. I've been going mad with it all.'

'You should be on the stage, Chris. Your natural talents are quite wasted here. It's true we've all been worried, even Miss Martin and Miss Fortescue.'

'Emily?' he said with a frown. 'I never wanted that, for her to worry.'

'What did you think would happen, when your friends all saw you seemingly falling into the schemes of a man like Thursby? Of course we were worried.' They came to the Pont Neuf and William paused to lean on the stone ledge, staring down at the boats drifting past on the river. 'But you have been doing good work here.'

'Do you think so?' Chris asked eagerly. 'I do enjoy feeling useful again. Thursby is a wrong 'un.'

'Truer words were never spoken. Thanks to you, we can be hopeful he'll be gone soon and you can take on a more open job at the Foreign Office. If that's what you want.'

'I think it is. Getting too old for such shenanigans, aren't I?' Chris also stared down into the river, a thoughtful frown on his face. 'Maybe our parents are right. Time to think about the future.'

William also considered the future and for an instant he pictured a home, a warm drawing room with music and laughter, and Diana standing there, waiting for him. Holding her hand out with a smile. It was all he could have hoped for—and all he couldn't have.

'I'm glad to hear you say that,' he said. 'Before we get to a settled future, though, we have to catch Thursby in the act. And I have a feeling this matter will get worse before it is resolved, even with you, Lady Smythe-Tomas, and the Maharajah on our side.'

'You're right about that. I've been spending far more time than I would like with the man lately. He's ruthless in his plans, but luckily for us not the most discreet.'

William remembered that Diana had run into the embassy garden when she thought Chris was there in trouble. 'Were you with him at the embassy ball?'

Chris shook his head. 'I know Thursby was meeting one of his contacts there that night, but I was late getting to the ball and he managed to shake off everyone else following him. I ran into one of his cohorts on the street and was warned off.'

William told him what had happened to Diana, that she had thought she saw Chris in trouble in the garden and had followed, only to be pushed and injured.

Chris looked utterly appalled. 'Diana was hurt? By Thursby?'

'She couldn't see anyone clearly, but I assume it was him, or one of his guards. Perhaps she was close to discovering some meeting.'

'She should leave. Her and Alex and Emily, they aren't safe here,' Chris said.

'My thoughts exactly,' William answered tightly.

Chris studied him closely. 'You'll miss her, though, won't you? I think you just might care about her.'

William gave a brusque nod. He couldn't talk

about her, couldn't even find words for how she made him feel, what she made him wish for. But neither could he deny it to his brother. Not entirely. 'We have to do what's best for those we care about.'

Chris nodded. 'So we do. The ladies need to be out of the way as we move in to arrest Thursby. Once he realises he's cornered, he'll be more dangerous than ever.'

William was sure Chris was right about that. He had seen it himself far too often. 'I'll see you back at the office this afternoon, then,' he said, turning away. He pulled around him that cloak of cold resolution that had served him so well in his work. Just as it had been before he met Diana, and how it would have to be again.

'Where are you going?' Chris called after him. 'We're supposed to meet Ellersmere at the Indian Pavilion later!'

'To finish what I need to do,' William answered.

Chapter Twenty-Two

William made his way to the winding stairs of Diana's building with a slow, solemn resolution. He had faced danger before, chased villains, fought them, dug out secrets no one ever wanted to see the light. Yet he had never dreaded a job more than he did at that moment.

He remembered holding her in his arms as they danced, heard her laughter in his ear, felt her kiss on his lips. The wonderful sweetness of it all. He hadn't seen the world the way he did with Diana in a very long time. Maybe he never had. She took everything that had been in the shadow and drew it into the sweet light. He had grown to crave it, need it. To need *her*. He didn't want to give it up, to live in the shadows again.

Yet for her sake, he knew he had to. It was dangerous for her to be near him now. It would probably always be dangerous, as long as he did his job, chased men like Thursby. If he cared about her, loved her, then he had to make sure she was safe and happy, even though that meant she would be far away from him.

Yes. Love. He loved Diana Martin.

He stopped in his path, stunned by the thought. The word. He, who had thought he could never be surprised by anything again, was brought up cold by the realisation. He loved Diana, for her merriment, her chocolate-coloured eyes, her laughter, her joy in the world. He *loved* her.

'Blast,' he muttered. So that was how love felt. Like he was floating. It was glorious. And a great nuisance. He had no room for love, no place for it, yet now that he had seen it, he needed it. Needed her.

Diana's door at the top of the stairs opened and she appeared in a burst of sunshine and lilac scent. She wore yellow and white, all warmth and light, and held a couple of paper-wrapped parcels along with a straw hat and a folded lace parasol. Her red hair glowed like a halo.

'Oh, Will,' she cried when she saw him, her brilliantly happy smile making his heart ache. 'Do come in!'

'You were going out,' he said. He wanted to find an excuse to leave, to not say what he had to say, but there was no escape.

'I don't have an appointment—I was just going to mail my new articles. Do come in, please. I can make tea again!'

He remembered the heat of their kiss the last time she had made tea and he knew that couldn't happen again. 'I can't stay long. I just realised there was something rather important I need to tell you.'

'Something important?' she said warily. She ushered him into her sitting room and gestured towards the chair where he had sat before. The window was open, letting in the warm breeze and the song of the tiny birds in their nest. When he shook his head, she stayed standing, too. She put down her hat and parcels on the table and watched him closely. Her open, welcoming smile had turned cautious. 'That does sound portentous.'

'Not at all. I just—feel that a misunderstanding has come between us and I felt I should make it right as soon as possible.'

Diana frowned. 'What sort of misunderstanding?'

William searched deep inside himself for the

right words, the words that would keep her safe. He knew had to stay strong, to do what he knew was right. 'I understand Alex and Miss Fortescue are to go home very soon, to see to my aunt the Duchess's health.'

'Yes, Alex sent me a note just today. They're leaving tomorrow. I shall miss them.'

'Do you not think to go with them?'

Diana laughed uneasily. 'I'm sure I have more articles to write.'

'But you must have enough notes to write such articles in London. I do feel I should urge you to return to England.'

'Why is that?' she asked, her face puzzled. 'You said I was doing well here.'

'And so you are. Some matters have come to light, though, which lead me to think your reputation will be in danger if you remain here by yourself.'

'My reputation?' She still looked puzzled, but now angry, too. Her fingers curled into a fist on the edge of the table. 'Whatever do you mean? You sound like Lord Thursby, with all his talk of how a lady's place is making a home for her husband. I've done nothing to make myself open to reproach.' She glanced away, her eyes widening. 'If you mean what happened at the embassy...'

'Not at all,' William said. He could feel his resolve wavering, the need to go to her, to take her hand and reassure her, but he made himself steel his resolve. 'You did nothing wrong there. But the unfortunate events did show me that both of us have been rather drawn in to the Paris enchantment and we have to remember the real world. Our real selves.'

'What do you mean?' Diana said, her voice thick, as if she was on the verge of confused tears.

'I think, though I hope I am mistaken, that I may have given the impression I harbour certain—feelings towards you.' As he did. And they were like a thousand stabbing knives now as he watched her baffled face. As he forced himself to stay where he stood, maintain his calm distance, and not rush to kiss her again. 'You are a very nice young lady, but I cannot think of marriage for a long time yet and when I do it must be to a certain—certain...'

'A certain *sort* of lady,' Diana said, her sweet voice hardening. 'Yes. I can see that.'

'I have much enjoyed our moments together and I hope you understand why they must now cease.

For both our sakes, I'm sure you'll agree returning to London soon would be for the best. Gossip
among a small community as here in Paris can be
ruthless and with the Waleses involved...'

'Yes. They do say the Prince dislikes any hint
of scandal in his friends,' she said. She turned
away from him, touching the parcels, the edge
of the table, her shoulders stiff. 'I, too, have enjoyed our time together, Sir William. I hope we
both know I never expected more. I'm sorry if I
gave that impression.'

'Of course you did not. I merely realised it is
best to always be perfectly clear and honest.' And
now he was a liar as well as heartbroken. For he
wasn't being honest with her at all. He loved her,
needed her. But he reminded himself that it was
all to keep her safe.

Diana gave a brusque nod. 'Perhaps you are
right. About returning to England. My parents
will be worried about me. My father has already
written asking when I am coming home.'

'Then it is as it should be.'

'Yes. Now, Sir William, if that is all, I must be
going on my errands. Perhaps we might see each
other again at a London soirée, before you are off
to Vienna.'

'Of course. I'm glad we can be friends. Good day, Miss Martin.'

'Good day.'

William bowed and hurried back down to the street, forcing himself not to look back, not to reach for her as he longed to do. It had only been a few minutes, but the hardest moments he had ever known. More than any battle, any fight. He felt bruised, exhausted, even as he knew he had only done what he had to do. That it was for the best, just as he had told her.

At the corner, though, he found he could go no further. He stopped and, out of sight behind the edge of the white stone wall, he watched until she emerged from the building. Her wide-brimmed hat hid her face, but he could see the glow of her bright hair, the soft curve of her cheek. She held her parcels tight against her and didn't look around her as she rushed away.

William wanted to run after her more than he had ever wanted anything in his life. But all he could do was watch her walk away, out of his life.

Chapter Twenty-Three

For several long, endless minutes after William departed, Diana found she couldn't move. She stood there frozen, staring at the light that streamed from the windows even though she couldn't see it. She was amazed it was still daytime, warm and bright, when she was so cold.

How could she have misread the situation so badly? It was true she had little experience with romance outside of books, but she wasn't such a terrible judge of people. Or so she had thought. But she had imagined William cared something for her, that their kisses and embraces had to mean *something*. That she had broken through his seemingly cold reserve and uncovered the passionate man beneath.

And she had liked that man so very much. Too much, she saw now. It had made her rush headlong into feelings she really had no business carrying for him.

'Fool,' she whispered, and her head pounded with the word. She had been a silly fool, imagining she saw things in William Blakely's heart that weren't really there.

She glanced down and saw the packaged articles she had to send to the magazine. Work. At least she had that, something she had built for herself, that she alone controlled. Work wasn't like the wild galloping of her unruly heart, running off after such dreams. It was real, solid, and she had to concentrate on that now, or she would weep.

She hastily wiped at her eyes and smoothed her hair, hoping the familiar movements would make her feel better. Feel more like the self she had been before William Blakely. It didn't, but she did feel as if she could at least take a step again. One after the other, she told herself, until he was quite left behind.

If only that could happen quickly! That she could just forget him and the ridiculous, wonderful hopes she had dared whisper to herself at night. But she was afraid forgetting him was a long way off.

She put on her hat and gathered up her parcels.

Surely, she thought, if she went off to the Exposition, had an ice cream, watched the acrobats, she would lose herself in all that colour and noise again. She wouldn't think about William. Surely he didn't deserve it.

She made her way down the street and turned towards the river. On the corner, she thought she saw a flash of movement, sensed someone watching her. When she peered closer, though, no one was there. Just the usual flower stall, a nanny with her little charges, a matron in satin and furs with her little dog tucked in to a velvet muff.

Diana turned the opposite direction and hurried towards the walkway along the river. She could hear music there, laughter and voices, the splash of the *bateaux* rowing past, but she couldn't quite escape the hurt, the longings, the feelings she still felt for William.

At the Champ de Mars, she went to send off her parcels, the articles about Parisian fashions and new dance steps the magazine wanted. How useless it all was, she thought now. She should write an article urging women to always guard their hearts, to tend only to their own concerns, whatever those might be. Cooking, embroidery, writing, party-planning, being a royal lady-in-waiting—they were all far more reliable than romantic emotions and far less likely to leave a lady feeling sad and hopeless.

She wondered if Princess Alexandra needed a new attendant. Or maybe Princess Louise. Surely a life at court would be a marvellous distraction? And there would be many gentlemen at court.

But none of them would be William.

Diana laughed at herself as she made her way under the arches of the tower into the Exposition itself. Her small allowance would never let her live at court, with all the copious numbers of gowns and jewels it took to keep up with the Marlborough House Set. Writing, at least, was cheap.

She mailed her parcels and emerged from the little post office back into the fair. It was as lively as ever, with throngs of laughing people, bubbles and balloons, but Diana didn't really see any of it. She drifted along the lanes that branched off from the Champ de Mars, trying to focus on the bright crowds. It didn't help her forget as she had hoped. The whole Exposition, all of Paris in fact, reminded her of moments with William. The light, laughing way he once made her feel—and the confusion and hurt she had now.

She stabbed at a potted shrubbery with the tip

of her parasol, cursing when it got stuck there and she had to yank it out. She couldn't even have a fit of pique properly! She finally freed it and hurried on until she came out near the Indian Pavilion.

It was still closed, the locked doors guarded, but that didn't keep away the curious onlookers gathered near the marble steps. It had grown into quite the scandal. The papers, having finally broken the news, printed every day for the Exposition screaming in their headlines about the mysterious jewel, the Waleses in danger. Warnings to everyone to guard their valuables, nay, their very lives.

Diana studied the pavilion, remembering the night of the theft. In the light of day, it seemed almost unreal that such a thing could have happened in a place as merry as the Exposition. Yet she had been right there when it did and the Star was still gone.

Who had taken it? And did what happened in the embassy garden have anything to do with it? What did William really know about it all?

She wandered slowly around the building, studying it from every angle. It was so quiet, so coolly elegant, it really was hard to believe there had been a theft there.

At the back was a high, narrow window set into

the white stone wall, standing out from the shadows. Unlike the rest of the darkened pavilion, a light shimmered there, pale gold in the shadows of trailing ivy. She remembered the newspapers' warnings of danger on the loose in the fair, remembered the fear of being pushed down in the embassy garden.

She told herself she should leave immediately, tell someone that there was a light where there should be none. But her blasted curiosity got the better of her, as it always did. She put down her parasol and found a sturdy-looking ivy trellis she could climb, just for a quick peek. Her leg still ached from the scrapes she had got at the embassy, yet she continued climbing to the top of the trellis to peer through the window.

It gave a view, albeit a small one, into the main exhibit room. And it wasn't as empty as it should be. Three men stood near the empty display case—the Maharajah, Lord Thursby, and Chris Blakely.

'Oh, Chris,' she whispered, her heart aching that he was in trouble, too.

They seemed to be arguing, Thursby waving his hands, the Maharajah with his arms crossed over his chest, Chris stepping back with his palms out, as if trying to calm everyone down. As Diana watched, on the edge of crying out, Thursby held out the Star, its deep blue facets caught in the light.

Diana scrambled back down the trellis and took off at a most unladylike run. She wasn't sure exactly what to do and like in a dream her feet felt frozen, not moving nearly fast enough. She wished William was with her.

At the corner, she realised she could think of only one place to run. She hailed a passing hansom cab and had it take her to the royal hotel. She only hoped it was not too late.

At the marble steps of the hotel, she leaped down from the carriage and ran past the astonished-looking ushers and into the Waverton suite just below the one occupied by the Wales party. Alex was in the sitting room, seated beside her mother who was prone on a *chaise*, sniffling into a handkerchief. The Duke was nowhere to be seen, but the Princess of Wales was there.

'Diana!' Alex cried, hurrying over to take her hand. 'What's the matter?'

'Miss Martin?' the Princess said, her sweet voice only sounding mildly concerned, as if wild-eyed ladies with untidy hair and half-unpinned hats were forever bursting in on her. And, with three daughters, maybe they were. 'Are you unwell?'

'Someone must go to the Indian Pavilion at once,' Diana gasped out. 'They have the Star!'

'My goodness,' Princess Alexandra said. She glanced over her shoulder. 'Did you hear that, Sir William?'

Diana spun around, mortified to find William Blakely there, standing by the fireplace. He watched her coolly, giving nothing away by his expression, and she wanted nothing more than to sink into the floor.

'Miss Martin is quite right,' he said calmly. 'We are in the process of apprehending the thieves. There is nothing to worry about at all.'

Chapter Twenty-Four

'Well, now, Blakely. That's another problem done and dusted right, eh?' Lord Ellersmere said, pouring out two generous glasses of port even though it was barely afternoon. Outside his office window, the London traffic bustled past, never slowing down no matter what happened around them. Time just kept sliding forward.

William sipped at the rich, spicy port and studied the grey sky, so different from the sunshine of Paris. Even though it was only days behind him, it felt like years. All that laughter and music, the bicycles and dances and cafés, the river, the Venus de Milo, it all seemed to belong to another, younger man. And William just felt old, hard, as brittle as those stones statues had been.

He was sure he had left Diana for her own good and he would do it all over again if he had to in order to keep her safe. Yet he hadn't anticipated what not having her in his life would really be like. How dry and grey the world was without her. Nothing was the same as it had been before.

'Another job done,' he said softly, answering Ellersmere's toast.

'Thursby did try to make a run for it, of course, but thanks to your work he was traced to Calais. He has confessed to the theft and of "being forced", as he described it, to knock Miss Martin over in his attempts to flee his rendezvous unnoticed. He will be dealt with accordingly. And the jewel is safely back in the possession of the Indian Pavilion, for now, anyway,' Ellersmere said with a smile of satisfaction. 'All finished up very neatly.'

'Thanks mostly to my brother's work,' William said. 'He was the one who put himself in danger.'

'Yes,' Ellersmere said, his smile turning thoughtful. 'I have to admit we weren't too sure about young Mr Blakely when he first offered his services. We didn't think he would have your admirable steadiness, what with his—background. But he wanted to a chance and he certainly proved his mettle.'

William smiled proudly. 'I think so. Does he have a future career here, then?'

'Very possibly. As you know, we always need watchful eyes in India. Or Egypt, or Mesopotamia, maybe. If he keeps on as he has, he should prove to be a useful chap indeed.'

William took another drink of his wine, thinking of Chris and all that had happened in Paris. Surely his brother wouldn't have to look out for an heiress now.

'In the meantime, though,' Ellersmere went on, 'he has asked to stay in Paris for a few days' holiday and I'd say he deserves it. We need to focus on *your* future now.'

The future. He hadn't even considered it since Diana. 'Is Vienna set, then?'

'Oh, yes, if that's what you want. The office there is eager to have you and there's much to be done. Europe is in a fragile state, you know, and that empire has become unwieldy. No chasing jewel thefts, maybe, but certainly no lack of work.'

William nodded. He found he no longer much cared where he went, or what he did. The coldness seemed to have settled in permanently. 'I'm ready to go where I'm needed.'

'Of course you are. You're our most reliable man.' Ellersmere poured out more wine, watching Will carefully. 'The Prince of Wales himself spoke very highly of your work in Paris. I'm sure after Vienna, there could be a place in the royal household, if you're interested in that sort of thing.'

'If His Royal Highness thinks I could be of use to him, I'm happy to serve.'

'Yes.' Ellersmere kicked his feet up on to the desk. 'Have you given any thought to what we discussed before? Concerning wives and such?'

Will had a flashing image of Diana's smile, her hand reaching out to him. 'I have thought about it.'

'Good, good. A lady at one's side can be such a help in any diplomatic household, organising entertainments and all that. You don't want a girl like my own daughter. She and her friends are too fond of reading ghost stories and then shrieking and fainting on the sofa. Silly things! But someone like my wife, so sturdy and practical—I couldn't have managed without her all these years.'

William frowned, remembering Diana on the grass at the embassy, the blood and fear. 'Our work is so dangerous sometimes.'

'You mean when you meet a rotter like Thursby? There is always that danger, sadly, even when we keep our families at a proper distance from it all.

My own wife is quite equal to it. She even killed a cobra with a kitchen knife, when we were newlyweds in Kenya! It's true we were young when we wed, foolish and romantic maybe, but we couldn't have done without each other all these years. She would say the same. What is life, after all, Blakely, without someone to fight it by our sides?'

'Indeed,' William muttered. Someone to fight by his side. Surely Diana had shown herself, like Lady Ellersmere, 'equal' to anything? Her bravery, her shining hope in life, it had made him feel new, as well. Had he been unfair to her, to them both? Had he tried to do the right thing, in the wrong way?

He felt hit over the head by such a realisation. He had faced so much in his work, but he had never faced love before and it made him feel all at sea.

'Anyway, the greatest danger in Vienna will surely be in remembering all their blasted rules of etiquette,' Ellersmere said. 'Those Hapsburgs are very fond of their court rules and they have a million of 'em. Your lady would have to remember them all. And after a year or two there, you'd be back here in London. Slippers and pipe time.'

William laughed, as he couldn't quite picture

Diana knitting by the fire, watching him puff at a pipe. He *could*, however, picture her waltzing in a Viennese palace, charming all the stuffy Austrian courtiers, then laughing with him over all the gossip in the carriage on the way home.

And then lying beside him in their bed afterwards, her glorious red hair falling around them in a shimmering curtain as she kissed him. Her touch on his bare skin, their breath mingled, the rest of the world forgotten. He could *definitely* envisage that.

'Any candidates in mind, then, Blakely?' Ellersmere said.

'Maybe one or two,' William answered. If she would ever forgive him for being such a fool.

Ellersmere chuckled. 'Yes. I imagine you have no difficulties with the ladies. Well, get a good wife soon, I say.'

As William left the office and made his way out to the crowded street, he kept turning those words over in his head. *Get a good wife soon.* How he wished it was that easy! That he could just grab Diana and haul her up the aisle like some Viking of old.

He had turned away from her because he wanted to keep her safe. Now he hoped he had more to offer her. A Viennese adventure, then maybe a royal career, hopefully with more journeys and a few children. Time for her to write, as well as a comfortable home. He hadn't realised how much he had come to need her. How grey every day was without her smile, how nothing seemed to matter if he couldn't talk it over with her.

He had sent her away, had hurt her. How could he win her back again? Persuade her they belonged together?

He glimpsed the teashop where they had sat together, remembered her laughter, the glow of her smile.

It wouldn't be easy, he knew that. But he also knew he had to try. It was the most important task of his life.

'William! Yoo-hoo!' he heard a fluting voice call as he walked down the street from the office.

He turned to see Laura Smythe-Tomas hurrying towards him, her bronze-silk walking suit shimmering. She waved to him. 'William, darling, do wait for me. I've been quite longing for a little word.'

'Of course,' he said, though really he longed to hurry on his way, to find Diana. But he owed Laura a moment, a word. He offered her his arm.

She took it and they strolled slowly along the pavement, past the busy cafés and the bright flower carts. The edge of her enormous feathered hat brushed against his shoulder.

'I do hope you aren't cross,' she said, 'that I kept the fact that we are actually working on the same side away from you. I was utterly sworn to secrecy.'

'Of course not,' Will said, surprised she would even have to ask that. 'Secrecy is a great weapon in our task. A necessary one.'

'Quite right. But—well, I *am* rather fond of you in my way. We did have a fun time once. I wouldn't want you to think ill of me.'

'I don't, not at all.' He smiled down at her, thinking of that 'fun' time. It felt so far in the past, as if it had happened to different people, but he couldn't help admire the work she did now. 'You're very good at this, you know. Even I was fooled.'

She gave a merry laugh. 'You needn't sound quite so surprised, darling. I admit, it was quite unpleasant to have to appear to be in such financial dire straits as to convince Thursby of my investment in the scheme. But we ladies can do all sorts of things, be every bit as strong and stalwart as you men. Maybe even more so. We're capable of so many tasks.' She peeked up at him slyly from under her hat. 'Like your Miss Martin.'

'Diana?' he said, surprised.

'Oh, yes. I used to think she was just a spirited little schoolgirl, a bit silly, but she's really a very plucky little thing, isn't she? Very brave. Talented, too.'

'She is certainly that.'

'And you're very lucky to have her.' Laura sighed. 'I only hope I can find such a match one day! Now, darling, I must run. *Modiste* appointment.'

She gave him an airy wave and rushed off through the crowd, but William stood still in the middle of the pavement, turning her words over in his mind. Women had a rare strength and Diana the most of all. Yes, she was very right about that.

He turned and made his way where he had intended to be all along, to Diana's street.

'Well, Di, you are quite the heroine,' Emily declared as she read the headlines of that day's *Ladies' Weekly.*

Villainous Jewel Thief Tripped Up in Paris by Ladies' Weekly *own!*

The article, *not* written by Diana, gave a very colourful account of the theft of the Star, with Diana herself, clad in her Worth gown, giving chase to the villainous Lord Thursby as he crept away with the jewel.

In fact, of course, she had been nowhere near when the man was arrested trying to escape. She was in England when he was found at Calais, the stone recovered and returned to the Maharajah, who had been working with the Foreign Office the whole time. The Maharajah had generously in turn put the Star on display at the Victoria and Albert Museum, for everyone to see. The Duke of Waverton, the Star's previous holder, had nothing to say about it at all, as he had been declared bankrupt and gone to Italy with the Duchess. Alex had taken her own refuge at Miss Grantley's and her letters to Diana and Emily were full of books she had read and games played with the students as she tried to find her own footing again.

Diana glanced at the paper, with the ink drawings of a lady much taller than her and with grander bosoms in an elaborate ball gown, chasing masked thieves from the Eiffel Tower. The article said little of the truth, of course, some of which she had learned from Chris after they returned home: Lady Smythe-Tomas's role as a spy as well as Professional Beauty, the part Will's own office had played.

And no one would ever know. That was the point of their work.

'I don't feel like a heroine,' she said. She glanced down at her desk, where she had started a new series of articles. It seemed silly to write about new recipes for Roman punch after all that had happened. London, her family's house, none of it had changed at all. They looked the same, moved to the same schedule, had the same concerns of housekeeping and parties. Yet she felt utterly different.

She missed Paris, missed being useful. Mostly she missed seeing William, seeing his smile, having his hand on hers. Would she ever feel that way again?

'Well, everyone thinks you are, so you should take advantage of every moment,' Emily said. 'I'm going back to Paris next week to do some more ordering for Papa. Why don't you come with me?'

Paris again. The rainswept cobblestone streets, the shops, the people. It sounded glorious. But would it really be the same again, if William wasn't there? 'I would like that, Em, very much. But I'm just not sure…'

Emily gave her a wide-eyed, sympathetic glance. 'Of course. Maybe not just yet.' She folded up the newspaper and tucked it away before she straightened her hat and reached for her gloves. 'Well, I am not leaving for a few days, so plenty of time to change your mind. Will I see you at the Portlands' tea tomorrow?'

'Yes, certainly. I'm supposed to write an article about their new solarium.'

After Emily left, Diana wandered over to the window and stared out at the grey, overcast London day. All she could see were umbrellas below her, a sea of black, and she thought of the bright flowers of Paris. Of riding a bicycle beside the river, feeling herself flying as a new world opened before her. A new ocean of feelings, of romance.

'You have to forget all that,' she told herself sternly. It was behind her. William had his own life to lead, one without her in it. She needed to do the same.

'Beg your pardon, Miss Martin,' a maid said at the door, carrying a large white box she could hardly see over in her arms. 'This just came for you.'

Diana studied it, puzzled. 'I don't think I ordered anything.'

'The man who brought it is waiting downstairs. He also left these and asks if he can come back at calling hours.'

The maid held out a small bouquet from under the box, a bunch of dark, velvety violets tied up in green satin. Diana slowly took them and saw the plain, dark engraved words on the fine cream stock.

Sir William Blakely

She turned it over, her heart pounding, and saw a message scrawled in pencil.

Please. I am sorry. Talk to me?

Diana hardly dared believed those words were real. 'This man is downstairs, you say?'

'Yes, miss. Waiting for a reply, he said.'

Diana glanced down at the box: *M. Worth—Rue de la Paix*. She pushed off the red bow and tore open the lid. There, nestled in fine tissue, was an exact copy of the gown she wore in the embassy garden on that dramatic night. She thought even the rustling folds of tulle and silk smelled just the same, of the lavender sachets of the Worth salon.

Startled, she whirled around to the doorway,

not sure if she was going to run to him, or away from him. Not sure what she felt in the confusing whirl of her heart. For an instant, she was sure she was dreaming again, seeing Will standing there as he had been so often in her dreams at night. When she was awake, she had to put thoughts of him away, to bury him under talk and parties and afternoon calls. At night, when everything was quiet, he wouldn't be put away. He was always there when she closed her eyes, his dark eyes, his smile, the way his touch felt.

Just as he was there right now, watching her from hooded eyes, his hat in his hands. Diana shook her head, wondering if she was really still dreaming, yet there he was.

She didn't know what to say, what to do. She had never felt such hope before and it frightened her.

'I hope the gown is right,' he said, his voice low and deep. 'The people at Worth said it was the one you ordered. And I did remember the blue. So very well.'

'I...' Diana swallowed hard before she could find her voice. 'I thought you would be in Vienna by now.'

'Not yet. Soon. I needed to talk to you before I left.'

She turned away, unable to look at him any longer. When he was so near, she just wanted to give in to the hope, to run into his arms. 'Really? I can't imagine why. Surely everything between us was resolved in Paris.' How she hated her tone! It sounded so quiet to her, so uncertain, just how she felt. She didn't want him to know how much she really cared, how much she had thought of him since they parted. She busied herself putting the flowers into the nearest vase.

'Oh, Diana. About all that...' He came into the drawing room and she saw his hand raise towards her, palm up, before he dropped it again. 'I must say something to you and it's not easy to know how to begin.'

Diana tried to push down the light touch of hope, but it wouldn't be banished. Not yet. Not entirely. 'Surely it's better just to say whatever it is and be done with it. I have a dinner to go to this evening. If you've just come to apologise again for giving the wrong impression...'

'I am,' he said quickly. He sounded so eager, so unlike his usual calm, deliberate self, that she was startled enough to turn and face him. He watched her closely. 'I am here to say I'm sorry, Diana. To beg your forgiveness, in fact. But not in that way.'

She was utterly confused. 'Then in what way? I don't understand you.'

He gently took her hand and led her to the sofa by the window. She wanted to snatch her hand away, but she also wanted more than she had ever wanted anything to stay with him. To make that moment last for ever.

'I mean I'm sorry for what I said that day, at your apartment in Paris,' he said, still watching her so closely. So—hopefully? 'I thought it was for the best then, that I was doing something that would keep you safe. My own parents had such a terrible marriage, such distance between them thanks to my father's work. I knew you did not deserve such treatment, that you deserved so much more out of life, and I thought I could only give you that by leaving. But I've regretted it ever since, have seen that instead I did something that hurt me deeply. And I will never forgive myself for hurting you, as well.'

'I—was very unsure,' she admitted. 'But how did you think it was for the best, if you didn't mean it? I don't understand you, William.'

He gave her a rueful smile. 'I don't understand

myself. After what happened at the embassy, knowing the Office was after Thursby, I was afraid my work would catch you in its net and you would be harmed. But by leaving you, I only left you more open to being hurt and myself, as well. I should have told you everything, knowing that you would be of great help to me and that I could trust you utterly. I see that now. I can't tell you how much I've missed you, Diana. How I need you by my side, always.'

'Oh, you—you fool,' she said, choking on a sob. Hope and fear were so mixed up inside of her, but hope was winning. Shining like the sun through the rain clouds.

'I know,' he said with a smile. 'I was indeed a fool. I should have seen your strength all along, your beautiful strength. You can withstand anything and by not being honest with you I could have hurt you even more. Every day since then, I've wanted only to talk to you about things. To tell you everything, hear your thoughts and just look at you. Be with you.'

'I've wanted the same,' she admitted in a rush, her hands tight on his. He couldn't escape her, not again. 'To be with you, that is.'

'I would never make such a mistake again,' he

said. 'If I can just call on you again, explain everything to you...'

'No,' she said firmly. 'I don't need to hear more.'

He frowned. 'You are sending me away?'

'No.' Diana laughed and squeezed his hand.
'Surely we've had enough of that between us?
Lost enough time. I forgive you for being foolish. You did it because you care about me. Just
as...' She took a deep breath and gathered all her
courage. 'Just as I care about you. So very much.'

He smiled tentatively and suddenly looked so
hopeful, so heartbreakingly young. He knelt down
beside her, holding her hands between his. 'Then,
my dear Miss Martin, may I beg for your hand
in marriage? I'm being sent to Vienna soon and
maybe after that a place here in the royal household. But we can go wherever you like, if you
can just forgive my foolishness and marry me. I
promise I will spend the rest of my life making
it all up to you.'

Diana laughed with a joy she couldn't have
imagined feeling before. 'Then, yes, I will marry
you. But there is nothing to make up any longer.
We only have to be happy for the rest of our lives.
Follow our new adventures together.'

'Truly?' he said hopefully.

Diana drew him up beside her on the sofa and wrapped her arms tightly around him so he couldn't ever leave her again. 'Truly. Oh, Will! I never knew there was happiness like this to be had.'

'Neither did I. Ever. Oh, Diana. I love you. I've wanted to tell you that for so long.'

'As I love you. So much.'

His lips met hers and it felt like the fireworks over Paris, bursting with light and heat. Until the door swung open with a startling bang, making Diana jump.

'What is going on here?' her mother cried, her face shocked beneath the feathered brim of her hat.

Diana and William looked at each other and burst into laughter.

'Exactly what is meant to be happening,' Diana said. What she had dreamed of for so long. *Love* was happening.

Epilogue

When it comes time to do one's duty, every lady must simply close her eyes and imagine the lovely children she will one day have and the good of the nation. It will be over soon and one's marital bonds will only be strengthened.

Diana looked up from the pamphlet on 'Marital Harmony' someone at *Ladies' Weekly* had given her and frowned. Her wedding gown was laid over the *chaise* of her new bedroom, all white satin and wreaths of silk orange blossoms. The sun had gone down beyond the blue-velvet curtains, the grand wedding was behind her and the trunks were closed and labelled, ready to leave for Vienna in the morning.

It was her wedding night, the moment she had longed for.

And now the magazines were saying she just

had to endure it? Diana sighed. They surely had to be wrong. Nothing that made her feel like William's kisses did could be so arduous, could it? So bad she just had to think of the nation. He would never hurt her. He was her husband now.

Her *husband*. The very word made her feel giddy. It was like a dream, a wondrous dream that had started when she floated up the aisle and took his hand, saw him smile down at her through her gauzy veil. His dark eyes glowing, her heart feeling like it was about to burst with joy.

The floating hadn't stopped all day—she spun and laughed all through the cake and champagne, the speeches and dancing. A wonderful day with her friends and family, William on her arm. Her husband at last and she his wife. All the foolishness and pain gone. Very soon, they would be joined in truth.

Diana firmly closed the pamphlet and put it in the dressing-table drawer. She had come to it seeking advice. She knew little enough of the marital act, just what she read in novels, or what the girls at Miss Grantley's whispered about. Her mother had tried to give her advice before they dressed for church, but it was so stammering and strange she was even more confused. Her mother had said much more than what the pamphlet did—marital love was something to be endured. Surely that wasn't true. She wished Emily or Alex could help, but they knew as little as she did. And what Alex *did* know, from her proximity to the Marlborough House Set, sounded positively terrifying. Diana hoped Will didn't expect anything like that.

She glanced at herself in the mirror and smoothed her loose hair, trying to forget all that. She and William were different. Surely their wedding night would be, too. It would be beautiful. Romantic.

And so what if she really had little idea what to do? Millions of people had done it before. It was natural. She reached for her brush and pulled it through her hair, still curled from the elaborate updo that had held her veil and wreath. She let the length of it fall loose, hoping he would like it. That he would think her beautiful.

There was a soft knock at the door. 'Diana?' he called quietly. She felt a jolt of nerves again and a wonderful, warm anticipation.

'Come in,' she answered.

William slipped into the bedroom, his dark hair rumpled, his lean body wrapped in a brocade dressing gown. She had thought him gloriously handsome in his suit at the church; now he was ten times more so, his eyes like dark, inky pools when he looked at her. She felt a quiver deep inside.

With that glimpse of his beautiful face, his familiar, gentle smile, all those fears vanished. She ran to him and he grabbed her up in his arms. His lips swooped down to cover hers.

She wrapped her arms around him, feeling the warm safety of him enveloping her until every fear vanished and there were no doubts at all. Only hope and desire. She was exactly where she needed to be. As he drew her closer, his hands around her waist, she felt that wonderful excitement that always fizzed and popped in her heart when she was near him, come back over her, stronger than ever. It was so wonderful and warm, like the force of life itself.

She couldn't believe that it, that he, was hers for ever now. And she suddenly knew exactly what to do.

She smiled up at him and wound her arms around his neck, feeling the warm silk of his hair on her fingers. She went up on tiptoe and kissed him again, pressing one swift caress to his lips, then another and another, knowing she could never satisfy this longing for his taste, the feel of him against her. He groaned and pulled her even closer, his tongue seeking hers, and they were lost in each other.

He whispered her name as he slowly drew back, pressing tiny, fleeting kisses to her cheek. She trembled at the cool feeling of his breath on her skin.

She laughed and clung to him, vowing she would never let go.

'Come with me,' he said deeply. He clasped her hand in his and led her to their waiting bed, the sheets turned back invitingly, flower petals scattered on the pillows. Her steps felt shaky, weak from their kisses, but she wasn't unsure at all any more.

'Diana, I…' he began, his voice hoarse.

'Shhh.' She laid her finger to his lips and smiled. Words could only shatter their spell. 'I know.'

She stepped back to unfasten the ribbon around her neck, letting the white gown pool at her feet before she could feel afraid again. As he watched her, his eyes narrowed and bright, she took a deep breath and took off her chemise as well, leaving herself bare to him.

She shook back her hair and smiled. 'I'm all

yours now, William,' she said, taking his hand. 'Your wife.'

'No,' he answered. 'No, I am yours.'

He kissed her again and all their words were swallowed, his lips soft and open on hers, hungry, not to be denied. It was a hunger that called out to her own. He groaned and his hands slid over her bare shoulders.

She untied the sash of his robe and pushed it away, some instinct guiding her fingers as she touched him eagerly. Her mouth tasted the damp hollow of his throat, the sharp curve of his shoulder. How smooth his skin was, how hot under her caress.

Twined together, they fell on to the waiting bed, the velvet canopy whirling dizzily over her head. She landed on top, pushing away his loosened robe. He was exquisite, she thought in breathless awe. So alive, so glowing, so full of desire and strength and heat. Her trembling touch traced the light, coarse hair of his chest. His stomach muscles tightened, his breath ragged from her touch.

She fell happily back into his arms as he reached for her, their lips meeting, hearts melding. There was nothing careful about their kiss now, it was all hot desperation, the urgent need that had built for so long bursting like the Paris fireworks into the night sky. She wasn't afraid at all any longer.

Still holding her close, he rolled her beneath him and she laughed as her hair spilled around them in a red curtain. She felt so free at last, so glorious! So exactly where she needed to be. He kissed her and all thought vanished into sensation.

She closed her eyes, revelling in his touch, the press of his mouth on her breast, her palms sliding over his strong back. Her legs parted instinctively as she felt his weight lower between them, the press of that heavy desire.

'I don't want to hurt you,' he gasped.

She smiled, her body aching for that final union that meant he was truly hers. 'You never could.'

She spread her legs wider, invitingly, and he slid inside of her. It did hurt; how could it not? A quick, burning ache, but then it was gone. Nothing to the sensation of fullness, of him joined with her at last. She arched her back into him, wrapping her arms and legs around him tightly.

'You see?' she said. 'I feel completely perfect.'

He laughed hoarsely, and moved slowly, so slowly, drawing back and sliding forward again, just a little deeper, a little closer, every time. Diana squeezed her eyes closed, feeling the ache ebb away until there was only pleasure. A tingling delight that grew and expanded inside of her, unlike anything she had imagined.

She cried out his name at the wonder of it all, the bursts of light behind her eyes, all blue and white and red, spinning and sparkling.

Above her, she felt him tense, his back arching. 'Diana!' he shouted.

And she exploded, consumed by those lights, by his voice. She held on to him and let herself fall down into the fire. After long moments—hours? Days?—she opened her eyes, sure she had fallen down into some strange fantasy. Yet it was the same bedroom, the same moonlight from the window.

But it was a new life, with a new sparkle.

She snuggled into his arms and smiled. 'You see?' she said. 'I didn't need to think of the nation at all.'

* * * * *

Author Note

I've had the most fun working on this series, and visiting my favourite place in the world—Paris! Even if it's only vicariously, on the page! I also love the Belle Epoque period, a time of such beauty and innovation and optimism. It seemed like the perfect place for a vivacious, enthusiastic lady like Diana and her handsome hero.

The Exposition Universelle ran from May the sixth to October the thirty-first 1889, celebrating the one hundredth anniversary of the storming of the Bastille, and was a highwater mark in modern Europe. It also gave us one of my very favourite spots, the Eiffel Tower!

Covering two hundred and thirty-seven acres, the Exposition featured pavilions and villages from countries all over the world, including Java, Egypt, Mexico, Senegal, and Cambodia, introducing Europeans to a wide array of music, food, art, and languages.

There was a railroad to carry the fairgoers between exhibits, the Galerie des Machines featuring modern inventions—including a visit by Thomas Edison to show off his new-fangled light bulb and gramophone—Buffalo Bill's Wild West Show, with Annie Oakley, and the art pavilion with works by Whistler, Munch, Bonheur, and Gaugin.

Another popular exhibit was the Imperial Diamond, also known as the Jacob Diamond, in the French Pavilion. It was one of the largest stones in the world, previously owned by the Nizam of Hyderabad and then by the government of India. I used it as my inspiration for the Eastern Star.

The fair's main symbol, of course, was the Eiffel Tower—the entrance arch to the fair. By the time the Exposition opened, workers were still putting in the finishing touches and the lifts weren't quite working, but people swarmed up its stairs to take in the dizzying views and shop at the souvenir counters and eat at the cafés.

It wasn't entirely loved, though. A petition sent to the paper *Le Temps* read:

We writers, painters, sculptors and passionate devotees of the hitherto untouched beauty of Paris protest with all our strength, in the name of slighted French taste, against the erection of this useless and monstrous Eiffel Tower.

The tower was meant to be temporary, but it grew on the population of the city and is now one of the most visited and beloved landmarks in the world—a symbol of the beautiful city itself.

One of my favourite aspects of researching historical backgrounds for my stories is looking into the fashions of the day! The end of the nineteenth century and beginning of the twentieth seems like a particularly elegant period to me and the most famous of all the purveyors of fashions of the day was the House of Worth.

Opened in 1858 by an Englishman, the house on the Rue de la Paix was soon *the* place for ladies of fashion to shop. Empress Eugenie, Sarah Bernhardt, Lillie Langtry, Jenny Lind, Princess Alexandra, and a variety of royalty and American millionaires patronised the elegant, comfortable salon, ordering their wardrobes for each season. Lush fabrics, unique designs and impeccable service made it famous and its designs are still well known.

I also had a lot of fun using the real-life visit of Edward VII—then the Prince of Wales—in my story! On June the tenth, Bertie, Alexandra, and their five children arrived at the Eiffel Tower. It was a 'private' visit—Queen Victoria couldn't countenance the celebration of a country throwing off its monarchy!—but Paris was Bertie's lifelong favourite city and he wasn't about to miss a look at something as grand as the Exposition.

They arrived at the Tower at ten-thirty in the morning, entourage and press in tow, with the Princess wearing a 'simple' blue and white silk gown and bonnet trimmed with lilies of the valley, and were conducted on a tour by Monsieur Eiffel himself. I've expanded the trip, with a few more parties and excursions for the royal group, but I'm sure the fun-loving Prince wouldn't mind!

I hope you enjoy exploring the beauties of Paris with Diana and William as much as I loved writing about it! Stay tuned for the next book in the series, when we see what's *really* going on with Lady Alexandra and her gorgeous millionaire department-store owner...

Here are a few sources I used in researching the period:

Jill Jonnes, *Eiffel's Tower* (2009)

Amy de la Haye and Valerie D. Mendes, *House of Worth: Portrait of an Archive* (2014)

Claire Rose, *Art Nouveau Fashion* (2014)

Jane Ridley, *Heir Apparent: A Life of Edward VII* (2013)

Richard Hough, *Edward and Alexandra: Their Private and Public Lives* (1992)

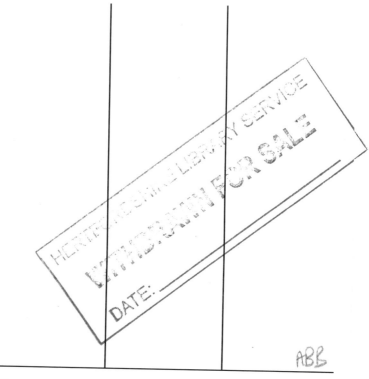

Please renew or return items by the date shown on your receipt

www.hertfordshire.gov.uk/libraries

Renewals and enquiries: 0300 123 4049

Textphone for hearing or 0300 123 4041
speech impaired users:

L32 11.16

Hertfordshire

52 454 026 3